MASTER OF CASTILE

Master of Castile

BY SAMUEL EDWARDS

WILLIAM MORROW AND COMPANY

NEW YORK, 1962

For John C. Willey

The right word, spoken at the right moment, is worth ten thousand lances. He who would be master of Castile must command an enormous vocabulary, yet must use it sparingly.

—Alvaro de Luna

1. The Boy

1

Toledo, proud capital of the independent kingdom of Castile, perched as haughtily as a Spanish eagle on her island of granite. Lazy boys fished in the Tagus River on three sides of the city; and on the north, where the water cut through a deep gorge, their younger brothers darted past indolent sentries stationed on the double walls of the ramparts, to throw stones down the precipice and listen to the echo. But only the soldiers were lethargic, and busy Toledanos were hurrying back to work after their siestas. Wool combers and weavers labored in dimly lit garrets, sword makers tested their superbly flexible steel near glowing hearths, using methods that had remained a closely guarded secret for more than one thousand years, and tanners, seated beneath the skylights of the tall buildings of the artisans' guilds, patiently kneaded cured leather to make it soft and pliable.

Prosperous merchants in velvet doublets walked to their shops through the narrow, twisting streets, preceded by pages armed with thick staffs, who ruthlessly cleared paths for their masters. Castilian peasants who had brought their produce to the city's markets and had sold their olives and grapes, haunches of lamb and coarsely ground wheat, resented the cavalier treatment and glared defiantly at the wealthy citizens. But the city dwellers, many of them *Mozarabs*, Jews and Moors who were allowed to live peacefully in Toledo and who were responsible in large part for the capital's artistic and intellectual domination of Castile, shrugged philosophically and flattened themselves against the stone walls and metal doors of the solid buildings. Lean and resilient, they looked contemptuously at the merchants who had grown fat on gluttony; the *Mozarabs,* who lived on the least nourishing cuts of lamb and boiled beans, could not afford to cook in oil and only on rare occasions could buy a handful of rice or a jar of wine.

Dominating the city was the Alcazar, the square-shaped castle that was the heart of the kingdom, its four turrets, one at each corner, soaring high above the tallest buildings, even dwarfing the spire of the great cathedral that had not yet been completed after more than two hundred years of patient work. A yellow and scarlet pennant rippled and snapped in the cold breeze that swept down across the northern plateau, indicating that King Juan II, the seven-year-old monarch of Castile, was in residence. Although the winter sun was shining behind a thin layer of Andalusian clouds that were drifting back toward the south, oil lamps and expensive, smokeless French tapers were burning in almost every window of the huge building.

Don Juan Hurtado de Mendoza, minister-in-chief of the royal council, sat in his plainly furnished office on the second floor of the castle, tugged thoughtfully at his pointed black beard and, dipping a quill into a jar of ink, wrote the date in a firm hand at the top of a page in his leather-bound official journal: "January 12, 1412."

A gale of laughter in the throne room at the far end of the corridor made Mendoza wince, and he threw his pen onto his desk. King Juan's mother, Catherine, the English Queen Dowager, was in a frivolous mood—there would be nothing to write in the journal. Burying his face in his hands, the minister wished that John of Gaunt's daughter had never come to Castile; she was always playful, shrank from responsibility and devoted herself exclusively to the pursuit of bizarre pleasures. Her co-Regent, Don Ferdinand, the king's uncle, was the only stable force in the land, but Mendoza knew he had been offered the throne of neighboring Aragon, a prize that no sensible man could refuse.

"May the Lord and all His saints preserve Castile," Mendoza said fervently to himself.

On the third floor of the Alcazar a group of busy, giggling ladies-in-waiting, members of Queen Catherine's suite, were clustered about a bewildered sixteen-year-old boy, who stood trembling, stripped to the waist, clutching his breeches of black wool. Alvaro de Luna, as stunned as he was outraged, would have known how to deal with men who tried to humiliate him, but he could not challenge a group of women to combat, and so much had happened within the past hour that he was dazed, incapable of thinking or acting rationally.

He watched in angry dismay as the women smoothed the stockings of finely woven silk in which they had encased his legs; he felt ill when they thrust his small feet into delicate, high-heeled shoes; and he blinked in helpless indignation when, laughing and chattering, they fastened two lace-edged petticoats around his waist, hiding his breeches. He protested in vain when they laced a dainty corselet around him, and when he saw two of the ladies approaching with a pale yellow gown of gauzelike silk, he made an attempt to break away. But the ladies, enjoying their game, held him firmly and slipped the dress over his head.

Alvaro wondered whether he was going mad, whether he was suffering a hallucination. He had returned to his native Toledo from the court of his natural uncle, Pedro de Luna, whom half of the Christian world recognized as Pope Benedict XIII, after ten years of study and hard work at Avignon, in France, where Benedict was defying the authority of Rome. In Alvaro's pocket had been a letter recommending him to Queen Catherine as a page, and the future had seemed bright to the orphaned, illegitimate boy. Then, without warning, he had been plunged into misery.

Catherine had received him in her apartments, glanced at

the letter and then studied him intently. "You are Castilian?" she had asked incredulously, examining his fair skin, blue eyes and sandy hair.

Alvaro, always conscious of his short stature and slender build, had strained in an attempt to make himself seem taller. "Yes, ma'am," he had replied in a Spanish accent far more cultured than that of the English-born Queen Dowager. "I am the natural son of the late lord of Canete, Alvaro de Luna the elder, brother of His Holiness of Avignon, who has allowed me to assume my father's name."

Catherine had thrown the letter aside, smiled languidly and turned to the ladies attending her. "Such beauty is wasted on a boy. It would amuse us to see him attired as a girl. There are no jugglers or ballad singers at the court today —the little de Luna will provide our entertainment. We will inspect your handiwork in the throne room."

One of the ladies came into the dressing room carrying a wig of dark red hair; another arrived triumphantly with a tray of cosmetics. Alvaro, clenching his fists furiously, swore under his breath in French.

A handsome young lady of approximately his own age who was helping to hold his left arm surprised him by whispering in his ear. "You speak the tongue of Paris?" she asked in French.

He nodded miserably.

"Then listen to me carefully. Submit to this masquerade with dignity and humor." It was obvious that his predicament amused her, and it was equally apparent that Catherine's caprice titillated her. She seemed to find it difficult to catch her breath, the color in her face crept higher and the gleam of excitement in her eyes made it evident that she was enjoying herself.

But Alvaro, trying to preserve his sanity, was aware of nuances, and detected a sense of compassion in the young lady, too. She felt no pity for him, which helped him to salvage the remnants of his battered pride, but she seemed to understand what he was feeling, and she was offering him at least a measure of sympathy. More important, she was trying to advise him at a moment when he was too bewildered to think clearly.

"How can I submit to this insanity with humor?" he demanded. "It's impossible!"

The girl controlled a desire to laugh and spoke solemnly. "Pretend you are enjoying the lark, and Her Majesty will take a fancy to you. All of us here are subject to her whims. If you displease her, you'll be sent from court. I've known her to banish nobles from Castile for offending her in some trifling matter."

"This is not trifling," Alvaro replied bitterly.

"Accept your situation with grace, and tonight you'll be Catherine's favorite. There is an old Castilian proverb you may have heard, 'He who is wise bends his knee when he must.' "

Pope Benedict had told him much the same thing before he left Avignon. "You have no protector at Toledo," his uncle had said. "You own no lands and, properly speaking, you are not a member of the nobility. Speak softly, therefore, ingratiate yourself with those who hold the reins of power; maneuver gently to establish a place for yourself."

Steeling himself, Alvaro compressed his lips.

The middle-aged lady-in-waiting who was holding the tray of cosmetics became indignant. "Hold still or I'll paint a crooked mouth on your face!"

Alvaro allowed her to daub rouge on his lips, draw a black line around his eyes and coat his lashes with a stiff black substance. He tried to think of other things as two ladies placed the wig on his head and fussed with the curls, and he shut out the sound of the high-pitched voices.

"Earrings," someone said. "We must have earrings."

"And gloves. Her Majesty loves those clinging silk gloves

from Aragon." The speaker became more enthusiastic. "A bracelet over the left wrist and a ring on the right hand. An emerald would provide the right touch with that hair and gown."

Rice powder was dusted on Alvaro's nose and chin, and he wanted to sneeze.

At last the women were finished and stood back to inspect him. Several frowned, others stared unhappily; it was obvious they were less than satisfied. Suddenly one of them shrieked with laughter and, seizing two scarves of thick silk, rolled them into balls. "We forgot the bosom!"

Alvaro's shame was complete. He averted his face as the scarves were stuffed into the bodice.

The ladies relaxed. "Perfect," one of them said fondly.

"Lovely," another murmured.

Only the young woman who had addressed Alvaro in French looked at him sympathetically and, aware of his suffering, moved to the rear of the throng.

"Here, my dear," one of the ladies said, thrusting a mirror in front of his face. "Admire yourself."

Alvaro forced himself to gaze into the mirror, and was shocked. It was difficult for him to remember his mother, but when he had been six years old she had looked as he did now. It was the supreme irony, he thought, that the ladies had chosen a dark red wig.

Two of the women took his arms, and the whole party trooped gaily into the corridor and down the broad stairs that led to the throne room. Alvaro, wobbling precariously on the high heels, unable to manage the ankle-length skirt and petticoats, would have tripped and fallen had his escorts not held him upright and pulled him to the entrance of the throne room.

Scores of magnificently dressed ladies and gentlemen filled the hall. Their jewels, their clothes, the drapes of heavy gold damask that lined the walls—all were dazzling to Alvaro, who had never seen any royal court except that of the austere Pope Benedict. At the far end of the chamber three thrones stood on a dais. The steps leading up to them were covered with a rug of thick purple velvet. Yet the figures seated on the thrones looked less than impressive. Queen Catherine had never been a beauty, and since her husband's death there had been no one to restrain her passion for cosmetics. Her rouged, powdered face reminded Alvaro of a harridan he had seen begging in the streets of Avignon. King Juan, a pale, thin boy of seven, squirmed in his seat, plainly bored with his surroundings, and with reason: he seemed to be the only child in the room.

Don Ferdinand, the co-Regent, was a prematurely bald, wizened man who stood out in the throng because he was wearing a suit of chain mail. His four sons stood on the steps below him, and Alvaro, who had studied the portraits of the royal family of Castile, recognized all of them. Don Alfonso, the eldest, was attired in chain mail like his father, but the other princes, Enrique, Pedro and Juan, wore suits with diamond buttons. The lace at their throats and wrists was worth a fortune.

Gradually the courtiers became silent, and Alvaro froze as he realized that he had become the center of attention. Apparently the Queen Dowager had told them about the entertainment she had planned. Everyone craned and jostled in an attempt to see the miserable creature in the entrance more clearly. As the ladies who held Alvaro's arms propelled him toward the dais, he lowered his head in mortification

"Curtsy to Her Majesty," one of the ladies whispered.

Alvaro was trembling too hard to obey.

"Enchanting!" Catherine exclaimed, clasping her hands in delight.

Don Ferdinand slapped the arm of his throne. "I will not be a party to such insanity," he said in a low tone to his eldest son. He rose and stalked out of the throne room, Don Alfonso following him.

There was an awkward pause, and Don Enrique took it upon himself to restore the atmosphere his father's abrupt departure had dulled. "I congratulate you on your superb jest, Aunt," he said, and turned to the courtiers. "Gentlemen, many of you were sad when Magdalena Ruminez died. But Her Majesty is a sorceress. Behold, the favorite courtesan of Toledo has been restored to us. This, dear friends, must be one of the careless Magdalena's whelps."

The laughter that welled up in the throng was quickly stifled. Alvaro, losing his temper, tore the wig from his head and threw it into the face of the startled prince. "I allow no one to insult my mother!" he shouted. "I demand satisfaction!" His rage mounting, he ripped off the jewelry and hurled it also at Don Enrique.

Several guards stationed about the hall started toward the base of the throne, their pikes lowered, but little King Juan, who had jumped to his feet on his throne, halted them. "We approve!" he said in a shrill voice. "Only a coward would refuse to defend his mother."

Catherine smiled at her son and patted his shoulder.

Don Enrique stared coldly at the ludicrous creature who had assaulted him. "Magdalena's spawn shall have satisfaction."

A gentleman standing in the front row of courtiers cleared his throat nervously. "If you please, Your Highness, let me remind you that duelling with members of the royal house is forbidden."

Don Pedro chuckled, but Don Enrique struck an arrogant pose and said venomously, "There will be no duel. I intend to rid the world of this effeminate vermin."

Alvaro's face remained expressionless behind his minstrel's mask of rouge and kohl and powder.

Queen Catherine, enjoying a far more exciting spectacle

than she had envisioned, laughed happily. Although she had spent her entire adult life in Castile, she had no understanding of the Spanish temperament and was the only person in the throne room who failed to realize that her nephew-by-marriage meant precisely what he said.

King Juan, who hated his adult cousins because they bullied him, jumped up and down on his throne gleefully. "I like him," he said, pointing at Alvaro. "I want to be his second."

Alvaro bowed to the younger boy. "I appreciate Your Majesty's friendship," he said earnestly, "but it would be unseemly for you to be a party to a fight in which blood will be shed."

The child was disappointed, and turned to his mother, pouting. "May I watch, Mama?"

Catherine stroked his head. "Of course, dear."

Don Enrique was exasperated. "The sooner we start, the sooner this farce will end. Meet me in the central courtyard."

"It will be my pleasure, Your Highness." Deliberately Alvaro turned his back on his tormentor, thus committing an unmistakable breach of etiquette, and after inclining his head to the Queen Dowager and King Juan, started to stalk from the hall. He had forgotten the skirt and petticoats that hampered his movements, and was subjected to the final humiliation of being forced to lift them in order to walk. A gale of laughter followed him up the stairs to the deserted dressing room.

He ripped off the women's clothes and, finding a basin of water and a dish of soft, pure soap on a low chest of drawers in a corner, scrubbed his face until his skin was raw. He could not rid himself of the scent of musk which the ladies-in-waiting had applied liberally to his arms and neck, but there was no time in any case. He dressed feverishly, pulling on his long black stockings and stamping into the cuffed boots that had been a farewell gift from his instructor in mathematics and finance at Avignon. He was lacing his doeskin shirt when the door opened and a white-haired courtier hesitated in the frame, then entered.

"Do you know me, boy?" he asked.

Alvaro stared at him for an instant, then embraced him. Juan de Olio, an influential member of the late king's court, had been his benefactor; it had been de Olio who had shamed Alvaro's father into recognizing his son and had persuaded Pope Benedict to take the child into his household. Emotion choked Alvaro. He couldn't speak.

The old man grasped his shoulders and gazed at him sorrowfully. "I'm afraid you've inherited your father's arrogance and your mother's temper, boy," he said. "I realize that you were placed in a situation of the utmost embarrassment and that Don Enrique taunted you unmercifully, but it's madness to cross swords with a prince of the realm."

"I allow no one to mock the memory of my mother, sir," Alvaro replied stubbornly.

De Olio shook his head. "Enrique is ten years older than you, and his reach must be at least nine or ten inches longer. Have you spent all these years receiving the finest education on earth only to be butchered, skewered like a wild boar?"

"Perhaps, sir, I can look after myself."

The youth's bland self-confidence was irritating. "Suppose the saints intervene on your behalf and you scratch Enrique. You'll probably hang for your insolence. Even if you should win a reprieve, where would you go? Don Ferdinand and Don Alfonso admire your courage, although they think you're foolhardy, but they couldn't welcome you to Aragon if you were to draw the blood of their close kinsman. Prince Juan is betrothed to Princess Bianca of Navarre," he continued heatedly, referring to the tiny Spanish kingdom in the north that was bounded on two sides by the Ebro River and on the other two by the Pyrenees Mountains. "You'd be refused admission there. And I assure you that His Holiness of Avignon would turn you away. The Spanish nations have been loyal to him, but if he offered you shelter, they might swear fealty to the other Pope, at Rome."

"I could go to Granada," Alvaro said defiantly.

De Olio's patience was exhausted. "You're a practising Christian, I presume?" he asked sarcastically.

Alvaro nodded.

"Then the Moors of Granada would enslave you. You'd spend the rest of your days in chains."

The boy buckled on his sword belt, pulled his broad-brimmed hat onto his head and picked up his doublet. "Our Lord forgave Maria Magdalena," he said, a faint tremor in his voice. "Shall I condemn Magdalena Ruminez? She was beautiful and very poor. The nobles took advantage of her. I blame them, not her!"

The old man, knowing he could not destroy Alvaro's illusions about his mother, sighed. "If I could, I'd help you, but I've retired from the active world. I visit Toledo infrequently, and I spend most of my time at my estate near Ciudad Real. There's nothing I can do for you."

Alvaro embraced him again. "I swear to you, sir, I can look after myself."

De Olio made no attempt to hide his pain and disappointment. "It might have been better, far better," he muttered, "if I had left you where I found you, living in the midst of *Mozarabs* and artisans and scum." Abruptly he left the room.

The boy stood quietly for a moment. Then he tugged the brim of his hat, squared his slender shoulders, and walked purposefully down to the large central courtyard of the Alcazar. Dusk was falling, and scores of torches lighted the cobble-stone-paved square. Alvaro was astonished to see that the entire court had gathered. The low murmur of conversation rose as he approached, and the ladies and gentlemen, most of them laughing and joking, made way for him as he walked resolutely to the center of the square. There Don Enrique, attended by two of his brothers, stood with folded arms. Don Ferdinand and Don Alfonso stood with Catherine and little Juan, and Alvaro could not resist showing off. Removing his hat, he bowed low, sweeping the stones with it.

"Lad," Don Ferdinand said brusquely, "you're a damned fool. Withdraw now, apologize to my son and I'll find a place for you in the royal entourage of Aragon when I go to Saragossa. Refuse, and even if you survive, I'll be forced to forbid you to set foot on the soil of Aragon as long as I live."

"I make the same pledge," Don Alfonso declared vigorously.

Alvaro bowed again, "I'm grateful to you, but it is Don Enrique who owes me an apology."

The future ruler of Aragon shrugged.

King Juan, who had been gazing at Alvaro with shining eyes, wrenched away from his mother and grasped the older boy's arm. "You're going to win," he whispered.

"Your Majesty's faith will protect me from harm," Alvaro replied.

Enrique gestured impatiently. "How long are you going to keep me waiting, son of a whore?"

Alvaro turned quickly, throwing aside his hat and doublet. He tested the cobblestones and, aware that they were slippery, kicked off his boots, even though his stature was thus reduced and his opponent towered over him by at least a head. He drew his sword and raised it in a crisp military salute. "I'm ready, Your Highness."

He had scarcely finished speaking when Enrique lunged, the point of his superb Toledo blade aimed at Alvaro's face.

Alvaro stood still and, deflecting the thrust with a deft, almost imperceptible bending of his wrist, caused Enrique's sword to slide harmlessly up the length of his own blade.

Surprised, the prince laughed. "That was lucky," he said loudly, and attacked again.

Alvaro continued to parry, his weight balanced effortlessly on the balls of his feet. When he refused to retreat in the face of a furious assault, a low hum of appreciation swept through the throng. Two generals of cavalry glanced at each other with raised eyebrows, and other grandees who understood the art of duelling were visibly impressed. They realized that the boy had been trained in the French style, that he depended on speed and a sharp eye rather than power, that he was compensating brilliantly for his short reach.

Don Enrique continued to press his attack, flourishing his sword, leaping and prancing. Alvaro parried every thrust calmly, with a minimum of effort, and even the ladies began to understand that he was superior to the prince, whose arm was unsteady and footwork clumsy. The child king cheered his favorite in a high, piping voice, but Catherine looked distressed. When Don Pedro and Don Juan, who were obviously worried, tried to intervene on their brother's behalf, their father restrained them with a curt gesture.

Alvaro, conscious of his mastery, remained on the defensive, deliberately making his opponent look like a fool. But when Enrique's lunges became desperate, he knew the time had come for him to change his tactics. A duellist who was aware that he was losing sometimes behaved recklessly—Enrique was now so angry that he would take any risk in order to kill his opponent.

Shifting his stance slightly, Alvaro struck, and inflicted a long, deep cut in the flesh of the prince's left cheek. Before Enrique could react, the boy's blade flicked again, and a second gash appeared on the prince's face. He would bear the scar in the shape of an "x" for the rest of his days.

"Let all who mention the name of Magdalena Ruminez in my presence speak of her with respect," Alvaro said loudly. He bent down and pulled on his boots.

The stunned Enrique's sword fell from his hand to the cobblestones with a clatter.

Alvaro, still stooping, scooped it up, along with his hat and doublet. "I'll keep this blade as a souvenir," he said lightly.

Simultaneously everyone in the courtyard started talking and shouting. Ladies and gentlemen forgot their breeding and began to shove each other in an attempt to reach the center of the arena. Alvaro was almost swept off his feet. Suddenly both of his arms were seized. He struggled to break free, then realized that the young lady who had befriended him was on his left, and that another girl, whose features he half-recognized, was on his right.

Exhilarated after his victory, he allowed himself to imagine that he had pictured her in his daydreams. Certainly he had never seen anyone so radiant, so lovely. In spite of her immaturity, she possessed a beauty that went much deeper than the perfection of her features, the budding, fresh excitement of her figure, the regality of her posture. She was little more than a child, yet she seemed already wise; the situation was tense, but she remained serene in spite of the turmoil around her.

Unlike her friend, who was enjoying the excitement of the occasion, she seemed to be concerned about nothing except Alvaro's immediate plight. Their eyes met briefly, and when she looked away, he felt cold, then hot. He had always hoped that some day a member of the opposite sex would understand him immediately, instinctively. Now this unknown young noblewoman had managed to establish a complete rapport with him.

Oddly, he felt he knew her, too. It was apparent that she was proud but lonely, more afraid of her own emotions than of offending others; and obviously she was capable of great daring when the occasion demanded. Allowing himself to be guided through the milling crowd, Alvero told himself firmly that he was giving in to a dangerously romantic notion; it was true enough that the young lady who fascinated him was taking a risk for his sake, but it was nonsense to

credit a total stranger with attributes of perfection. It was
enough to know that, for whatever her reasons, she and her
companion were helping him. Forcing himself to concentrate
on what was real, he continued to grasp the hilt of the sword
he had captured, ready to use it again instantly.

"Trust Her Highness and me," the French-speaking young
lady said.

He looked again at the tall, aristocratic girl of about four-
teen on his right, and suddenly remembered having seen her
portrait in Avignon. She was the Infanta Catalina, King
Juan's older sister.

"I wish you had killed Enrique," the princess murmured.
"Mama thinks he's amusing, but ever since he learned that
Uncle Ferdinand has been offered the crown of Aragon, he's
become impossible. He abuses everyone. Until you stood up
to him, no one dared to oppose him."

The other girl was guiding them toward a side gate, where
two sentries in armor were on guard. It was quieter there,
and dark, but the men recognized Catalina and, standing
stiffly at attention, raised their lances in a formal salute.

"Hide somewhere in the city," the princess whispered.
"They'll send troops to search for you, and you'll be sentenced to death if you're caught." She reached into a leather
pouch hanging from her velvet girdle.

Alvaro saw a gleam of metal, realized she was trying to give
him a gold *dolar* and drew back, but she pressed the coin into
his hand.

The black-haired girl who had first befriended him leaned
toward Alvaro impulsively, and her lips brushed his cheek.
"Go with God," she said.

One of the sentries grinned and the other winked broadly
as the slender youth slipped through the partly open gate.
Obviously they had heard of his victory and felt under no obligation to serve the interests of Don Enrique. The sudden
panic that assailed Alvaro subsided when it occurred to him

that he and the guards understood each other. Like him, they were commoners, and like him, they secretly hated the haughty grandees who lived in luxury, supporting themselves by imposing crushing taxes on the poor. If the men who were sent to hunt for him shared the same sentiments, there was at least a slim chance that he might escape.

Sprinting down the high hill on which the Alcazar was perched, Alvaro knew his judgment of the aristocracy had been unfair. The Infanta Catalina was the second lady of the realm, the daughter of a king and the sister of a king, yet she had helped him. And her companion was necessarily of noble birth, too. It was wrong to damn the entire upper class. He recalled a saying he had heard as a child: "One rancid lemon does not prove that all fruit on the tree is sour."

Instinct rather than memory guided Alvaro when he reached the narrow, dark streets of the crowded city. It would be extremely dangerous to take lodgings at an inn, he knew, for the story of his duel would be common knowledge by morning. He felt certain that a reward would be offered for his capture, and tavern-keepers were notoriously venal.

He darted through one narrow lane, made his way down another and, after passing the deserted bazaar, entered the one district of Toledo he could never forget. Garbage littered the streets; houses were flimsy and were built close together; there were deep holes in the cobblestones underfoot. He slowed his pace lest he stumble, but continued to walk rapidly until he reached a square he remembered vividly. A small church stood on one side. Facing it was a synagogue and on the far side was a mosque, its minarets shrouded. Pausing for a moment, Alvaro smiled, then hurried past the mosque. He took a short cut through an alley that seemed even narrower than he remembered it, and at last emerged onto a street lined with high stone buildings. Here Castilians, Jews and Moors lived peacefully as neighbors; here talented artists copied and illuminated books, and skilled craftsmen transformed strips of leather into superbly tooled belts, gloves and boots. Every man was accepted or rejected here solely on the basis of his abilities.

Seven or eight small boys, all of them armed with sharp, pointed sticks, appeared suddenly from the shadows of a house. They crept toward Alvaro to encircle him. Apparently nothing had changed in the *Mozarab* quarter in ten years, and he understood the children's intentions even better than they did. "It is truly magnificent," he said in the vernacular of the district, grinning broadly. "Never have I seen such valiant young fighters." Brandishing Enrique's sword and drawing his own, he cut the air above the boys' heads. The blades whistled ominously, and the startled children paused.

Alvaro sighed and pretended to groan as he stabbed at an imaginary foe. "I suffer from rheumatism," he declared solemnly. "But I will try to defend myself if any valiant ones lay their hands on my aged body."

The boys scattered, dropping their sticks, and he chuckled; the years seemed to fall away, and he felt as though it had been only last night that he had been a member of such a band. Sheathing his sword but still gripping Enrique's, he briskly resumed his walk, and at last knew his destination. He walked to the end of the street, turned a corner onto another and halted abruptly.

A four-story house with a badly tarnished metal door loomed up in the dark. He could see that the small garden in front of the building had not been tended in years, the wooden stoop had rotted and some of the shutters were broken. He hesitated for an instant, taking a deep breath, then leaped over the stoop and raised the latch. The rusty hinges creaked. A small animal scurried away as he walked into the empty, damp house, but he paid no attention to it. He made his way through the small entrance hall and climbed the stairs.

His mother's sitting room and bedchamber had been located on the second floor, and he tried to avert his eyes when he reached the landing, but the temptation was too strong. He paused to stare at what had once been the center of his world, a place he had loved and hated. A broken blind flapped aimlessly. As Alvaro's eyes became accustomed to the gloom, he finally saw the rooms more clearly, now stripped of their furnishings. It was difficult to believe that he had been born here, that he had spent the first six years of his life in this place. His mother's personal suite had been a privileged sanctum to which he had been admitted only on special occasions, but he remembered every detail of the sitting room—the satin-covered divans, the tables inlaid with mosaics, the thick, tasseled drapes that had felt so rich and smooth when stroked surreptitiously. He could almost smell the strong scent his mother had worn, a perfume that had seeped into every corner of the suite. Then he remembered the enormous canopied bed that had dominated the inner chamber, and he turned back to the staircase furiously.

Scarcely aware of what he was doing, he ran to the top floor. Gasping for breath, he swept a spider's web away as he groped for the latch. He opened the door and walked into the tiny cell in which he himself had slept. The oiled paper that had covered the window was gone, and a cold breeze blew through the chamber. He looked around the room slowly and, feeling very tired, sat down on a broken crate that stood in a corner. Laying Enrique's sword across his knees, he cursed himself for his weakness. He would not be feeling so desolate if he hadn't paused to look at his mother's private suite, he thought, but he knew better. Nothing could erase the memory of his final visit to her sitting room from his mind; he would remember every word that had been spoken, every gesture, every nuance, as long as he lived . . .

. . . Alvaro, six years old, opened the back door of the house carefully. He hid his pointed stick under some dusting rags in a linen cupboard, then climbed the servants' staircase to the top floor. He heard voices in his mother's sitting room, and he cringed when a man's hearty laugh echoed through the house, but he continued to creep silently toward his own chamber. He would be punished if either of the serving maids caught him, as he was forbidden to go out after nightfall, but experience had made him crafty, and he reached the last landing without difficulty.

"There you are!" The old woman who donned the black lace of a duenna when she accompanied his mother on public outings, stood before his door, grim-faced.

Alvaro tried to duck back down the stairs, but the woman caught him and held him firmly. "Stop struggling or I'll whip you. Doña Magdalena has been waiting all evening to see you."

The boy's inevitable annoyance at hearing his mother mentioned as "doña," a term reserved for ladies of the nobility, was tempered by his surprise. He was never summoned to the apartment on the second floor after sundown, and on the few occasions that he had gone to the suite when his mother had been entertaining a man, he had been punished severely.

"You look frightful," the old woman said angrily, half-dragging, half-carrying him down the stairs. "Your clothes are torn and you look as though you'd been rolling in mud."

Alvaro had already learned the value of silence. He would receive a worse beating if he admitted that he and some of his friends had been fighting a band from the opposite side of the *Mozarab* district. He said nothing.

The old woman tapped on the gilded sitting-room door, opened it and announced, "He's here."

Alvaro was shoved into the room with such force that he sprawled on his mother's favorite rug, a splendid gift that one of her admirers had brought her from Byzantium.

Magdalena Ruminez astonished her son by laughing lightly, musically.

The child pulled himself to his feet and glanced obliquely at his mother. She was reclining on her white divan, propped on a mound of silken pillows. She was wearing one of the audaciously low-cut gowns for which she was notorious. Gems glittered on her arms and a huge diamond comb sparkled in her dark red hair. She held out a hand in a gesture as sweet as it was graceful, and when Alvaro approached her tentatively, ready to bolt if she tried to slap him, her perfume was deliciously subtle.

"You've been very naughty, dear. Mama was so worried about you." A tiny frown line appeared between her eyes for an instant, then vanished, and she looked serenely beautiful again.

A deep laugh from the opposite side of the room made it unnecessary for the boy to reply. A spendid gentleman in pale satin, wearing the broad ribbon of the Military Order of Santiago across his chest, was seated on a mahogany chair, sipping a mug of Magdalena's famous spiced wine. "You've been fighting, boy, by the looks of you."

Alvaro studied the man carefully, saw a twinkle of amusement in his eyes and decided not to dissemble. "Yes, sir. And we won."

The man slapped his leg and laughed loudly. "Always fight to win, boy."

"I do."

Plainly bored, Magdalena shifted her weight a trifle. "Don Juan de Olio has come here to see you, child. He's been waiting for more than an hour."

It was inconceivable to Alvaro that any member of the nobility should seek him, and his eyelids lowered suspiciously. Wise as only a boy of the *Mozarab* streets could be wise, he knew why the great men of Castile came to the house; there was no need for his mother or her lovers to dissemble in his presence. "Now that you've seen me," he said stiffly, "I'll go."

"Not so fast, arrogant one." The man extended a long leg to block Alvaro's exit.

Swallowing hard, the child halted.

"Now, then. Do you know your name, boy?"

"Of course," was the contemptuous reply. "I'm Alvaro."

"Alvaro? Have you no surname?"

Magdalena's huge blue eyes widened, and the droop of her shoulders suggested that she was hurt.

Her son said nothing.

"Your father," de Olio declared, speaking slowly, "served in my regiment in our last war against Granada."

The boy felt numb. "You know my father?" he asked incredulously. He glanced obliquely at Magdalena, whose face had become a lovely mask.

"I've spent many hours with him discussing you."

A sudden rush of blood to Alvaro's head made him feel giddy.

"By the merest chance I saw you with your charming mother on the day we rode off to war. You stood in the crowd, cheering. Your resemblance to your father was so marked that I noticed you immediately."

Alvaro dug his dirty, broken fingernails into the palms of his hands. A boy disgraced himself if he wept.

"I've persuaded him to acknowledge his paternity," de Olio continued. When he saw that the child didn't understand, he reached into a pocket and drew out a parchment bearing an imposing red seal. "This is an official paper that says you're his son."

Magdalena reached for the document languidly.

De Olio's smile faded. "You've seen it, my dear. I'm taking it to the royal archives, where it will be placed on file. Boy, from this day forward, you are entitled to call yourself Alvaro de Luna."

The child's lower lip trembled. "When will I meet my father, sir?"

It became imperative for de Olio to blow his nose. He stared out of the window and took his time stuffing his fine linen handkerchief into his cuff. "I'm afraid that Don Alvaro's duties at court occupy all of his time. He's a conscientious servant of the crown, and has no personal life."

Alvaro blinked away scalding tears and made an effort to stand erect.

"However, I've persuaded—that is to say, he has volunteered to make you a financial contribution that will give you a start in life." The nobleman fumbled with the strings of a purse that was tied to his belt, and handed the pouch to the child. "He has given you two hundred gold *dolars,* a handsome gift."

The purse was surprisingly heavy. Suddenly it was snatched from Alvaro's hands, and Magdalena, swinging it with careless charm, returned to the divan. "Congratulations, my friend," she said to de Olio. "I tried for three years, but he wouldn't give me a copper for the boy." She sounded almost pathetically grateful, and smiled gently. "I hope you'll stay for a bite of supper with me, Juan, so that I can express my gratitude to you."

The man's voice was hard. "That money," he said, "was given to me for your son."

"As his mother, I should take charge of it for him." Magdalena continued to smile.

De Olio sighed and turned back to the child. "The thought occurred to me that you wouldn't be permitted to keep the money—"

"Oh, I don't want it myself," Alvaro interrupted, knowing that if he failed to protest vigorously, his mother would take him to task later. "Mama will take good care of it for me."

"I have no doubt she will," the nobleman replied dryly. "Come here, boy."

"Yes, sir?"

"Your father isn't your only relative. There's another who shows great interest in you. Have you ever heard of someone named Pedro de Luna?"

Alvaro shook his head, but was startled when he saw his mother sit upright, lower her head as she did in church and cross herself.

"Once he was a famous professor of law, and then he became Archbishop of Toledo," de Olio said patiently. "Now he's in Avignon, a city in France, and is known as Pope Benedict XIII. Many nations, Castile among them, recognize him as Pope, although some do not. It is our hope that the cardinals at Rome will make their peace with him and accept him as the Holy Father of all."

Stunned, Alvaro found it difficult to catch his breath. "The Pope is my uncle?"

"Yes, boy, and as you are Don Alvaro's only child, His Holiness has agreed to raise you at his court, if your mother is willing. You'll receive the finest education on earth there, boy, but you'll work all day, every day. You'll have to make up your own mind."

"He'll go," Magdalena said brusquely.

The bewildered child nodded.

De Olio stood and looked sternly at the woman.

Alvaro, who had always seen admiration in men's eyes when they had gazed at his mother, became even more confused.

"He'll need suitable clothes and a proper escort. The journey through Aragon and Navarre is long." The nobleman's smile was tight. "You'll have to spend some of those gold *dolars* after all."

Magdalena became petulant. "If His Holiness wants to educate his nephew, the very least he could do would be to send a purse to cover traveling expenses and a wardrobe."

Controlling his temper, de Olio made no direct reply. He

patted the child's head. "Bless you, boy. May you become wise and strong." He took his hat and cape from a chair, bowed distantly and departed.

Magdalena, forgetting her son's presence, lay back on the cushions. She threw the purse into the air and caught it with one hand. Then she held it close to her ear, rattled the coins and sighed quietly, with deep satisfaction.

Alvaro crept out of the room and ran up the stairs to his own chamber and stood inside the door, shivering. The sudden change in his fortune dazzled him, but at the same time he was reluctant to leave the only home he had ever known. Even more important, he realized dimly that he had always nourished the hope that some day he would win his mother's affection. Now, he knew, there would never be an opportunity for her to learn to love him . . .

. . . The adolescent Alvaro sat on the upturned crate, shivering. Not until he saw the light of a single candle burning in a small lantern and caught a glimpse of a shadowy figure on the threshold did he realize that someone had disturbed his privacy. He snatched up Enrique's sword and leaped to his feet.

"Peace to you." The voice was that of a young man, and when he came into the room, Alvaro saw that he was wearing the biretta and robe of a priest.

The sword wavered uncertainly.

"You don't know me, it seems." The priest started to cross the room.

"Don't come any closer, Father!"

Ignoring the warning, the latter smiled gently. "I knew I'd find you here."

"If you're one of Enrique's spies—"

"Be quiet. You forget the shutters are broken. Do you want to awaken the neighborhood?" The priest halted and, raising the lantern, held it near his own face. "Look at me closely."

Alvaro, still gripping the sword, studied him intently. "You're a stranger to me."

"It was too much to hope that you'd recognize me. We shared this room until the seminary accepted me as a novice. You were three at the time, as I recall."

Stunned, Alvaro forgot to maintain his guard.

"I was in the throne room at the Alcazar this afternoon when that depraved woman tried to mock your manhood. And I saw the duel, of course." The priest's smile became bitter. "You don't know how fortunate you are, Alvaro. Magdalena Ruminez was the most notorious strumpet in Castile. Ever since the archbishop sent me to the court as the child king's confessor, I've heard her reviled and abused and ridiculed." He touched a silver crucifix that hung on a chain around his neck. "A man who wears this symbol can't challenge princes—or even lascivious minor grandees—to duels."

"Who are you?" Alvaro asked hoarsely.

"You're more fortunate than I in more ways than one. Mother never told me my father's identity. I suppose she really didn't know which of her lovers sired me . . . I call myself Francisco Ruminez."

Alvaro embraced his half-brother fiercely. Then, overcome by emotion, he began to weep.

"I know how you feel," Francisco told him, patting his head. "You've walked a lonely road."

Alvaro wiped his eyes savagely on the back of his sleeve. "You must hate her, too," he whispered.

The priest shook his head. "I hate no one, and I pray for the salvation of her soul. She didn't know she was wicked. She was born in the heart of *Mozarab* Toledo, and she was so beautiful that men took advantage of her when she was very young. She knew no other life, and she was greedy because she had to fight and scheme for every copper she ever earned."

Ashamed of himself, Alvaro kicked one boot with the other. "I love her," he said defiantly.

"Of course, just as I do. But we'll have to talk about her another time. A regiment of foot soldiers and two troops of cavalry are scouring the city for you. There's a price of four *dolars* on your head, you know."

The youth drew himself up proudly. "I'm worth more! Don Enrique will be scarred for the rest of his life!"

The priest laughed heartily. "The name they're calling you seems accurate. You've become known as 'the little panther.' "

"I haven't finished growing," Alvaro retorted.

"His Holiness of Avignon must be a very patient man, a saint. Perhaps if I write to him, he'll tell me how he learned to tolerate your belligerence."

"I'm sorry," Alvaro said quickly, and felt his face grow hot.

Francisco placed his lantern on the crate and stared at his half-brother curiously. "I've just told you that more than one thousand soldiers are searching for you, but you show no fear. Aren't you afraid?"

"Certainly not! They won't capture me alive, and I'll teach them swordsmanship before they kill me, I promise you."

"I've made other plans for you," the priest said calmly. "You've already given Toledo a demonstration of your skill as a duellist, thank you, and you've created more than enough problems for me this evening. Had you fought Don Alfonso, there would be nothing I could do for you—Aragon would have declared war on Castile if the future heir to her throne had been attacked. Luckily for you, Enrique and his other brothers are thoroughly unpopular. The monsignor at the church of Santa Margarita will make certain that the troops who come into this district aren't too diligent, and at daybreak, when the city gates are opened, you'll leave Toledo."

"No matter how much the soldiers may sympathize with

me, the officers are loyal to the royal family," Alvaro protested. "I'll be arrested at the city gate."

"Even though I'm your brother," Francisco said, "I'm not totally mad. You'll go in disguise, of course, dressed as a priest and riding a donkey. All of the arrangements have been made. One of my colleagues is waiting downstairs with the habit. Had your crime been a minor one, it might have been possible for you to remain here, on your own property, but you've made too many enemies in high places."

The boy had heard only one phrase. "My own property?"

"When our mother died, she left this house jointly to you and to me. I pay the taxes to the royal collectors each year, but I can't afford to have repairs made. Weren't you surprised to find it empty when you came here?"

Alvaro flushed and stared in embarrassment at the dirty floor. He had been so proud of his cleverness and skill that he couldn't admit the thought hadn't crossed his mind that someone else might be occupying the only home he had ever known. Forcing himself to forget his shame, he straightened; he was a property owner, and for a moment he felt important. Then he became conscious of the dilapidated state of the house, and smiled bitterly. "So this," he said dramatically, gesturing toward the open window, "is my heritage."

"Part of it, yes." Francisco's fingertips touched the cross that rested against his chest. "In time, I hope, you'll learn that Magdalena Ruminez left you more than a shell of a building. When you've learned to forgive her," he continued, speaking more to himself than to the boy, "you'll inherit her natural courage, perhaps, and her inner dignity that no man could destroy. You may even laugh at adversity, as she did, and hold your head high when the whole world despises you." He broke off abruptly, aware that his words were wasted. "We'll speak of her again, if you wish, when you're older. Right now you must leave Toledo and go into hiding."

Alvaro gestured impatiently. "You're very kind, and I'm

grateful for the risks you're taking. But escape is useless. There's no place I can hide."

The priest shook his head. "Although you seem to possess a talent for creating disturbances, you have more friends than you know. The Holy Father has corresponded with the Archbishop of Toledo about you, and all of the Castilian cardinals are interested in you. You'll be protected and given the chance to complete your education. The Pope says you show great promise . . . The grandees grow wealthier every year, the poor cry for help, and there is none. Castile needs someone who has your ability and courage, provided you learn self-discipline."

"I have no wish to become a clergyman."

"That possibility didn't occur to anyone." Francisco smiled faintly. "Nevertheless you'll be trained by the fathers of the Sanctuary of Santo Domingo."

"You're sending me to Madrid?" Alvaro asked in dismay.

"I'll admit it's a dreary place, but no one would think of searching for you in an unimportant provincial town. And Santo Domingo is the most unusual retreat in the world. Some of the priests there are philosophers, others are former members of the royal council, and you'll even find a few who can teach you a few tricks in riding and swordsmanship and jousting."

"How long must I stay there?"

"It's strange," Francisco said, "how much you resemble our mother when you show impatience." He paused, then added firmly, "You'll remain until the sons of Don Ferdinand have forgotten you, and until the abbot of San Domingo believes you're prepared to serve our people."

2

The mountains of the Sierra Guadarama range were a tantalizing mirage. Alvaro, who had now spent two years in Madrid, knew better than to stare toward the north at the cool, green slopes and snow-capped peaks. Madrid was reality, and the town was hot and dry and drab. Clouds of brown dust rose from the ground in the huge outer yard of the Sanctuary of Santo Domingo, coating the stunted pines and the drooping olive trees that stood outside the limestone wall of the retreat. The dust choked Alvaro, making it difficult for him to swallow or inhale, and he looked enviously at the priests in their long black robes, drinking watered wine from goatskin sacks.

He felt a surge of resentment, stifled it and tried to ease the weight of his heavy armor by planting his feet apart. Father Ramiro, the abbot, kept a short donkey whip beside his desk and didn't hesitate to use it when one of the youths who were being given shelter and training at the Sanctuary complained. Those who were wise held their tongues. Alvaro told himself, as he did many times each day, that he was fortunate, that nowhere else on earth could he learn so much. At the same time he realized that nowhere else would he be compelled to work so hard, but he pushed the disloyal thought out of his head, removed a heavy gauntlet of chain metal from his left hand and wiped the sweat from his forehead. Natives of Madrid claimed it was so dry in the town that no one ever perspired, but their boast didn't apply to hot-blooded southerners.

"Look at Father Sebastian." Roderigo Pinar, a burly young man of nineteen, leaned toward Alvaro, his armor creaking. "He must have been a great general before he retired from the world, eh?"

Alvaro watched the tall, grey-haired priest, clad in shining plate armor, who was riding slowly across the yard, the padded tip of his lance held before him, the shaft perfectly balanced. Students at Santo Domingo were forbidden to speculate on the fathers' past life, and Alvaro shrugged. "I was sent out into the fields to gather hay at dawn this morning.

I've had a class in the principles of taxation from Father Ramiro and another in diplomacy from Father Fidelio. One of us is going to win the prize in the jousts this afternoon, and I'm too tired to wonder who Father Sebastian may have been before he came here. I'd rather conserve my strength."

Grinning, Roderigo swung his visored helmet idly in his right hand. "Myself, I'd rather have a drink of that wine than a silver hilt for my knife."

Alvaro sighed quietly and shook his head. He liked Roderigo, but the older boy's inability to grasp essentials, to understand what was important and what was not, sometimes exasperated him. "If you drink anything before a tournament, you'll be sick. Anyway, the hilt is solid silver. It must be worth at least three *dolars.*"

He broke off abruptly as Father Sebastian pointed his lance at a youth on the far side of the yard, and he watched, completely absorbed, as the young man was helped onto the broad back of a horse, took his place at one end of the field and then rode rapidly toward the center of the arena to meet the iron-clad priest, who approached from the opposite direction. The combat ended almost before it started; the young man lost his padded lance, his balance and his dignity. He lay helplessly on his back in the dust, his heavy armor immobilizing him, until two novices helped him to his feet.

Roderigo laughed coarsely.

"Too fast," Alvaro muttered. "He should have approached more slowly."

Father Sebastian, cool and unperturbed, raised his visor and spoke in a loud voice for the benefit of the eight young men in armor who awaited their turns. "Diego forgot that one takes the measure of one's opponent carefully," he said in a deep, resonant voice. "Walk your mount, and when you are four lance-lengths from your foe, trot. But canter only when you are very sure of yourself. You don't want your necks broken in battle—remember what I say to you." He lowered his voice and his tone was sympathetic as he glanced at the youth whom he had unseated. "You're entitled to a second chance if you wish, Diego."

The young man, who had removed his helmet, smiled ruefully. "Thank you, Father, but I need more practice before I face you again."

Father Sebastian's lance was suddenly pointed at Roderigo. "Pinar! You were amused when Diego fell. We shall put your sense of humor to the test."

Roderigo pulled his helmet over his head and walked out onto the field, unable to conceal his reluctance. Alvaro knew how he felt. It had been wrong to laugh, and Father Sebastian was a strict taskmaster. Alvaro braced himself and, as he waited for the inevitable, couldn't help wishing he were as tall and broad-shouldered as Roderigo. At least it was a relief to know that he was endowed with more common sense. Perhaps he shouldn't judge his friend too harshly, though, for Roderigo de Pinar the elder had incurred the enmity of Queen Catherine, and as a consequence had lost his life and estates. It was understandable that his son, who had been given refuge at Santo Domingo, should have adopted an air of reckless indifference. However, it was remarkable that he had remained so obdurate, for he had been disciplined repeatedly and obviously was going to be taught still another lesson.

Alvaro caught a glimpse of Father Sebastian's lined face, thin lips and coldly detached expression and, even though the sun was shining in a cloudless, pale-blue Castilian sky, he shivered. He watched Roderigo being hoisted into the saddle by several novices, but he closed his eyes as someone handed the brash young man a padded lance. Hoofbeats sounded on the hard ground, then there was a heavy thud and Alvaro forced himself to look at the still body of the youthful gladiator.

Father Ramiro, who stood apart from the other priests,

fingered the dark-red sash that identified him as a senior abbot. "Remove Pinar to his cell," he said in a voice as dry and bleak as the cracked earth. "When he recovers consciousness, let him work in the stables grooming horses until sundown. Also he has been deficient in his studies of finance and Latin—he will be given a special examination on both subjects at daybreak tomorrow."

No one spoke as Roderigo was carried past the chapel to the building that housed the refectory and the students' quarters. Father Sebastian, showing no emotion, pointed his lance at another armor-clad figure, and the practice tournament continued.

Alvaro was the last to be called, and he wondered whether he was being rebuked subtly because he had demonstrated an eagerness to demonstrate his skill. Perhaps, he thought, one of the fathers had heard him confide to his comrades over bread and cheese at noon that he believed he had acquired sufficient experience to hold his seat in any competition. His confidence vanished as he adjusted his visor, and when two novices had helped him mount a sturdy grey gelding he looked through a slit in the steel mask at Father Sebastian and his heart sank.

The warrior-priest was a menacing figure in his silver armor, and Alvaro knew he had been foolish to talk so freely. He had won competitions in duelling, philosophy and mathematics within the past month, but he certainly knew that no one had ever knocked Father Sebastian to the ground in a tournament. The defeated young gladiators were watching him, grinning broadly, but he paid no attention to them. Accepting a heavy, padded lance, he concentrated his full attention on his foe.

Father Sebastian raised his left hand in a signal, and both horses started simultaneously toward the center of the arena. Alvaro, riding easily, maintained a slow pace until the last possible moment, then urged his mount to a trot and, raising his lance, first feinted at his opponent's head, then dropped the heavy ramrod a few inches and aimed it at the priest's chest. Before he could complete the maneuver, however, a savage thrust caught him in the diaphragm, lifted him into the air and sent him sprawling.

He landed on his back, swallowing dust, so giddy that for a horrible moment he was afraid he would lose consciousness. Several of the spectators laughed quietly. But Alvaro's pride was greater than his misery, and he sat upright, struggled for breath and jerked up his visor.

Father Sebastian was gazing down at him, wooden-faced. "It would appear, de Luna," the priest said calmly, "that you forgot this was a jousting match, not a duel. What is the first rule of the joust?"

Still gasping, Alvaro waved away the novices who were coming across the field to help him and, having painfully hoisted himself to his feet, limped closer to the powerful stallion. "You've taught me, Father, that I must never feint. 'Don't strike until you're ready, then hit hard and true.' That's what you've taught me."

"I wonder," Father Sebastian said softly, "whether I've been wasting my time. It would seem that you're another of these fair-weather gallants."

Stung, Alvaro clenched his fists so hard that the chain mail of his gloves dug into his flesh. "I swear to you that I'm not!"

"Like the others, you're entitled to your second chance." The priest sounded indifferent.

"I accept with pleasure!"

Father Sebastian and the abbot exchanged a long, significant glance, and finally Father Ramiro nodded. Priests, novices, students—everyone started speaking simultaneously, but Father Sebastian merely smiled coolly. "Would you care to take the final step, de Luna? You won't be granted knighthood while the English queen is regent, but you can try to qualify for your spurs."

Alvaro's heart pounded against his rib cage, and for a moment he was too startled to reply.

"Are you afraid, boy?"

Recovering his poise, Alvaro stared up into the man's steady grey eyes. "No, Father."

"Very well." Father Sebastian raised his voice. "Take away that gelding and bring de Luna a stallion. You, there. Go to the armory and bring two lances with steel tips and two combat shields."

Word of the test spread quickly through the monastery, and twenty or more priests who had been engaged in various activities hurried out to the yard. Someone led a strong white stallion onto the field, and a young priest who assisted Father Sebastian in teaching swordsmanship inspected Alvaro's armor, helmet and gloves carefully. Diego, the student who had lost the first match of the afternoon, dropped to his hands and knees so that Alvaro could stand on his back while mounting, and two other students helped him into the saddle. The young priest carefully adjusted the stirrups for Alvaro's short legs, took a circular shield emblazoned with a golden cross and fastened it on Alvaro's left forearm.

"Remember, de Luna, hold your shield high. You aren't tall enough or heavy enough to carry a long one. You'll have to make your final judgment quickly, and when you raise your shield into position, keep it there."

Alvaro nodded.

"Test this lance."

The shaft was perfectly balanced, and the steel tip gleamed in the bright sunlight.

"May God watch over you and protect you from harm." The young priest gathered his robes around him and walked to the shade of the patio at the far end of the yard.

Alvaro pulled his visor over his face, raised and lowered his left arm several times in order to accustom himself to the weight of the shield and, turning slowly, grasped the lance tightly, letting it rest on the metal webbing between the thumb and forefinger of his right glove.

Father Sebastian, who had been waiting patiently, looked formidable behind a rectangular shield bearing an impressive crest. He had lowered his visor, too, and his lance was pointed at his opponent; his mount, sensing the growing tension, was pawing the ground, and the armor plates on the horse's head rattled as the animal waited for the signal to advance.

A cold stream of perspiration ran down Alvaro's spine. At the last moment he remembered to wind his stallion's reins three times around his left hand.

"Are you ready, de Luna?" Father Sebastian's voice sounded remote and muffled behind his thick visor.

"Ready, Father."

There was a long pause; then suddenly the priest lifted his shield. His horse started to advance, and Alvaro moved forward, too. The stallions walked toward each other across the parched field, their gait steady, their bearing sedate. They began to move at a slightly faster pace, and Alvaro, inhaling deeply, tried to remember all that he had been taught. His lance would take care of itself until he needed it, provided that he continued to hold it parallel to the ground. He sat upright in his saddle but let his horse carry his full weight, and he kept his left arm close to his body so that he could shift the position of his shield at the last possible instant.

He stared fixedly at the lance that could, even in a trial, take a man's life; and knowing that Father Sebastian showed no mercy in battle, he braced himself for the shock of physical contact. Although the maneuver was one that he had practised many times, Alvaro discovered that there was a vast difference between rehearsal and real combat, and for an instant he wondered if he had been rash to accept the challenge. But it was too late now to decide that he should have waited another six months, another year. Putting all thoughts and fears out of his mind, he continued to ride toward his foe.

The two horses started to trot simultaneously. Alvaro, studying the long lance aimed at him, concluded that his opponent would try to strike him on the chest. In the last moment available to him, therefore, he lowered the shield a trifle, leaving his head exposed, and, as the lance jabbed at him, thrust his own weapon at the tall man confronting him.

Metal crashed against metal, wood splintered. Alvaro slipped, regained his balance and, as his stallion swept across the field, discovered that he had managed, miraculously, to keep his seat. He pulled his mount to a halt, turned and started back, then stopped abruptly when he saw that Father Sebastian carried only the stump of a lance and that there was a jagged hole in the left side of his helmet. Alvaro gripped his own lance so hard that his fingers throbbed, afraid for an instant that he had injured his instructor. But Father Sebastian raised the splintered end of his lance in salute, removed his visor and, beckoning several students, told them to help him to the ground. He walked slowly, stiff-legged in his heavy armor, across the yard toward the youth who had defeated him, and his eyes were bright as he said in a loud, triumphant voice, "Victor, you have beaten me in fair combat."

Eager hands lifted Alvaro to the ground and stripped away his armor; he pulled off his helmet, tugged at his gloves and, scarcely conscious of the dirt that had caked on his face and neck, embraced his instructor. "I thank the Almighty that you aren't hurt, Father," he said, his voice husky.

The priest laughed dryly. "I've survived many battles, de Luna, but I'll think carefully before I meet you in a real jousting match again. You've won your spurs, and when you're granted the right to be called Don Alvaro, I shall give

you the pair that I wore in three campaigns against the Moors
of Granada."

Tears filled Alvaro's eyes and he blinked them away angrily, ashamed of showing his feelings.

Father Sebastian patted him on the shoulder. "We'll prac-
tise together often. I'll recommend to the abbot that I give
you special instruction in military strategy and tactics. I've
hoped for a long time that you might become a great soldier.
Today you've begun to justify my faith in you."

A sense of pride almost overwhelmed Alvaro, but after two
years at the Sanctuary he knew what was expected of him.
He dropped silently to one knee. Father Sebastian placed a
hand on his bare head and prayed quietly in Latin; Alvaro,
eyes closed, remained motionless, trying unsuccessfully to
curb the elation that welled up in him. He knew he should
listen to the blessing, but it was impossible to think of anything except his moment of triumph.

When he stood again, he saw that the abbot had joined
Father Sebastian. Father Ramiro smiled broadly as he held
an engraved silver dagger hilt in the open palm of his left
hand. "No one will deny that you've won today's competition, de Luna," he said gently.

Alvaro accepted the prize and lowered his eyes respectfully.
"I'm grateful to you, Father."

"Be grateful to God, to whom all glory is due." The abbot
paused, and his tone was still serene as he added, "Only last
month I delivered a sermon on vanity. Do you remember my
quotation from the Book of Ecclesiastes, de Luna, the teaching that I used as my text?"

"No, Father." It was useless to lie.

"I was afraid of that." Father Ramiro smiled again, sadly.
"After your exploit of this afternoon, vanity will tempt you.
We must remove the serpent from your path. Take your
prize to your room, and then go to the south field. Father

Aldo needs someone young and healthy to spread manure in the vegetable patch before vespers."

The Puerte del Sol, the largest plaza in Madrid, was crowded with merchants and artisans, peasants and soldiers, walking arm-in-arm with women in starched, frilly white blouses and full, embroidered skirts. Wine vendors who had set up their carts on two sides of the square were doing a thriving business, carpenters were putting the finishing touches on a platform at the far end of the plaza, and a group of musicians, already surrounded by an eager throng, were testing their castanets and tuning their lutes. The town was beginning to celebrate its most important festival of the year, Carnival, which preceded Lent, and the Puerte del Sol was the magnet for most of the merry-makers.

Citizens who lived and worked in the buildings surrounding the square leaned out of windows, calling greetings to pretty girls, then quickly sobered when their wives appeared beside them. Young women, the majority of them accompanied by duennas in black, paraded circumspectly around the square, pretending to be unaware of the glances and comments they were trying so hard to attract. An elderly man selling sausages at a booth that almost blocked the road leading to the Portillo de Sol, one of the town's oldest bridges, was kept busy cutting chunks from a seemingly endless supply of his wares. A woman who looked enough like him to be his sister was roasting chestnuts over a charcoal brazier nearby.

Small boys ran through the crowd, members of the constabulary patrolled the plaza in pairs, keeping a sharp watch for cut-purses, and a squad of soldiers kept the east end of the square empty. Members of the nobility would come to watch the festivities for a time from the seclusion of their carriages before riding on to the large houses near the royal hunting lodge that had not been used for almost fifty years. The soldiers encountered no difficulties in keeping the area clear, for only a few nobles lived in Madrid, the most unfashionable town in Castile. The lords and ladies who would watch the celebration were themselves rustics, the owners of relatively small holdings, and there was little friction between them and the commoners. Most of the large estates belonged to absentee landlords, great princes and dukes who rarely bothered to visit such a dull, provincial town when they could relax in Toledo or Cordoba, Avila or Salamanca, Valladolid or Zamora, all of them centers of sophistication and culture.

It had been a custom for hundreds of years to grant a temporary amnesty to fugitives and criminals during Carnival. Schools and academies closed, and the abbot of Santo Domingo had given his students a night and a day to wander where they pleased, provided they did not leave Madrid. The Puerte del Sol was a natural magnet, and the young men, eagerly seeking relief after their gruelling months of unrelieved study, hurried to the center of the town in small groups. Alvaro, his somber black clothes brightened by the silver dagger hilt at his belt and a green feather in his hat, tried in vain to match the longer stride of Roderigo Pinar, who was magnificently attired in a brocaded suit, silk stockings and shoes with gold buckles.

Alvaro was conscious of his own drab appearance, but refused to let a sense of inferiority spoil his pleasure. In his purse he carried one *dolar* and eighty *centavos,* money he had earned on the Sanctuary farm, and he was determined to obtain the maximum enjoyment for each copper he spent. This was one evening when he didn't have to think about deploying battalions and bringing up siege guns in a theoretical battle, when he wasn't forced to struggle with long columns of figures or the intricate grammar of foreign languages; and when morning came he could sleep as late as he pleased instead of attending mass at dawn and then laboring in the fields.

Roderigo could not forget the monastery of Santo Domingo, however, and spoke of nothing else as the two youths made their way across the flat streets of the town to the Puerte del Sol. "I felt sure that Father Sebastian would come to Carnival, but I looked into his cell as we were leaving, and he was reading his Prayer Book."

"Why should he bother with Carnival?" Alvaro asked indifferently, turning to look at a band of amateur masked minstrels who were serenading a group of portly men and women gathered on the balcony of a large stone house.

"I'd scarcely call it a bother," Roderigo replied with unaccustomed stiffness. "Madrid may be the most backward place in Castile, but even a grandee who visits the royal court no more than once a year at the annual meeting of the *Cortes* would recognize the Father and invite him to a splendid dinner this evening."

Alvaro was amused. "Are you still trying to discover who Father Sebastian was before he came to Santo Domingo?"

"I know," Roderigo replied with satisfaction, lowering his voice. "I copied his handwriting one day, and when we were studying the rebellion in Leon that broke out ten years ago—"

"Eight."

"Very well, eight. What does it matter?"

"A great deal, in Leon."

"Stop distracting me, Alvaro. I saw some orders written by the commander-in-chief of the Castilian army, and the handwriting was identical. I've made copies of the field orders, too, and I can show them to you."

"Some day," Alvaro said with a laugh, "your talents as a forger are going to cause you great difficulty. Mark my words, you'll go to prison instead of winning back your family's estates. As to Father Sebastian, he's made peace with himself and with God. I don't intend to pry into his past."

"What a strange fellow you are," Roderigo pulled off his

hat and ran a large hand through his thick, black hair. "You aren't like the rest of us."

The charge was true, but it would be immodest to admit that he considered himself set apart from everyone else. Alvaro remained silent.

"I've watched you studying," Roderigo declared, necessarily raising his voice because of the noise as they drew nearer the plaza. "I'll swear that you actually enjoy it!"

"As a means to an end." Alvaro halted and looked at the crowds milling about happily in the Puerte del Sol. Their abandon was infectious, and he felt his own ever-present inner tension lessen.

"What end?" Roderigo demanded.

Alvaro had been unable to put his ambitious dreams into words, and had not revealed his hopes to anyone. Even Father Sebastian, who had become his confessor, was only vaguely aware of them, and he certainly didn't intend to confide in a verbose young former aristocrat. "At the moment," he said, grinning, "there's nothing I want more than a chunk of that sausage." He walked quickly to the vendor and paid three *centavos* for a large piece of the meat, which he speared on the end of his dagger. "Let me treat you to some, too, Roderigo."

"Your generosity overwhelms me." The tall youth shuddered. "There will be a smell of garlic on your breath for the next two days."

Alvaro bit into the sausage, thought it was delicious and raised his hat in a polite salute to the vendor. "What's wrong with garlic? Everyone here will smell of it before the night ends."

"I won't, and neither will they." Roderigo nodded in the direction of the occupants of two carriages that had moved into the space reserved for the nobility. He would have pursued the subject, but an attractive young woman accompanied by a duenna caught his attention. He eyed her speculatively and she, aware of his interest, swung her skirt frivolously but lowered her eyes. "There's a pretty one," he said with a deep sigh. "What a pity she belongs to the merchant class."

"What difference does it make?" Alvaro glanced casually at the girl, who was simpering, and decided instantly that she didn't appeal to him.

"A gentleman never permits himself to lower his standards, as you well know," Roderigo retorted. "One makes love to either a lady or a strumpet, but never to the daughter of a merchant or a peasant."

Alvaro stiffened. He had never mentioned his mother to the other students at the Sanctuary, and he always refrained from participating in their conversations when they discussed girls.

"You're odd, all right." Roderigo sounded puzzled, but suddenly he chuckled and jabbed his friend in the side with his elbow. "Maybe you don't care much about women, but there's one who is interested in you."

Looking up, Alvaro saw a girl of about his own age standing at the edge of the crowd. She wore a bright-red flower in her hair, her lips were heavily rouged and her long lashes were stiff with black paste. She was tiny but voluptuous, and her glance was bold. Alvaro felt his pulse quicken, but he thought of his mother and his fingertips became cold and numb.

"Not bad at all for a trollop," Roderigo said judiciously, winking at the girl, who ignored him and continued to stare at Alvaro. "She's making it plain enough that you can have her if you want her."

"I want a drink," Alvaro said curtly and, deliberately turning away, started toward the nearest wine cart.

Roderigo caught his shoulder. "You'll be sick if you touch that stuff. There's a fairly decent inn near the Puente de Segovia that serves an excellent wine. Their mead is as good as you'll find in Toledo or Barcelona. And their calavados," he continued, referring to the grape brandy that was the strongest drink in Castile, "is palatable. It wouldn't be served to a prince of the blood, but it won't choke you or bring tears to your eyes."

Alvaro made no attempt to hide his annoyance and, walking to the nearest cart, bought a cup of calavados for two *centavos*. The cup was made of the cheapest pewter and a long chain was looped through the handle. The other end was nailed to the cart. The chain rattled as Alvaro belligerently thrust the cup under his friend's nose. "What's wrong with this?"

Roderigo grimaced. "Some traveling players gave a performance at my father's castle when I was about eight, and I was fascinated by one man who ate firebrands. When I asked him how he did it, he told me that he had trained himself by drinking the calavados that's distilled for ordinary people."

Alvaro's blue eyes became cold. "I am an ordinary person," he said, and drained the contents of the cup in a single gulp. The dramatic effect was spoiled when he gasped and coughed, and Roderigo, laughing, pounded him on the back. Wrenching free, Alvaro glared at his companion.

"Your palate is more refined than you think, little rooster."

"My palate is that of the people." Alvaro's throat still felt raw, but he ignored the discomfort and, his indignation mounting, reached for his dagger.

His fellow students had learned to respect his temper, and Roderigo apologized quickly. "I meant no offense. If you choose to kill yourself by drinking the calavados of peasants and whores, that's your affair."

Alvaro's retort was drowned by a loud cheer, and the plaza seethed with excitement as hundreds of flares were lighted. The flames leaped toward the stars that were appearing in the sky, plumes of smoke drifted high over the rooftops, and suddenly the musicians on the platform nearby struck up a lively air. Scores of men and women climbed up onto the stage to dance. Others clustered around the base of the platform to watch them, and everyone in the audience seemed to be singing, stamping and clapping hands to the tune of the familiar song.

"You and I," Alvaro said, regaining his dignity with difficulty, "have no reason to fight, my friend. It is I who must apologize, not you. My eyes are open, but you're blinded by the sort of life you've always led."

"If I knew what you meant," Roderigo replied, laughing, "I'd probably become very angry."

"It doesn't matter." Alvaro shrugged and changed the subject. "What are your plans for the evening?"

Roderigo looked toward the carriages of the nobles. "I hope I'll see someone who was acquainted with my father in one of those coaches. Then the evening will take care of itself. The son of Don Roderigo de Pinar and his friend will be driven to a villa near the royal hunting lodge for a good dinner and fine wine. There may be a young lady or two with whom we can flirt—discreetly, of course—and then we'll be driven back to Santo Domingo in style."

The song the musicians were playing was one that Alvaro recalled from his childhood. He couldn't remember his mother singing it to him, yet he recalled the words. *Her eyes are black as darkest night, her bosom fair and white; swear to her that true you'll be, and her love you'll win tonight.*

"Your evening will be more pleasant if you go alone," Alvaro said, refraining from adding that he wouldn't enjoy a formal dinner.

"What will you do?"

The musicians increased their tempo, and Alvaro's left foot, encased in a worn leather boot, tapped on the cobblestones. "I like it here."

"You'll be safe?" Roderigo asked dubiously.

"Of course! Who would harm me? There are only Castilians in the plaza."

Roderigo continued to hesitate.

"No one is allowed to carry a sword tonight, and Father Ramiro has sworn that any of us who are arrested by the constables will spend the next six months working in the fields from dawn to dusk as a penance. I don't enjoy that kind of labor. Go, my friend. I see that several more carriages have arrived."

Torn between friendship and his own desire, Roderigo finally made his decision and moved off. Alvaro watched him as he sauntered past the line of coaches, paused beside the door of one and removed his hat. An elderly gentleman wearing a huge lace bib over a black velvet suit shook his hand enthusiastically, two old ladies in old-fashioned, dome-shaped mantillas engaged him in conversation and he climbed into the carriage. He had found his own kind and was happy.

Alvaro turned away and, feeling unexpectedly lonely, gave in to a sudden impulse and paid two *centavos* for another cup of calavados.

The brandy burned, but he felt strangely light-headed as he drifted closer to the platform to watch the dancing. It was not true, he thought, that he belonged in this world of coarse artisans, but neither did he feel at home with glib aristocrats. He had spent the better part of his life at the court of Pope Benedict and at the Sanctuary, but he had no desire to become a priest. His head was bursting with knowledge, but he had rejected the suggestion of several of his teachers that he become a professor. The cloistered existence behind high university walls was as sheltered as the career of a clergyman, and Alvaro reflected that to an extent, at least, he had told Rodcrigo the truth: he had no desire merely to observe the life of Castile. He wanted to take part in it.

The dance on the platform ended; some couples climbed down to refresh themselves at the wine carts and others took their places. The music began again, and Alvaro became aware of a commotion in his immediate vicinity. Without realizing it, he had edged close to the stage, and several men near him were shouting, gesticulating and pounding their chests as they tried to attract the attention of a young woman who stood alone above them, searching the throng for a suitable partner.

"Take me, señorita!" a soldier called. "I'm the best dancer in my regiment!"

"Choose me!" a thick-shouldered blacksmith in shirtsleeves and a leather apron shouted. "You won't regret it."

Alvaro recognized the girl who had flirted with him, and as their eyes met she deliberately removed the rose from her black hair and threw it to him. He was so surprised that he fumbled with the flower for a moment, almost dropping it; then, before he quite knew what was happening, several men had hoisted him onto the platform. Still clutching the rose, deeply embarrassed, he removed his hat with his free hand and bowed. The girl smiled as she curtsied, then stood and moved closer to him.

"Your manners are elegant," she said in a husky, challenging voice. "I hope you can also dance."

Stung, he returned her gaze steadily as he opened the top button of his doublet and thrust the stem of the flower into the buttonhole. "You've made your choice, señorita. You'll have to take your chances," he said and, giving her no chance to speak again, caught hold of her right hand, raised it above her head and twirled her around.

His strength surprised her, but she pirouetted gracefully, and, facing Alvaro again, placed her hands on her hips. He followed her example, and stamping their feet in time to the music, they moved in slow circles around each other, twisting away when the music became softer, swinging toward each other again when the song became more demanding. They continued to watch each other closely, and when Alvaro moved around the girl, stamping, their shoulders touched for an instant.

"I knew you'd dance with me," she murmured.

"You're very sure of yourself," he replied in the same bantering tone.

"Don't you think I have the right?"

"Yes, you're very beautiful."

"Then why did you snub me earlier this evening when I smiled at you?"

The intricate formalities of the dance required them to move apart, snap their fingers in time to the music and weave through a maze of other dancers, so that Alvaro thought he had been saved the necessity of replying. But when he and his partner met again at the far end of the platform and stood close together, with only a few inches separating their swaying bodies, the girl pouted.

"You haven't answered me."

"Perhaps I prefer not to discuss my reasons."

"You were ashamed because your companion was a gentleman. You didn't want him to see you talking to someone like me."

Alvaro twirled her around savagely. "I would be proud to present all of my friends to you," he said when they faced each other again. "I wouldn't be ashamed to take you to the court of King Juan."

His vehemence surprised the girl, but she said nothing as she clicked her high heels. The musicians were playing rapidly now. Many of the older dancers had discovered that the pace was too fast for them, and only fifteen couples remained on the platform. Alvaro danced furiously and the brunette, her long hair streaming down her back, kept step with him, advancing and retreating, moving first to one side and then the other. Their efforts inspired the musicians, and the rhythm became so wild that only their instincts enabled them to maintain the same tempo.

A sharp crash of cymbals ended the song, and Alvaro laughed breathlessly, triumphantly. The girl joined him, and after he had jumped to the ground, he reached up, placed his hands around her supple, tiny waist and lifted her down. Their faces were close together, her red lips were parted and tempting, and he leaned forward to kiss her, but stopped abruptly when he realized that the crowd was applauding them.

"We might earn a good living entertaining at the villas of the grandees," the girl said slyly.

Alvaro did not reply.

She took his arm. "I'm thirsty."

"Forgive my rudeness." He escorted her to a wine cart, and they drank cups of calavados, but were still parched and each took a long swallow from a goatskin sack of wine.

The girl introduced herself briefly: her name was Maria, she said, and she lived in the neighborhood. She felt no need to add any details.

Alvaro was even more terse. "I am a student and I am called Alvaro."

She studied him covertly. "You are a grandee?"

"No!" He realized he had shouted, but didn't care.

Maria continued to scrutinize him. "It is very odd. One moment you act like a great noble, and the next you might be one of those goatherds or butchers." They had drifted away from the crowd and stood near one of the houses at one side of the plaza. "Your clothes are those of a poor man, but only someone who is very wealthy carries his knife in such a lovely case." She reached out and ran her fingertips across the silver hilt.

"I won it," Alvaro said curtly.

"Why do you become so angry when I ask you about yourself?" The girl was hurt. "Most men like nothing better than to talk about themselves."

He drew in his breath. "I am not like most men."

"So I am learning." She hesitated for an instant. "Yet you would like to come with me?"

"Very much," he replied candidly.

Maria was relieved, shook her hair free and laughed. "First we must share another cup of calavados to cement our friendship."

They drank the brandy, and when the girl took Alvaro's arm he felt distinctly dizzy. He thought of his mother as Maria led him down a dark, narrow side street, but he forced himself to concentrate on the present. He could not permit the ghost of Magdalena Ruminez to haunt him all of his life.

The music in the Puerte del Sol sounded softly in the distance as the girl approached the stoop of a narrow building. An old woman with penetrating eyes and a thin mouth was sitting on the step, her arms folded tightly, and Maria whispered, "Pay her ten *centavos* and she'll leave us in peace."

Alvaro reached into his purse for a coin, and the woman extended a grimy hand, took the money silently and then folded her arms again. A sense of distaste enveloped Alvaro, but he ignored it and tried to shut out the image of the filthy staircase, the rotting boards and the unpainted walls as he followed Maria to the second floor.

Dawn was breaking as Alvaro left the house. The stairs creaked beneath his boots, but there was no other sound in the silent, sleeping building. Perhaps he was a coward to run away before Maria awoke, but he didn't want to face her. Too sleepy to analyze his own emotions, he knew only that he didn't belong in this place, that he had allowed himself to be drawn into a world that he hated. The musty, stale odors seemed to choke him.

He raced down the last flight, ashamed of himself but unable to control the desire to breathe the fresh air of early morning. Closing the front door behind him, he stood for a moment on the stoop, trembling, then told himself firmly that he was behaving like a child. Gradually his panic subsided, and he looked around slowly, realizing that the gay celebration had ended. Now the town was incredibly ugly. The street was deserted, and the cobblestones were littered with the refuse of Carnival, broken wine jugs, bits of ribbon and, in the gutter near a pile of garbage which a grey cat was sniffing cautiously, a flimsy, torn mask.

Alvaro couldn't remember the precise route that Maria had taken when she had brought him to her house, but he knew that the Puerte del Sol was off to his left, and he made his way there slowly through the strange neighborhood. The platform had not yet been dismantled, and a peasant was sprawled on one side of the stage, snoring. A dozen or more women were washing wine stains and sausage skins from the cobblestones, scrubbing vigorously with long-handled brushes and splashing water onto the street from thick wooden pails. Two soldiers leaned against a wall, eating bread and cheese. The sight of the food made Alvaro realize that he was hungry.

He approached the soldiers, who glanced at him indifferently. "Where will I find the nearest baker's shop?"

One of the men wiped his mouth with the back of his hand, jerked a thumb over his shoulder and stuffed a chunk of bread into his mouth.

"Thank you," Alvaro said courteously and, his appetite mounting, walked rapidly down the broad avenue. He saw the baker's sign, and, grinning happily, decided he would treat himself to some hot, spiced sausages as well as a loaf of fine-ground wheat bread.

Drawing near the bakery, he untied the thongs of his purse, flipped the cover back and reached inside. His fingers explored the inner recesses and he stopped short, feeling ill. Maria had robbed him during the night. But it would be a waste of time to protest to the royal governor of Madrid that a strumpet had emptied his purse; he could prove nothing and the authorities would only laugh at him.

His fingers trembling, Alvaro mechanically tied the thongs of his purse; then he raised his head and laughed, loudly and savagely. Maria's cunning was worthy of Magdalena Ruminez. Pulling the feather out of his hat, Alvaro broke it, threw it into the gutter and started on the long walk back to the Sanctuary of Santo Domingo.

Hunger and chagrin sharpened his mind, and after he had recovered from his first sense of shock, he found himself engaging in a painful self-examination, a habit that Father Sebastian had taught him. It was important that he know himself, and the more he probed, the unhappier he became. But he continued the process of self-searching relentlessly. When a tooth rotted, it had to be pulled, and there was something inside him that could destroy him if he refused to face reality.

He had gone with Maria, he knew, because she had reminded him of his mother and he had hoped to capture some of the gay warmth that Magdalena Ruminez had dispensed so lavishly to the men in her life. The gaiety had been an illusion, he knew now, and the warmth a façade for greed. He had always felt cheated because his mother had treated him coldly, but now he understood, for the first time, that she could not have behaved in any other way. It would have been impossible for her to give him love when she hadn't known the meaning of real affection. She herself had been a pauper, and he had craved something from her that she had never possessed.

Rather than hate Maria, he thought, he should be grateful to her. The money she had taken from his purse had been a small price to pay for his freedom. Never again would he idealize his mother, never again would he let the shadow of her selfish beauty dominate and haunt him. The experience of a single night, he felt, had removed a weight from his shoulders, a burden he had carried since early childhood.

Weary but rejoicing in a sense of liberty that was so new it exhilarated him, he walked with his head erect, smiling. Now, at last, he could live his own life.

The winter of 1414–1415 was the most severe that Madrid had known in a generation. Snow had fallen on three occasions, which was unusual, the ground was frozen hard and a steady, piercing wind blew down from the Guadarama mountains across the plateau. It was bitterly cold at the Sanctuary, and even in the abbot's office, where a fire of pine logs burned in a huge open hearth, the chill crept in everywhere. Father Ramiro believed that the pampering of the body corrupted the spirit, but eventually he was persuaded to wear a shawl over his cassock, and by the latter part of February he had grown so accustomed to draping it over his shoulders that he sometimes forgot he wore it.

He sat one afternoon, his thin fingers playing absently with the black fringe of the shawl, and looked up at the young man who stood before him. "You wanted to see me, de Luna?"

"Yes, Father, I—"

"Sit down. I know your reasons." The abbot smiled faintly. "You're nineteen years old, you're restless and you're tired of your studies."

"I hope I'll always be a student, Father," Alvaro replied cautiously as he seated himself on the stool opposite the desk, "but I'm spending my best years in idleness."

The old man sighed as he ran his hand through his thin white hair. "It would be a waste of breath to tell you that your life hasn't yet started. But there is one thing I will say to you. We don't engage in idle pursuits here, de Luna, as you should have learned by now. We aren't spending our best efforts training you only to see you ruin our plans for you."

"What plans, Father?"

It was the abbot's turn to speak carefully. "I send reports

on your progress to Avignon regularly. The Holy Father is interested in everything that you do."

"I can't accept a position at the Pope's court," Alvaro said bitterly. "I won't have everyone pointing a finger at me and whispering that I'm being shown favor because I'm his nephew. I'd be useful to him only if I became a priest, and if you'll pardon my bluntness, Father, I have no wish to take holy vows, even if I were certain that some day I'd become a cardinal."

"We've observed you for three years, de Luna, and we've formed our own ideas about you. Your instructors agree with me that you're not suited for the Church." The abbot paused imperceptibly, then added in a dry voice, "You may set your fears at rest. No one will try to persuade you to become a priest."

Alvaro curbed his temper. "Then why am I still here? Haven't I learned everything that the fathers can teach me?"

"You have yet to learn patience," Father Ramiro said sternly. "What would you do, boy—go to Toledo and submit meekly when Queen Catherine sent you to prison?"

"No, Father." Alvaro grinned ruefully. "I've seen enough of Her Majesty to satisfy me for the rest of my days on this earth. I've been thinking," he continued, his voice becoming strident, "of offering my sword to the king of France. With any luck I might make my fortune in Paris."

The shawl slipped from the abbot's left shoulder as he leaned forward. "Obviously you've never heard that the French feel contempt for mercenaries. They'd regard you as a renegade, and at most they'd offer you the command of a company of foreign troops. In ten or fifteen years, if you survived, you might be given a battalion. But Charles VI hates foreigners, and even if you should drive the English legions invading his realm into the sea, he wouldn't reward you with as much as a knighthood."

There was a silence and Alvaro, unable to meet the old

man's eyes, buried his face in his hands. "What shall I do, Father?"

"Wait, conserve your strength and trust in God. Do you suppose you were given the best tutors at Avignon because His Holiness enjoyed humoring an illegitimate nephew? Do you think that the wisest and most competent of my priests have tested your wits and endurance because they have nothing better to occupy their time? Castile needs you, Alvaro de Luna, and when she calls you to duty, you must be prepared to respond."

"What can I do for Castile, Father?" Still hunching forward on the stool, Alvaro spoke through clenched teeth.

"The poor, who are everywhere, cry for help, and no one hears them." Father Ramiro stood, and his voice soared, as it did when he delivered a sermon. "The grandees bicker in the *Cortes,* maneuver for position and increase the taxes of those who can't afford to pay. Aragon stands aloof when she should be united with us just as Leon was absorbed a few years ago, and Navarre, which shares our language and customs and faith, remains independent and saps our strength. The Moors in Granada threaten our borders and urge the infidels of the East to join them in a war that will convert our homeland into a Moslem wilderness. Yet you ask what you can do for Castile!"

Alvaro's inner turmoil subsided and he spoke quietly. "All I've ever wanted is the chance to serve, Father. When shall I begin?"

The abbot's eyes became softer. "In God's time, my son. Wait for His sign and pray for the strength to endure the trials that await you."

It was hot in the hole twenty feet below the surface of the earth, but Alvaro, filling a bucket with clay, dug energetically with his spade and consoled himself with the thought that at least he wasn't standing in the sun. The summer was as suffocating as the winter had been cold, and everywhere in Madrid people were being forced to dig new, deep wells in order to obtain water. The smaller of the Sanctuary's wells was dry, only a trickle appeared at the bottom of the larger and the students, working under the supervision of Father Sebastian, had spent the better part of a day preparing a new one.

Alvaro, the smallest member of the group, could maneuver in the pit more easily than any of his colleagues, and he had been digging steadily. His arms and back ached, but there would be no respite until the task was completed. He pulled sharply on the rope attached to the bucket, guided it as it was pulled up and emptied, and then caught it when it was lowered again. Bare to the waist and covered with grime, he wiped a film of perspiration from his forehead and upper lip, then started to dig again methodically.

A face appeared at the top of the hole. "Have you struck water yet?"

"I'm not staying down here because I'm enjoying myself." Roderigo had a remarkable talent for asking stupid questions, Alvaro thought irritably, digging again.

"Well, Father Sebastian wants you to come up."

"Why didn't you say so? I hope he sends you down here to take my place!"

Roderigo laughed. "I'm too big."

Alvaro threw his spade into the bucket and caught hold of the rope. "Haul me up, and be gentle. I'll thank you to remember that I'm not a load of dirt."

He clung to the rope, and when he reached the surface the sunlight was blinding. Shading his eyes, he was surprised to see that all of the students except Roderigo and Diego had vanished.

"You look like a mole," Roderigo declared solemnly.

"Or a miner," Diego said, chuckling.

Alvaro glared at them venomously. "You won't laugh quite

so loudly when you're sent down there, my friends. Where is Father Sebastian and what does he want?"

Before either could answer, a pale, small boy of eleven ran across the field and threw himself into Alvaro's arms. "I'd have known you anywhere," the child shouted.

Disentangling himself, Alvaro realized that the boy was wearing an expensive velvet suit trimmed with lace. "Be careful, young one, or you'll get filthy. There's nothing as sticky as the clay of Madrid." He stared at the boy for an instant, gasped and dropped to one knee. "Your Majesty!"

King Juan beamed. "You knew me, too!" Reaching out, he grasped Alvaro's hand. "You're my friend, so I grant you a right I've given no one else. You don't have to kneel before me, ever."

Alvaro started to thank him, but saw Roderigo and Diego hastily backing away across the field. They were looking behind him, and when he glanced around he was dismayed to see Father Sebastian, who was accompanied by two exquisitely dressed young ladies. He recognized the Infanta Catalina and beyond her the girl who had befriended him at the castle in Toledo. Conscious of his dirty, naked torso, his grimy hair and his filthy breeches and boots, he was tempted to climb down into the well again.

"Forgive us for embarrassing you," the princess said. "Doña Teresa and I would have waited in the refectory until you could make yourself presentable, but Juan was too impetuous."

"I wanted to see my friend," King Juan retorted, and grinned again at the filthy well-digger.

Alvaro had never been so mortified. "Your Highness, Doña Teresa," he murmured, bowing, but in spite of his humiliation his mind continued to function and he realized that until now he had not known the name of the lady-in-waiting.

Father Sebastian came to his student's rescue. "Perhaps His Majesty would like to go with you while you make yourself more presentable, de Luna. I'll show the ladies around the grounds, and we'll meet you in the refectory."

"You're still the accomplished diplomat, General," Doña Teresa said, deliberately refraining from looking at Alvaro.

"I am known only as Father Sebastian," the priest declared firmly.

Alvaro muttered apologetically, backed away a few paces and then started toward his quarters at such a rapid pace that the little king had to run in order to keep up with him. Water was precious, but he used it prodigally, scrubbing himself until his skin felt raw.

Juan, perching on the foot of the narrow cot in the cell, looked more like a curious child than a monarch. "You aren't much taller than you were the last time I saw you, but you must be very strong."

Alvaro dried his short, blond hair with a rough towel and, walking to the chest of drawers in the corner, took out his one good doublet, his only pair of velvet breeches and his newest cuffed boots.

"You have muscles in your back." Juan was still studying the young man. "I don't, but when you come to Toledo to live, you can help me to grow stronger."

"Of course, Your Majesty." Paying little attention to the boy's chatter, Alvaro dressed with frantic speed. "What brings Your Majesty to Madrid?"

"Cousin Juan married the Infanta Bianca of Navarre last week, and we're traveling back to Toledo after the wedding. You remember Juan—Enrique's brother."

"I remember him." Alvaro realized that the king's cousin had won more than a bride. The king of Navarre was old and weak, and Prince Juan would soon be a king in his own right, as Bianca had no brothers. The sons of Don Ferdinand were ambitious, and it was uncomfortable knowledge that, with Alfonso on the throne of Aragon and Juan ruling Navarre, the future of Castile was endangered. Only the frail child perching innocently on the bed stood between the throne and Don Ferdinand's other sons, Enrique and Pedro.

"Enrique's face is still scarred," the king said, and giggled.

Alvaro finished buttoning his shirt and pulled on his boots. "Has Her Majesty come to Madrid with you?" he asked, tactfully changing the subject.

"Mama stopped at Valladolid to rest and sent us ahead." A sly, triumphant smile crossed the boy's face. "She doesn't like you, and she'd be very angry if she knew we came to see you, but Catalina will keep the secret, and so will Teresa. They were pleased when I suggested the idea to them. Teresa's face became very red, and Catalina teased her."

Alvaro decided he had heard enough confidences. He picked up his belt, and although no one at the Sanctuary was permitted to carry arms, he attached his silver sheath to the leather and slid his knife into the case. As the circumstances were extraordinary, Father Sebastian would be unlikely to punish him for breaking the rules. "Is Your Majesty ready to leave?"

"No!" Juan pouted and clung to the iron bedstead. "I know what will happen. You'll be so busy talking to Catalina and Teresa that you won't pay any attention to me."

Anyone who dared to touch the person of the king of Castile could be sentenced to death, but Alvaro threw an arm around the boy's shoulder and hugged him. "Your Majesty," he said, "you took my part when the whole court laughed at me, and you won my complete devotion for life. I am at your command, now and always."

Tears appeared in Juan's eyes. "They told me you had forgotten about me, but I knew they were wrong."

"Who told you?"

"My cousins. Enrique and Juan and Pedro."

"They lied, Your Majesty." Perhaps it was unwise to speak so candidly to a child who didn't know how to hold his own tongue, but the words slipped out before Alvaro could check himself.

"Everybody lies to me. People tell me what they think I want to hear." It was evident that, in some ways at least, Juan was wise beyond his years.

"I won't lie to you, Your Majesty."

The boy stood and stared at Alvaro intently. "You'll tell me the truth, even if it's something I don't want to hear?"

"I will, Your Majesty, and I'll begin right now. Both of us will be considered very rude if we keep the ladies and Father Sebastian waiting too long."

Juan laughed heartily and made no further protest as Alvaro opened the door. They walked down a roofed, arched passage, and through the gates of the monastery Alvaro caught a glimpse of scores of horses, men in uniform and several gentlemen in civilian attire. "Is that Your Majesty's escort?"

The boy nodded.

"They'll know you've come to see me."

"You're wrong. They think we've stopped to visit Don Sebastian de Goeda."

Alvaro wondered how he could have been so stupid. Father Sebastian was the former Grand Master of the Order of Santiago, the commander-in-chief of the Castilian army, and his dispute with the queen dowager had shaken the kingdom.

"Mama will be annoyed, but she won't lecture us too severely. Don Sebastian was Papa's friend, and Mama is still afraid of him. She'd send him out of the country if she dared, but she has no authority over him any more."

They reached the refectory and Alvaro stood aside to let the king precede him into the cool, high-ceilinged hall. Father Sebastian and the two young ladies were sitting at the abbot's table, drinking cups of non-alcoholic fruit punch, a concoction that the Moors had introduced into Castile. Alvaro removed his hat with a flourish and bowed, and Juan addressed himself to the priest. "When I rule Castile in my own right, will you come back to Toledo and command the army, as you did for Papa?"

Father Sebastian shook his head. "I'm sorry, Your Majesty, but I serve the King of Kings now, and He is a jealous Master."

"Then I'll make Alvaro my general."

Catalina laughed and Father Sebastian smiled, but Teresa's face remained serious. "I'd be surprised if he weren't a very good general."

Alvaro was embarrassed. "I have yet to fight in a single battle."

"No matter," she replied firmly. "You'll get whatever you want."

"She always talks about you that way," Juan declared.

Teresa realized she had said too much, and flushed.

Father Sebastian intervened smoothly by offering cups of punch to the king and Alvaro. The conversation became strained, and the priest did most of the talking. Alvaro found it difficult to avoid staring rudely at the young ladies, and couldn't resist comparing them. Both were unusually attractive and both were refined; if Catalina seemed the more self-assured, it was because she was a princess. There was little opportunity to speak to either girl, however, for Juan made frequent demands on the young man's attention and Alvaro, conscious of the king's fear that he would be ignored, sat beside the boy and carefully answered every inconsequential remark he made.

Catalina became restless, and refusing to let either the old man or her brother dominate the meeting, she turned and faced Alvaro. "You've changed, Señor de Luna."

He tried to meet her gaze, but felt as he had at their first, brief meeting. Her beauty dazzled him, and he wondered angrily how he could have thought her no more attractive than her friend. Teresa was pretty, well-groomed and aristocratic, and any man would be proud to act as her escort, but Catalina was a princess in every sense of the word. It was painful to think that some day she would become the consort of a king. Irritated, Alvaro grimaced; it was absurd for a pauper who had no title, no lands, no future, to let himself think in terms of a romance with an Infanta of Castile.

Teresa saw his expression, and there was a hint of amusement in her voice. "You've embarrassed him, Your Highness."

"Have I? I'm so sorry." Catalina's concern was genuine.

Alvaro wanted to relieve her distress. "Forgive my clumsiness, Your Highness, but I haven't learned the art of making gallant conversation."

"I hope it's something you'll never learn." Catalina leaned forward slightly, her eyes bright. "I despise meaningless talk, and I meant what I said as a compliment."

Alvaro inclined his head awkwardly. "Thank you." He took a deep breath and plunged into dangerous waters. "May I compliment you in return by saying that you haven't changed? You're exactly as I remember you."

Color rose in the princess' face.

Teresa laughed, and there was a slight edge in her voice as she said, "I do believe, Señor de Luna, that you're more of a courtier than you're willing to admit."

Her acidity was disturbing, and Alvaro felt compelled to defend himself. "I spoke the truth."

Catalina opened a fan with a snap of her wrist and used it vigorously.

Juan squirmed in his seat, and Father Sebastian frowned, making it obvious that he disliked the turn the talk had taken. But he thought it better to let Alvaro extricate himself, and glanced sharply at the young man.

"It would be difficult," Alvaro said slowly, "for me to forget either of you. I'm sure that no one else in Castile has ever been rescued from death by two such lovely ladies."

Teresa was mollified, and Catalina smiled politely, but the expression that appeared in her eyes for an instant indicated that she wished there were some way to pursue a private conversation.

Alvaro felt his temples pound, and instinct told him that the princess was drawn to him. But he could not let himself forget the vast difference in their stations, and he knew that one brash word would result in his expulsion from the country. It was the prerogative of a princess to bestow her friendship with discreet candor, but a commoner could not reciprocate.

In self-defense, Alvaro turned to Teresa. "I've often thought of writing to thank you for your kindness to me."

She flicked a triumphant glance at Catalina, then turned back to Alvaro with a broad smile. "That wouldn't have been wise."

"I know. I'm just trying to explain why I may have seemed like a boor to you."

"Oh, I understood." She studied him covertly, her lashes lowered. He had given her the opportunity to arouse his interest, and she was quick to seize and exploit it.

"I have been admiring your silver scabbard," she said, smiling boldly.

Father Sebastian generously explained how Alvaro had won it, and the princess was deeply, honestly impressed. "He beat you in a jousting match?" she asked incredulously.

Juan looked as happy as though he himself had been the victor.

"I'm not surprised," Teresa murmured.

Alvaro, enjoying the praise but ill-at-ease, removed the dagger from the sheath, took the scabbard from his belt and handed it to her.

Teresa examined it carefully, turning it over in her slender hands. At last she returned it to him, and looked straight into his eyes. "I have no doubt that you'll win many wonderful and valuable prizes in your life."

Alvaro knew she was inviting him to pay court to her, even though she was undoubtedly aware of the fact that he was a penniless commoner. He grinned at her, but before he could reply, Catalina, glancing at the hour glass over the hearth, quickly adjusted her mantilla and stood, forcing the others to rise, too.

"Mama will be certain we've joined the general in a conspiracy if we stay here too long. I'm sure the hunting lodge has been made ready for us by now—we must leave." She gave Alvaro her hand, and he bent low to kiss it.

Juan hung back, but when Catalina started toward the door, accompanied by Father Sebastian, he was forced to follow them. "When I rule in my own right," he said petulantly, "I won't allow anyone to leave a room without my permission. Don't you agree, Alvaro?"

"I'm confident that Your Majesty will rule wisely, " was the cautious reply, "and that you'll consider every problem carefully before you solve it by issuing an edict."

The king's sister rewarded him with a smile, and Father Sebastian nodded approvingly. "Wait for me here, de Luna," he said, and escorted Juan and Catalina into the open.

Alvaro and Teresa were alone for a moment, and he lingered over her hand an instant longer than was polite. "I'm sure we'll meet again," he said.

"So am I." She sounded a trifle breathless as, the color high in her cheeks, she swept out of the refectory without a backward glance.

A trumpet sounded, spurs jingled as the escort formed, and hoof-beats echoed through the monastery. When they faded in the distance, Father Sebastian returned to the refectory, his grim features relaxed. "You stand in high favor, de Luna," he said. "King Juan has formed a strong feeling of friendship for you, the Infanta Catalina admires you, and it appears as though you've conquered the heart of Doña Teresa de Robres."

It was unnecessary now for Alvaro to inquire about the girl's identity. He had heard Roderigo gossiping about members of the court, and knew that she was the orphaned niece of Don Fernando Alonso de Robres, the minister of finance and second most important member of the royal council.

"It would appear," the priest continued, "that I may have been right when I urged you to wait patiently for your chance to serve. Fortunately, that time hasn't yet come."

Alvaro looked at him in bewilderment.

"All that you've learned here, all that you were taught in Avignon, will be wasted unless you act humbly and exercise self-discipline. Today you did neither, but gave in to temptation." Father Sebastian pointed grimly at the dagger and silver sheath. "You know the order against carrying weapons at Santo Domingo may not be violated without the written permission of the abbot. You may be the friend of the king, de Luna, but you'll spend an extra hour in the chapel every night for the next month, and you'll work alone digging the new well."

The majority of the Sanctuary's students left the monastery early in 1416 when Queen Catherine, whose unpopularity with every class was mounting, responded to the urging of Don Juan Hurtado de Mendoza, the minister-in-chief, and granted an amnesty that applied to most of the young men. Several others went into exile in Portugal, and only Alvaro and Roderigo Pinar remained. The queen, unable to maintain friendly relations with anyone for more than a short time, soon became involved in new, vindictive feuds, and by midsummer the students' quarters were filled again. Most of the newcomers were in their early teens, and Alvaro, who was now twenty, felt more like an instructor than a pupil.

He became desperate again, and was tempted to follow

Diego and some of his other friends to Lisbon, but conquered the desire by devoting all of his waking hours to his
studies. He rarely retired before midnight. Late one evening
in September he sat beside an oil lamp in his cell, reading the
autobiography, in Latin, of Alfonso VI, the great twelfth-
century king of Castile. It was surprising how little the country had changed in three hundred years, and Alvaro was so
absorbed in the illuminated parchment volume that he failed
to hear a tap at the door of his cell until it was repeated.

A novice stood in the frame. "You're wanted in the abbot's
office, Señor de Luna."

"At this hour?"

"If you please. And hurry. Father Ramiro and Father
Sebastian are waiting for you, and so is a stranger."

Alvaro marked his place in the book, picked up the lamp
and made his way down arched passages to Father Ramiro's
office. The abbot and Father Sebastian greeted him tersely,
and Alvaro saw another priest in the shadows at the far side
of the room. The man approached him, and he recognized his
half-brother, whom he had not seen since he had left Toledo.
They embraced warmly.

"What brings you here, Francisco?"

"You," Father Ruminez replied, wasting no words. "The
English woman died as she was dressing for dinner tonight."

"You've ridden here from Toledo after dark?" The news
that Queen Catherine was dead had not yet penetrated.

"The regency," Father Ramiro said, interrupting, "is
ended. King Juan is now twelve—Mendoza and Robres want
to announce that he'll rule in his own name. He won't, of
course, but they'll maintain the fiction, if they can move
quickly enough."

"A new royal council will be formed tomorrow, immediately after the queen's funeral," Francisco explained, "and
the *Cortes* will be summoned late in the day to approve the

change. There are enough members in Toledo to form a quorum."

Alvaro's mind was functioning more clearly now, and he frowned slightly as he asked. "Isn't the haste unseemly?"

"It's essential," Father Sebastian said flatly. "Through God's grace the king's cousins are out of the country. Don Pedro is visiting Navarre, and Don Enrique is in Barcelona, but both of them will hurry home when they hear the news. If they can, they'll insist that they be confirmed as co-Regents, and within a year either one or the other will see to it that the king meets with an accident. There will be a race between Pedro and Enrique to see which can crown himself first."

"Mendoza and Robres are old," Francisco added. "So is the Duke of Lerma, the third member of the council. They want to appoint someone to watch over King Juan and protect him from harm. When the Infanta Catalina proposed your name, everyone agreed that you were the perfect choice."

Alvaro knew his life as a student had come to an end, but he tried to conceal his elation as he asked, "Who was consulted?"

"The members of the council, naturally. Juan himself was enthusiastic, and His Eminence thought it fitting that a nephew of Pope Benedict who has spent his whole life preparing for such a role should take an active part in the affairs of state."

Alvaro looked at the abbot and Father Sebastian, who had guided him for so long, and both nodded gravely. "You'll ride to Toledo tonight," Father Ramiro said. "Try to remember what you've learned here, and, above all, don't forget the old saying, '*Acometa quien quiera, el fuerte espera.*' The weak man is impetuous, the strong is patient."

Father Sebastian picked up a small, heavy package from the desk. "Here are the spurs I promised you. I've prepared a letter saying that you've passed all the tests necessary to qualify as a knight."

Accepting the gift with a bow, Alvaro stared at his mentor. "What are your instructions?"

"I don't intend to meddle, or to use you as my mouthpiece. Be vigilant, listen to your own conscience and when you draw your sword for King Juan, remember that through him you stand guard over all Castile."

2. The Grandee

1

Torches flared and sputtered in the sockets set at intervals in the stone walls of the Hall of Nobles, and the members of the *Cortes* chatted with each other in low voices as they strolled toward their places. Great dukes, arrogant in doublets of cloth-of-gold and cloth-of-silver, their beards trimmed to fashionably sharp points, their hair sprayed with sweet-smelling scent, moved to the padded benches in the first rows, and behind them walked the counts and barons, elegant in velvets and silks. Alvaro, who had been created a knight only a day and a half earlier, made himself inconspicuous on a bench in the rear, ignoring the whispered advice of Roderigo, whose title and family estates had been restored to him in a private ceremony.

"We're both land-owners of consequence," the tall young man muttered. "We're entitled to sit closer to the throne."

Alvaro found it difficult to think of himself as a man of property. "I've never seen my father's lands or his houses. I prefer to tread softly."

Sighing, Roderigo sat down. "This bench is as hard as the pews in the Santo Domingo chapel."

"Your backside hasn't become accustomed to luxury yet. Don't complain." Alvaro grinned absently at his friend, and studied the grandees who were moving toward the front of the chamber.

"If it weren't for you, I wouldn't be here at all. I'll stay with you, but I think you're wrong."

Alvaro gestured sharply, interrupting the young baron who

had been transformed overnight from a bankrupt refugee to a person of consequence. "Who is that?" he asked, inclining his head in the direction of a heavy-set, bearded grandee who wore a coat of chain mail and carried a long, two-edged sword in his belt.

"Don Carlos, Marquis of Ensenada."

Alvaro looked carefully at the commander of Castilian infantry and, his lips thinning, rose to his feet. "It was decreed yesterday that no one may carry a naked weapon into the king's presence. The marquis' sword isn't sheathed."

Roderigo was alarmed. "Don't argue with him," he said urgently. "There's no one in the country stronger, and he enjoys the friendship of Don Pedro and Don Enrique."

Alvaro brushed aside his friend's restraining hand. "All the more reason to do my duty. Don Carlos!"

The grandee halted, turned slightly and waited, his dark, thin face expressionless.

"I am Alvaro de Luna, His Majesty's personal chamberlain."

Don Carlos continued to look through him, but the two nobles who accompanied him smiled in open contempt at the young man in plain black wool.

"I'd like to refresh your memory, milord. Apparently you've forgotten the announcement made yesterday regarding the carrying of arms. Your sword is unsheathed."

The marquis remained calm. "Do you propose that I leave it with the guards at the door?" he asked acidly, speaking with a cultured, patrician lisp.

"If you wish, milord," Alvaro replied politely. "Or you might send a servant for your sheath."

"And if I refuse?" Don Carlos rested his right hand on the jeweled hilt of the blade.

"In that case, milord, I shall be compelled to request you to leave the Hall of Nobles." Alvaro, aware that others were listening, deliberately raised his voice. He had hoped to avoid difficulties, but felt sure that the marquis was forcing an issue; he had to meet the challenge.

"I have sat in the *Cortes* since my twelfth birthday," Don Carlos declared haughtily, "and I have no intention of taking orders from a bastard upstart whose spurs haven't yet adjusted themselves to the shape of his boots."

"With all due respect, milord," Alvaro said, controlling his temper, "I speak not in my own name but in that of His Majesty."

"A child who does what he's told by anyone who happens to be in a position to influence him at the moment!"

"King Juan is twelve, milord, and I feel confident his wisdom is as great as yours was when you first took your seat in this body." Alvaro stepped around the marquis into the aisle, and when Don Carlos tried to push past him, he planted his feet apart. "It would grieve me to summon the guards, milord."

"Call them!"

"If you insist." Alvaro beckoned to a sergeant wearing the yellow and red plumes of the royal household guard in his helmet. "Escort the Marquis of Ensenada into the corridor."

Don Carlos glowered at the soldier. "I can have you reduced in the ranks or dismissed from the army."

"Begging your pardon, milord," Alvaro said firmly, "you cannot. Two days ago, during the reign of Queen Catherine, it might have been possible for you to ruin a man's career with a snap of your fingers. But His Majesty rules in his own name now, and he is as loyal to the men of his army as they are to him. Sergeant, you will proceed."

The soldier's eyes were bright. "This way, your lordship."

The marquis hesitated, saw that five other guards, all armed with pikes, were forming a solid line behind the sergeant and, glaring at them, made a brief speech for the benefit of his sympathetic colleagues. "Do you take your orders from the general of infantry or from a creature who has sprung from nowhere to act as the lackey of Mendoza's new council?"

An elderly duke cheered as he stroked the ermine edge of his cloak, and several other nobles joined him.

Alvaro was furious, but his tone was civil as he said evenly, "The general of infantry holds the King's commission, and so does His Majesty's chamberlain. All authority is vested in the crown, and has no other source. Sergeant, I'm waiting."

The soldiers surrounded Don Carlos, and the sergeant saluted courteously. "I'll follow you into the corridor, your lordship."

The marquis was pale, but, realizing he had suffered at least a temporary defeat, he tried to hide his chagrin by lowering his head for a moment as he unbuckled his sword belt and handed it, with his blade, to the burly guard. "As I have been given to understand that an emergency of some sort is pending, I prefer to attend this meeting. You may wait for me outside the entrance." Dismissing the soldiers with a wave, he hurried down the aisle, not glancing again in Alvaro's direction.

"You've made an enemy of Ensenada," Roderigo whispered as Alvaro took his seat, "and nearly everyone of consequence in the hall takes his part."

"It's better," Alvaro replied defiantly, "that every grandee in Castile understand from the beginning where I stand." He was a complete outsider, and the hostile faces he saw on every side confirmed the opinion he had formed since arriving in Toledo that, no matter how high he might climb, the members of the *Cortes* would be unwilling to accept him as an equal.

A trumpet fanfare made further conversation impossible, and a score of soldiers in yellow and red plumed helmets filed into the Hall of Nobles, followed by an officer carrying a mace and a golden orb. King Juan, his face still drawn and pinched after the ordeal of his mother's funeral, walked slowly behind them, dressed in a suit of deep black. He was followed by Don Juan Hurtado de Mendoza, the principal minister, and the other two members of the new council, Miguel de Mateo, Duke of Lerma, and Don Fernando Alonso de Robres.

Juan, trying to behave with dignity, mounted the dais at the front of the chamber, and after he had seated himself on a throne draped in black, Mendoza, who took his place on the king's right, addressed the assemblage. "Gentlemen," he declared somberly, "I was not mistaken yesterday when I urged you to make haste in approving the formation of the new council. News that has just reached the city confirms my fear that Castilian blood may be shed in the near future."

No one seemed surprised.

"Prince Pedro, His Majesty's cousin, has crossed the border of Navarre with an escort of five hundred cavalry and three hundred pikemen. The courier who brings us this information says there is reason to believe that His Highness wishes to establish himself as regent."

"Who has a better right than a member of the royal family?" a marquis called.

Mendoza looked meaningfully at the king, and Juan knew he was being required to assert himself. "It is not our wish," he said painfully, "that anyone act as regent. We have assumed the rule of our realm, and have appointed our advisers."

The grandees were afraid to defy him in an open meeting of the *Cortes*, but Alvaro, looking at the sullen, contemptuous faces of the nobles, realized that virtually every man present was a potential conspirator who would not hesitate to help either Don Pedro or Don Enrique gain the throne.

"The council," Mendoza said in a hoarse, tired voice, "has decided it must meet this threat of force with force. A column of troops will march north today to meet Don Pedro and persuade him that his ambitions are not sound."

Don Carlos of Ensenada was on his feet immediately. "As general of infantry, I refuse to lead Castilian troops against a prince of the blood."

"I agree with the marquis," shouted the white-haired Duke of Estremadura, the cavalry commander.

Alvaro was horrified, but apparently the members of the council had been expecting a rebuff, and none looked perturbed.

"His Majesty," Mendoza said calmly, "accepts the resignations of His Grace of Estremadura and His Lordship of Ensenada."

He signalled to Juan, who nodded.

"His Majesty requires the services of a volunteer to lead the column," the minister-in-chief continued.

There was a long, painful silence.

Alvaro, unable to curb his emotions, leaped to his feet. "Sir!" he called.

Heads turned, and a count's prolonged laugh was derogatory.

"Don Alvaro de Luna," the principal minister said, recognizing the speaker.

It still felt odd to be addressed as "Don" and Alvaro flushed. "I propose, sir, that His Majesty lead the column in person. If the gentlemen who have just retired from the army were reluctant to lead Castilians against a prince of the blood, think how such a prince will feel when he learns that His Majesty himself has taken the field. If Don Pedro is a patriot, he will disband his force. If he is a traitor, he will reveal his true stand, and will be punished accordingly."

Here and there a grandee smiled approvingly, the members of the council were obviously pleased and the cardinal-archbishop of Toledo, who sat in the first row on the right side of the hall, surrounded by prelates, beamed at Alvaro.

"We agree!" Juan declared shrilly, not waiting to take his cue from Mendoza.

Don Carlos, aware that the clever suggestion would spoil the plans of the ambitious prince, made a desperate appeal. "Don Pedro is a loyal subject of the crown. He will be insulted if an army marches out to meet him."

Alvaro knew it was not his place to reply, that the minister-in-chief was the chairman of the meeting, but he was so aroused he became reckless. "If His Highness is loyal," he said angrily, "let him prove it by coming to Toledo alone. No man who marches on the capital of his king with an escort of eight hundred armed men can be considered loyal."

The marquis tried to reply, several others began speaking simultaneously and Mendoza knew that a fight might break out in the hall unless he acted swiftly. "The council," he said loudly, making himself heard above the tumult, "has noted with pleasure His Majesty's agreement to lead his troops into the field. As the king has expressed his own desire, the confirmation of the *Cortes* is not required, and this meeting stands adjourned."

The royal guards started out of the chamber, marching down the center aisle, followed by the king and his elderly advisers. Juan halted at the rear of the hall, smiled at Alvaro and said distinctly, "You shall ride north, too."

Roderigo sighed lugubriously as the royal party left the chamber. "At the Sanctuary," he said, "I complained because life was so quiet. I'm beginning to wish I were back there, in a world where nothing ever happened."

The minister-in-chief looked at the men seated around the table and his expression was bleak. "I can find no officer who will consent to command the troops. Pedro and Enrique have corrupted the grandees even more than I had suspected, and every noble to whom I've spoken has given me an answer identical to Ensenada's refusal."

Cardinal Torello, who, as archbishop of Toledo, was the head of the Church in Castile, rubbed his chin, then clasped and unclasped his hands. "Prince Pedro must not be permitted to reach the city, or Castile will be destroyed. Alfonso of Aragon has no ambitions to swallow us, but if his brothers act like jackals, he'll behave like one, too. Juan of Navarre is supporting Pedro, of course, and it wouldn't surprise me to learn that Enrique is leaving Aragon to put in his claim."

Alvaro, sitting silently at the foot of the table, looked at each of the great men in turn and realized that all of them were frightened. They had honored him by allowing him to listen to their deliberations, but now he felt compelled to speak his mind. "Some day, gentlemen, Castile and Aragon and Navarre must be united, and the Moors must be driven out of Granada, which is our territory. The people of the Iberian nations have wanted to be united under one king and one flag for many years. We can expect the princes to cater to that craving. They'll claim that as their brothers already rule Aragon and Navarre, one family will reign everywhere if they take Castile, too. They'll prey on the longings of the common people for peace, but there will be no peace in the peninsula if they depose King Juan. The moment that Pedro or Enrique seized the throne, all four of the brothers would start fighting among themselves."

"You express my own views," the cardinal replied, "and it pleases me to find someone who can think clearly. Father Ramiro was right when he wrote to me that you show extraordinary promise, and I shall take care to inform His Holiness that he has reason to be proud of you. Don Juan," he added, turning to Mendoza, "before too many years have passed you may find it helpful to give de Luna a full seat on the council."

"There will be no council unless I can find someone to lead the expedition against Prince Pedro," the principal minister said gloomily.

Don Fernando de Robres tugged at his white beard. "I'm too old to flee into exile. I'll send my niece to Lisbon, but I'll stay here and let Pedro throw me into prison. Perhaps Your Eminence will be good enough to intervene to prevent them from torturing me. And as my palate is refined, I'll appreciate an occasional basket of fruit and wheat bread."

The Duke of Lerma twisted a huge emerald ring on the little finger of his left hand. "One of my nephews is in Enrique's camp and the other is riding with Pedro, but both of the princes would think carefully before taking my lands from me. There is no family in Castile older than mine. There were dukes of Lerma when the ancestors of the present royal family were shepherds."

Mendoza was startled and Robres glared at the duke. "If I understand you correctly, Your Grace, you're hinting that you'd make your peace with Prince Pedro."

Lerma shrugged and sighed. "I have no wish to see him on the throne, but my own survival is more important to me than a squabble over the throne. Like His Eminence, I must enjoy a working relationship with anyone who happens to wear the crown."

"Our situations are not similar," Cardinal Torello replied stiffly. "Although it is true that the Church must be prepared to negotiate with the king, neither I nor any of my fellow cardinals nor any of my bishops want to see Pedro or Enrique as master of Castile. Our duty is the salvation of souls, and we try, to the best of our ability, to ease the suffering of the poor while they are on this earth."

Mendoza smiled cynically. "*Al sastre pobre, la aguja que se doble,*" he said, quoting an old Castilian saying. "The poor must adapt themselves to circumstances." His smile became broader, but there was no mirth in his tone as he added, "We who are allegedly favored by fortune will hang from a gibbet in the castle courtyard, but the vintner and the leather-worker who don't have a copper between them will stand at the side of the road and cheer King Pedro as he rides past them. Then Enrique will put a blade between his brother's shoulders, and they'll raise their voices just as loudly for King Enrique."

The hopelessness of the old men infuriated Alvaro, but he knew his presence would be tolerated only if he spoke diplomatically. "May I be permitted to quote a proverb, too? *A' Idos de mi casa, y, Qué queris con mi mujer, no hay responder.* There is no reply when one says, 'Out of my house,' and 'What do you want with my wife?' "

The cardinal, who was the son of a stonemason and had spent his childhood in the *Mozarab* district of Toledo, chuckled at the blunt humor, but the patrician members of the council looked coldly at the young man.

"You fail to make your meaning clear," the minister-in-chief said frigidly.

"Gentlemen, you are experienced in the arts of statecraft and I am a mere novice," Alvaro replied, hoping he sounded sufficiently humble. "All the same, it seems to me that you accept Prince Pedro's victory as an accomplished fact. He marches with only eight hundred men, and a strong show of force would quench his thirst for conquest. Send four brigades of cavalry, two thousand men in all, to meet him. Don't bother with infantry, for they march too slowly. Let Pedro see the king—at a distance, of course, where he can't hope to capture Juan—and let him be given an order to disperse. If he refuses, he will be branded as a traitor, and surely two thousand horsemen can smash his little army of Castilian adventurers and mercenaries from Navarre."

There was a long silence, and Mendoza drummed the table slowly with the long, graceful fingers of his left hand. "Your idea is sound, Don Alvaro, except for one difficulty. You've forgotten the heart of our problem. Our junior officers are loyal enough, but even if we can find someone of ability who will command the column, how do we know that he won't negotiate with Pedro at the critical moment and join the enemy? Such arrangements have been made at one time or another in our unhappy past."

Alvaro gripped the arms of his chair so hard that his knuckles turned white, and although he tried to speak calmly, his voice was hoarse. "I can imagine no circumstances that would induce me to join Prince Pedro, and no offer he might make me, no matter how dazzling, would tempt me to desert His Majesty and Castile."

"Do you offer yourself as commander of the expedition, Don Alvaro?"

"I do, milord, in the absence of someone better qualified."

Robres and Lerma exchanged dismayed glances. "You've never fought in a battle, de Luna," the duke said unhappily.

"True, Your Grace, and I would have preferred to act as adjutant to the commander or to gain experience as the leader of a brigade, perhaps. But I've spent my whole life preparing for such a day as this, and our only alternative is surrender."

"But the king will ride with you," Robres said breathlessly. "Suppose he should be killed?"

"If it is God's will that he die," Alvaro replied, "is it better that he be killed in battle, beneath the royal ensign, or that he wait cravenly for an assassin to stab him in his feather bed while he sleeps between silken sheets?"

Again there was a silence, and Cardinal Torello leaned forward in his chair. "A fresh breeze blows across Castile," he said softly.

Deep furrows appeared between the eyes of the minister-in-chief. "You are only twenty years of age, Don Alvaro?"

"I regret, milord, that I have no grey hairs, and I fear that if Prince Pedro's coup is successful, I'll have no opportunity to grow any."

The members of the council looked at each other uncertainly, then turned to the cardinal. "It isn't my place to tell you what to do in temporal affairs," he said blandly. "I act as your spiritual adviser, as the conscience of His Majesty's government. I can only say," he added casually, suppressing a smile, "that the greatest general Castile has known in a generation, he who is now known simply as Father Sebastian, has unlimited faith in his protégé."

2

Lightly armored horses of the royal household guard milled about in the great courtyard of the castle; lieutenants shouted commands and tried to establish order out of seeming chaos. Adjutants and supply officers, carrying sheets of parchment filled with long lists, conferred with each other and rode in and out of the main gate, their expressions harried. A number of grandees had gathered on the steps of the castle and watched the military preparations with broad smiles, occasionally saying something derogatory to each other in quiet undertones.

Don Roderigo de Pinar, who had been appointed Álvaro's deputy, hurried from one end of the courtyard to the other, his armor clanking as he walked. The commanders and adjutants of the brigades that were mobilizing outside the gates of the city and would meet the household troops on the road sent couriers to tell him of their progress, and he received their reports with the confidence of a veteran. He, like Alvaro, was inexperienced, but any man who had been a pupil of Father Sebastian understood the mechanics of preparing for war.

King Juan appeared in the main entrance and made his way slowly down the steps to the courtyard, encumbered by his suit of heavy armor. He was followed by his personal standard-bearer and escorted by ten young gentlemen-at-arms, all of them selected because they had reason to dislike Prince

Pedro and Prince Enrique, not because of their loyalty to the boy king; there was, as yet, no group devoted to Juan.

Trumpeters sounded a fanfare, and all activity ceased as the officers and men saluted. Juan made his way in silence to the bay gelding that was being held for him in the center of the yard, Roderigo approached him to pay his compliments to the king and two equerries helped Juan to mount. The grandees spoke more cautiously now, and when a group of ladies, all in black mourning, appeared at the opposite side of the steps, the nobles quietly scattered.

Roderigo glanced repeatedly toward the entrance to the castle and tried to curb his impatience. The expedition could not leave without its commander, and Alvaro was being detained by the members of the council, who were giving him final, contradictory and confusing instructions at a hastily summoned meeting. At last he emerged from the building, surrounded by the old men of the council, and the grandees smiled derisively when they saw that he was wearing a suit of light armor. As any veteran knew, an officer who wanted to survive a battle always clad himself in the strongest and heaviest uniform of overlapping silver-coated steel plates.

Alvaro saw the ladies and walked toward them. The Infanta Catalina came forward, and he removed his helmet, dropped to one knee and kissed her hand. "I've made preparations for your protection during our absence, Your Highness," he said. "You have nothing to fear. Five hundred cavalrymen and three regiments of infantry are being brought to the city from the south, and a like number are coming from the west. Don Fernando de Robres, who is loyal to you and who was a good soldier before he became a statesman, will command them. I'll grant you that he's elderly, but he won't be required to campaign in the field."

The princess stood immobile, listening intently.

"The garrison will prepare for a siege," Alvaro continued, "and any grandee who conspires against the throne will be imprisoned. But the possibility that something unpleasant might develop is very slight. Only Enrique might try to stir up trouble, and when he learns there are enough troops stationed in the city to throw him back across the border of Aragon, I doubt that he'll act rashly."

"Obviously you understand Enrique," Catalina replied, her eyes darkening contemptuously when she mentioned her cousin's name. "He never takes unnecessary chances."

"Then your peace of mind regarding your own safety is assured. I give you my word that you needn't worry about His Majesty, either. I realize he's been bragging about the valiant acts he intends to perform, but I won't let him risk his life in battle."

"Thank you, Don Alvaro. I know I can depend on you." The princess hesitated for an instant, then smiled. "It's strange that you should have become so important to all of us, and so quickly. Juan and Teresa have been praising you for years, without real cause, and suddenly you're fulfilling all of their extravagant hopes. You've become our strongest supporter at a time when our supposed friends are deserting us."

Alvaro knew she had crossed an invisible border and addressed him with a familiarity unbefitting their differences in station, but he had to pretend her attitude was that of a great lady who was grateful for the loyalty of a retainer when trouble threatened. It was true that a great deal had happened in an incredibly short period to change Alvaro's status, but even a knight, royal chamberlain and temporary general could not permit himself to dream of winning the unattainable hand of a princess of Castile. Holding his helmet in the crook of his left arm, he bowed stiffly. "I'll try to justify Your Highness' faith in me."

"I'm sure you will." She smiled warmly, then her attitude changed abruptly. "You'll want to say good-bye to Teresa." Turning, she walked away quickly and rejoined her ladies.

Doña Teresa detached herself from the group and moved forward slowly, aware that scores of people were watching her.

Alvaro, bowing, felt sorry for her. If she weren't over-shadowed by Catalina, she would be regarded by everyone as the great beauty of the court.

Teresa honored him by sinking to the stones in a deep curtsy.

"I don't deserve that," he said quickly, offering her his hand and turning red.

She rose gracefully, with the ease of long practice. "The king's general deserves the homage of the whole country."

"I'm not really a general," Alvaro replied truthfully. "I'm leading the troops on this march because the council can find no one else who'll accept the assignment. But I hold no permanent commission, and I'll become a civilian again after I've persuaded Don Pedro that he's making a mistake."

The girl's eyes were shrewd and bright. "Who can say what the future holds in store? I believe, as I have for a long time, that you're destined to become a great man."

Embarrassed, he made a self-deprecatory gesture.

Teresa refused to yield. "Would you have imagined as recently as one week ago that you'd be in your present position today? Neither you nor anyone else can predict where you'll stand in another week. But I beg you," she added, her voice becoming husky, "take no risks that might endanger your life."

Her obvious concern was flattering, but he couldn't lie to her. "If Pedro is sensible, there will be no risk for him or for Castile. If not, I'll do what I must."

"I'll pray for your safe return," Teresa murmured, speaking so softly that it was difficult to hear her.

Roderigo interrupted them, mounting the steps from the courtyard noisily, glancing at Teresa in open admiration and then, remembering his training, saluting with a flourish. "Sir,

the brigades have assembled outside the city and are waiting
for us. The baggage trains are moving, and His Majesty's
escort is in place."

Teresa was conscious of Roderigo's interest, but continued
to look steadily at Alvaro.

It was tempting to show off for her benefit, but Alvaro
addressed his deputy quietly. "Tell the trumpeters to sound
the assembly, and inform the adjutant that I'll ride with the
vanguard."

"Yes, sir." Roderigo looked obliquely at Teresa again,
saluted and moved off down the steps.

The trumpets blared, horsemen moved into formation and
Alvaro, knowing he couldn't keep the men waiting, spoke
quickly, impulsively, "I have no right to ask a favor of the
niece of a council member, but I shall be honored if you'll
give me a token to carry north with me." He didn't dare let
himself glance at Catalina, whom his good sense told him to
forget.

Teresa caught her breath, fumbled with the strings of the
purse she carried at her belt and drew out a perfumed handkerchief, a large square of green silk.

Alvaro took this from her, and heard the ladies' sudden
outburst of excited chatter. He tied the handkerchief to the
hilt of his sword, then bent over Teresa's hand; she made no
protest when he turned it upward, and for an instant, as he
pressed his lips against the palm, they forgot the existence of
everyone else. Then he straightened, drew his sword and
raised it first to Catalina, then to the members of the council.

"I'll return," he said firmly to Teresa.

"Go with God," she whispered.

Speed was essential, and Alvaro broke rules that had been
followed for centuries. He ordered the men to shed their
heavy armor and strip their horses, and the column advanced
so rapidly that the baggage trains were left far behind. Loot-

ing was strictly forbidden, and the peasants, long accustomed to seeing their cheese and bread and olive oil stolen by raiders in uniform, were astonished when quartermasters paid them in silver *dolars* for everything the army needed, even the horses' fodder.

Unencumbered by heavy gear, the column covered forty to sixty miles each day, and Alvaro plotted the route of march carefully, avoiding cities and mountain ranges that would force him to travel more slowly. He took the road to Navarre that lay on the north bank of the Tagus River, then cut across open countryside to the town of Alhama, where he learned from a courier that Pedro had crossed the Ebro River from Navarre and was marching toward the Sierra de Gudar range. The column swung toward the east to cut him off. Another messenger brought word that the prince was spending a few days as the guest of the Duke of Cuevas.

Since the town of Cuevas was heavily fortified, Alvaro was afraid the king would be held a prisoner if he entered the gates, and the army camped in the foothills of the mountains about sixteen miles west of the place. Strong sentry outposts were established, and two days later, after the baggage trains arrived, Roderigo was sent to Cuevas with word that King Juan was in the area and requested his cousin to pay homage to him in person the following morning.

It was customary for nobles of every rank to swear fealty to a monarch who had just ascended a throne, but although Juan had been king since his father's death, the ordinary civilities did not necessarily apply in his case. However, as he was now presumably ruling Castile in his own right, the demand was reasonable. Nevertheless, each side was aware of the other's belligerent potential, and shortly before dawn Alvaro mustered his troops on a ridge overlooking a valley road that led to the town.

He had spent a sleepless night and, in an unexpected command issued before the units mobilized, ordered the men to wear only their light armor. When several subordinates protested, he called a council of war to explain his tactics. The loyal troops held the heights, he said, and if a battle should develop they could sweep down the slopes of the ridge to attack the enemy. Therefore, he felt, mobility and speed were more important than sheer strength, and if a fight developed, it would be preferable to win a decisive battle quickly than become involved in a long, exhausting series of individual jousting matches that would probably continue until sunset. There had been too many such battles in the past, he argued, and they usually ended in a draw, which settled nothing. Should hostilities develop, it was essential that the king's forces win a total victory.

Accompanied by Roderigo, an adjutant and several equerries, Alvaro inspected his squadrons and then returned to the center of the line, where the royal ensign had been raised. Juan, wearing full armor, was surrounded by his gentlemen-at-arms. The horsemen moved aside to let Alvaro approach and salute the king. Juan promptly raised his visor, and his eyes were sullen, his lips petulant.

"Why can't I wear a steel doublet and chain mail like everyone else?" he demanded, not bothering to greet his commander formally.

"You're the king, and I'm responsible for your life," Alvaro replied.

"But how can I fight when I'm weighed down by all this armor? If the rest of you charge down the hill, you'll reach the bottom before I've been able to gallop more than one hundred yards."

Kings, Father Sebastian had always said, were a special breed and required delicate treatment, but Alvaro, facing his first battle, forgot diplomacy. "You won't take part in the battle," he said bluntly.

The boy blinked at him. "That isn't fair!"

"I promise you that if circumstances permit, you'll have a

chance to win personal glory," Alvaro declared. "But you seem to have forgotten, Your Majesty, that I haven't had an opportunity to teach you the refinements of jousting. Until you learn them I believe it would be a frightful error for you to ride into combat against men who would like to win immortality by cutting off your head."

Juan smiled feebly, unconsciously raised a hand to the flaring band of steel that protected his throat and tried to recover his dignity. "I suppose you're right," he conceded. "But I'm going to hold you to your promise."

"I'll never break my word to you," Alvaro said earnestly and, removing his right glove, startled the members of the king's suite by clasping Juan's hand.

"They're coming!" someone shouted.

Alvaro stood in his saddle and addressed the gentlemen-at-arms. "Remember your instructions, and obey them faithfully. No man may approach His Majesty. If affairs go badly for us, escort him to Toledo, and permit no one to detain you." Raising his hand in salute, he pulled down his visor and rode off a few yards to join his staff.

"Their strength is about equal to ours," Roderigo said as they watched a long column of cavalry and infantry kicking up clouds of dust on the road that crossed the valley below. "Two scouts have reported independently of each other that Pedro has been reinforced by the Cuevas garrison."

"How many are horsemen?"

"Seven hundred, perhaps eight hundred. The rest are pikemen, in the main, and they have a few small units of artillery."

Through the slits in his visor Alvaro could see three huge catapults, each being hauled by a team of eight oxen, bringing up the rear of the opposing column. He laughed, and felt Roderigo staring at him. "What good will catapults do Pedro? Apparently he hasn't stopped to think that we're meeting him in the open. There are no walls to be breached, and at most his artillery can dig furrows in the hills and splinter a few harmless scrub pines."

"That hadn't occurred to me."

Father Sebastian had been right, Alvaro thought, when he had said that the grandees, as a class, were the victims of their own rigid formulae and were incapable of developing techniques of war to fit changing situations. Even Roderigo, who should have known better, allowed himself to be hampered by outmoded traditions and conventions.

The cavalry vanguard of the long column halted, and while the horses pawed the ground nervously, a small group moved out into the open to the tune of a trumpet flourish and ruffle of drums. Leading this band was a knight in full armor who carried a white flag, and behind him were several other men, accompanied by standard bearers. Roderigo studied the pennants carefully. "The yellow flag with the slanted black bars is Pedro's. Duke Domenico of Cuevas has a green ensign with a gold border, and the plainer green one beside it is that of his half-brother, the Marquis de Almanzora."

"Shall we have words with them?" Alvaro signalled to a page, who raised a white banner.

. Juan, so excited that he almost fell to the ground as he stood in his stirrups, called anxiously, "I want to come with you, Alvaro."

"Castile would never forgive me if Your Majesty suffered harm. With your permission," Alvaro added, observing the amenities by pretending to defer to the king's wishes, "I shall learn what Prince Pedro is thinking, and will report my conversation to you. Then you'll be in a better position to decide what action to take."

Not waiting for a reply, he started down the slope behind the page who carried the flag of truce. Roderigo rode beside him, and two adjutants, junior officers who held no important titles in their own right but had been granted commissions in the army because they were related to great nobles, brought up the rear.

"I wish," Roderigo said, "that there had been time to have our personal ensigns sewn before we left Toledo. We look like a band of mercenaries."

"I have no flag," Alvaro said cheerfully, "and I don't care if I never fly one." This was not the moment to explain his conviction that complicated, meaningless rituals were destroying the foundations of the code of chivalry. Even the greatest warriors were encumbered by insignia, heraldic devices and coats of arms, and the original purpose of these symbols, the identification of a man hidden beneath a suit of armor, had become lost in the competition between men of high station, who spent vast fortunes trying to impress each other with the magnificence of their crests.

Dismissing these thoughts from his mind, Alvaro studied the party at the foot of the ridge.

Pedro, Cuevas and the marquis all carried two-edged swords, shields and, hanging from their saddles, the curved scimitars of the Moors. Their aides were even more heavily armed: lances rested in saddle sockets, and heavy battle-axes were suspended from broad belts that also held sheathed knives. It was significant that the herald who carried the flag of truce wore a suit of German armor which was so heavy and thick that he could scarcely lift his arms. It was obvious that the prince and his allies were prepared for heavy fighting.

Nevertheless, Alvaro was determined to give no unnecessary offense. Raising his visor as his stallion reached the bottom of the hill, he held up his right hand in a gesture that indicated his peaceful intent. "On behalf of His Majesty, I bring you greetings," he called.

Pedro and Cuevas, who was only a year or two older than Alvaro, lifted their own visors, and the Marquis de Almanzora followed their example more slowly.

"We see the royal ensign up there," the prince replied unpleasantly, "but we have no proof that the king is actually here. Why hasn't he come to parley with me himself?"

"His Majesty has seen your arms," Alvaro retorted, "and doesn't wish to be captured and imprisoned by someone who may have evil designs against him. The size and strength of Your Highness' escort leaves your motives in some doubt." Although his words were blunt, his smile was friendly.

Pedro bristled, and the Duke of Cuevas leaned forward in his saddle. "Why has the king ridden into my domain with so many followers?"

"Your domain, Your Grace?" Alvaro demanded. "Has Cuevas seceded from Castile, or is Juan still the master in his own house? He goes where he pleases in his realm, accompanied by as large or as small a suite as he deems proper, and he is responsible to no man for what he does."

The duke flushed and tugged at his small, pointed beard. "I stand corrected," he said in an undertone.

Pedro stared hard at Alvaro, then at Roderigo. "Who are you? You speak in the name of the king, yet you carry no crests on your shields and you fly no pennants."

Roderigo drew himself to his full height proudly. "Don Roderigo de Pinar, lord of Montalban and nephew of the last constable of Castile, the late Don Ruy Lopez d'Avalos."

The grandees bowed to him, and the duke smiled. "Accept my congratulations on your return to royal favor, Don Roderigo."

Pedro pointed a mailed hand at Alvaro. "And you, who act as spokesman for King Juan?"

"Don Alvaro de Luna, royal chamberlain and commander of His Majesty's escort."

The prince and Cuevas exchanged uncertain glances.

It would be foolish, Alvaro thought, to remind Don Pedro of their previous meeting. Eventually the prince would remember that he was confronting the man who had humiliated and permanently disfigured his brother.

"Lord de Luna of Canete left no legitimate heir." Don Pedro was clearly puzzled.

Domenico of Cuevas coughed delicately. "A man need not be inferior because he is a bastard, Your Highness."

"My apologies, Cuevas. I had forgotten that you're illegitimate."

The Marquis de Almanzora shifted in his saddle and bit his upper lip. It was no secret that, although he was the son of the late duke's wife and should have inherited the senior title, his father had shown a marked preference for his older son and had been granted the right to leave the duchy to an illegitimate offspring.

Pedro was studying Alvaro again, and suddenly a light of recognition appeared in his eyes. "I know you now." He set his jaw firmly.

"Now that we have settled these minor questions," Alvaro declared, speaking calmly, "His Majesty wants to know your intentions."

"I shall tell them to His Majesty," Pedro replied rudely.

"He has ordered me to obtain a complete explanation from Your Highness."

The prince was silent.

"If you can give no satisfactory account of your reason for riding into Castile from Navarre with an army of mercenaries and securing the additional services of the household retainers of His Grace of Cuevas, you are instructed to disband your troops at once." Alvaro looked steadily at the prince.

"Suppose I refuse?" Pedro asked, and laughed contemptuously.

"In that unfortunate case, Your Highness, it would be my duty to perform the task for you."

The Duke of Cuevas was agitated. "One moment," he said. "What does the king intend to do about my estates?"

"I'm afraid I don't know what you mean, Your Grace." Alvaro sensed tensions he couldn't define.

"Is it his aim to deprive me of my lands and my title?" the duke demanded.

"Only if you take up arms against him," Alvaro replied flatly.

"Then he hasn't come to Cuevas in order to dispossess me?" The thought amused Roderigo.

Alvaro remained alert, however, and saw Almanzora glance at the prince for an instant, then turn away hastily. Suddenly the whole scheme was clear. "I think, Your Grace, that His Highness and the marquis may wish to retract some statements that I suspect they have made to you. Let me assure you that His Majesty holds you in high regard, that he believes you to be a loyal and honorable subject and that he has not contemplated taking either your title or your estates from you."

Cuevas reached into his helmet and wiped a film of perspiration from his forehead. "Then why have you brought thousands of horsemen into my duchy?"

"We have been seeking a meeting with His Highness. It's accidental that our paths should have crossed on your land. Had we left Toledo a day earlier, which I grant you would have been physically impossible, we would have met him somewhere to the north, closer to the border of Navarre."

The duke twisted in his saddle and looked at his half-brother.

"No, Domenico!" Almanzora cried.

"I see now," Cuevas said in a tight voice. "Very clever. I would have been killed in battle, and you would have taken my title." Not waiting for a reply, he turned to Don Pedro. "Your Highness, I withdraw from your force. Don Alvaro, I regret any inconvenience I may have caused His Majesty and you. I gladly place myself at your disposal, and beg you to accept my services. My retainers are yours to command." Slowly, deliberately, he rode to Alvaro, removed his right glove and extended his hand. Then, after glancing again at the marquis, he moved to a position beside Roderigo.

Alvaro made no attempt to hide his elation. His force, augmented by Cuevas' troops, could overwhelm the prince's little army—the battle had been won without a single charge, without a single casualty. "Perhaps," he said softly, "Your Highness will choose to reconsider the king's instructions. If you will disband your escort, he will be happy to show you how highly he regards his kinsman."

"I prefer to return to Navarre," Pedro said harshly.

"As you wish, Your Highness."

Several men were looking at the hill, and Alvaro was dismayed and annoyed to see Juan, surrounded by the gentlemen-at-arms, riding down the slope. The danger to the king was diminished, but the situation would have been easier to handle had he remained on the ridge. Now, however, there was no alternative, and Alvaro raised his right arm in a stiff salute. The Duke of Cuevas, Roderigo and most of the attendants followed his example, but it was significant that Don Pedro and the Marquis of Almanzora sat motionless.

"You've been conferring for a long time," Juan said as he approached the group. Although his visor covered his face, it was obvious he felt he had been ignored.

"There was a misunderstanding, Your Majesty," Alvaro said.

Cuevas dismounted, approached the king on foot and told his story quickly.

Juan raised his visor, blinked and looked mildly disappointed. "There won't be a fight?"

"Your Majesty has won a victory without a battle," Alvaro said emphatically.

The boy's expression became brighter. "Then you've won it for me, Alvaro!"

Domenico of Cuevas agreed heartily. "All credit is due to Don Alvaro, Your Majesty."

Don Pedro shifted in his saddle impatiently. "You choose strange companions, cousin, now that your mother is no longer here to protect you," he said with heavy sarcasm.

Juan looked as though he would burst into tears, but managed to control himself. "We permit no one to criticize our choice of friends," he said stridently.

Pedro bowed elaborately, his smile mocking.

Alvaro was relieved when the Duke of Cuevas mounted his stallion again. He felt certain that Almanzora had been tempted to ride down his half-brother and trample him.

"For the present, cousin," the prince said contemptuously, "I won't dispute your choice of friends. I am returning to the court of my brother in Navarre."

"Give our love to our cousin and namesake," Juan replied, displaying surprising vigor.

"With Your Majesty's permission," the Marquis of Almanzora said, "I shall accompany Don Pedro."

"Go where you please," Juan retorted.

Alvaro remained silent, but made up his mind to recommend, in the strongest terms, that the council proscribe the marquis, brand him as an outlaw and expropriate his property.

"I hope to find you consorting with gentlemen when we meet again, cousin," Pedro said to the king, "and perhaps I can help you, in a small way, before I take my leave." He faced Alvaro, his eyes cold. "You accused me of lying to the Duke of Cuevas in order to further my own ends."

"I made no accusations, Your Highness," Alvaro replied formally. "The facts were plain."

"My father was king of Aragon, my grandfather and his father before him were kings of Castile," the prince said proudly. "My mother was the daughter of a king, and could trace her royal ancestry through eight generations. Who are you, son of a bawd, to call me a liar?" Not waiting for a reply, he removed the steel-plated glove from his right hand and threw it on the ground in front of Alvaro's stallion.

"I'm the one he tried to trick!" Domenico of Cuevas shouted. "It's my right to avenge my honor!"

Roderigo tried to intervene, King Juan raised his voice excitedly and several of the attendants pressed forward.

"Move aside, all of you," Alvaro said, his tone so uncompromising that the others halted and stopped speaking. Drawing his sword, he leaned down, ran the point through the heavy leather webbing of the gauntlet between the thumb and forefinger and, after spearing the glove, deposited it on his saddle. He stared at it for an instant, then laughed. "It seems to be my destiny to fight the members of your family in duels, Your Highness," he said pleasantly, then hurled the gauntlet into Don Pedro's face.

The prince did not flinch. "Will you dismount?"

"Certainly, when you do."

Watching each other carefully, they lowered themselves to the ground.

"You demonstrated a measure of skill with a sword several years ago," Pedro said, "but I wonder if you happen to be familiar with other forms of personal combat."

"He challenged you, Alvaro," Roderigo said anxiously. "You have the right to choose the method of duelling."

"Don't joust with him," Cuevas added. "No one in Iberia is his match."

Angry and consequently reckless, Alvaro waved his right hand to quiet his supporters. "Although I have the right to select any form of combat I choose, I have no preference." He realized he was disregarding Father Sebastian's patient instructions, that he was foolishly relinquishing a natural advantage, but he was too aroused to care. "If you consider yourself an expert in jousting, Your Highness, I shall be happy to meet you here and now on the field. If you prefer swords, perhaps I can give you a beauty mark such as Don

Enrique wears." He bowed disdainfully. "As your ancestry is so distinguished, I defer to you."

Roderigo scowled and muttered under his breath, but King Juan was delighted and applauded his favorite's brave words.

Don Pedro's smile was bloodless. "You're so sure of your skill and strength you'll accept any type of combat I name?"

"With great pleasure and even greater anticipation."

"Then let your second confer with mine." Turning his back, the prince walked to Almanzora, and the marquis leaned out of his saddle to speak with him.

Roderigo dismounted quickly. "Don Alvaro is my friend," he said belligerently, daring anyone to contradict him.

Alvaro beckoned, and the adjutants rode closer. "Tell the commanders of the squadrons to be prepared for a charge," he said, speaking loudly and distinctly so that the grandees from Navarre could hear him. If the prince was hoping to launch a surprise attack, the royal cavalry would be waiting.

The adjutants saluted and cantered up the slope.

"Your Majesty," Alvaro said, "your safety is my first concern. I insist that you withdraw."

Juan was shocked and outraged. "No! I've never forgotten how you scratched Enrique, and I'm not going to be cheated now." He pulled his visor over his face and settled himself squarely in his saddle.

Alvaro tried to think of some way he could persuade the boy to ride at least a few hundred feet up the hill, where he would be out of harm's way.

Cuevas obviously understood his anxiety and sympathized with his dilemma. "Don Alvaro," he said earnestly, "you have little cause to trust me, I know. If it weren't for your shrewd thinking, I'd be a traitor to Castile at this moment. But I want to make amends, and I beg you to grant me permission to help the gentlemen-at-arms protect His Majesty. If any man dares to approach King Juan, I swear to you in the name of Saint Paulo, my patron, that I'll kill the rogue, no matter who he might be. Please, give me a chance to earn my self-respect."

Neither the tutors at Avignon nor the long years of study at the Sanctuary in Madrid had prepared Alvaro for such a situation, and he studied the duke in silence. He saw an opportunity to win a devoted friend for the crown and himself, but he was taking a terrible risk, and he weighed the question carefully. Unable to find a solution analytically, he relied on his instinct, smiled and extended his hand. "I place His Majesty in your keeping."

"You won't regret this, Don Alvaro, nor will the king." Cuevas moved closer to Juan and the gentlemen-at-arms, then ordered his own adjutants to detach his retainers from the Navarre contingent, march them up the hill and place them under the command of the forces loyal to the king.

Don Pedro, still talking in a low voice with Almanzora, who had dismounted, was unbuckling his armor. Alvaro glanced at Roderigo, who frowned and shrugged. Cuevas seemed to have no idea of what the prince had in mind, either, and even the knights from Navarre looked perplexed when Pedro removed the steel plates that covered his boots, handed his helmet to an equerry and then stripped to the waist.

At last Almanzora turned, and Roderigo, unable to conceal his curiosity, joined him. The marquis spoke softly for some moments, and Roderigo protested, but Almanzora seemed adamant. Alvaro, trying to appear unconcerned, waited near the king and Cuevas until his friend hurried toward him.

"Pedro thinks you're afraid to fight an old-fashioned Moorish duel," Roderigo said tensely, "and he won't consider any other kind of combat."

"Does he mean a duel with whips?" Alvaro felt a painful, familiar dryness in his mouth.

"No, with battle-axes, and he insists that each of you wear only breeches and boots. It's barbaric!"

Cuevas was distressed. "Don Pedro spent a year in the Alhambra as a prisoner of the Moors when his father's campaign against Granada failed, and I've often heard him boast that he was taught many of the arts of the Muslims."

Juan, whose faith in Alvaro was unlimited, was disturbed, too. "He wants to murder you. He's a butcher!"

A spasm of fear shook Alvaro, but he forced himself to think coolly. He had been taught to use a battle-axe at Avignon when he was a small boy, and had strengthened his arms and wrists at the Sanctuary by swinging a heavy axe occasionally. Father Sebastian had instructed him in the art of fighting with a scimitar, too, and he thought he knew enough to defend himself creditably. It was plain that the prince considered himself a master duellist and that he hoped to kill his opponent, but it was impossible to plead inexperience and refuse without losing all honor and dignity.

"Inform the marquis," Alvaro said thickly, "that I accept His Highness' proposal."

"Don't do it!" Roderigo replied in a low, urgent voice.

Alvaro saw Pedro watching him expectantly. "Tell the marquis I accept," he repeated loudly, and began to remove his chain mail.

The duel was delayed while the Duke of Cuevas' cavalry and pikemen marched in formation from the column in the valley and climbed the hill. Word of the impending duel spread, and officers on both sides controlled their men with difficulty. Troops pressed forward to obtain a better view, and lieutenants were forced to use the flats of their swords to restore order. Grandees from Navarre left their posts, and several officers who were members of Alvaro's staff rode down the hill. At least one hundred men were gathered at the site. Alvaro, pulling off his shirt, became annoyed.

"Clear the area!" he said sharply, betraying his nervousness.

"This is going to be a personal duel, not a public spectacle."

The loyal adjutants and Cuevas sent the cavalrymen up to the ridge again, and the gentlemen from Navarre, unwilling to let their foes appear more gallant, reluctantly withdrew, too.

Almanzora obtained two battle-axes from armored members of the prince's party, and Roderigo examined both weapons carefully, then returned to Alvaro, who felt cold, even though a hot sun was beating down on his bare head and back.

"You have your choice of axes."

"Is there any difference between them?"

"Their weight is equal, as nearly as I can judge." Roderigo tried unsuccessfully to hide the loathing he felt for the whole procedure. "One is an inch longer than the other."

"I'll take the shorter, then."

"But Pedro is taller than you, and his reach is longer. You can compensate, in part, if you take the longer axe."

"No." Alvaro was recalling Father Sebastian's advice in handling a scimitar. Balance, the priest had told him, was more important than any other factor in selecting a weapon, and it was obvious that a man with small hands and short arms should choose the smaller axe. "I know what I'm doing, Roderigo," Alvaro added when his friend hesitated, and tried to grin confidently.

His fear lessened somewhat when he gripped the smooth, polished oak handle of the murderous weapon. The head was double-edged, and the blades had been honed until they were as sharp as razors. Alvaro tested the axe, swung it experimentally a few times and surreptitiously wiped the palm of one hand, then the other, on his breeches. Pedro, he saw, glancing obliquely at his opponent, was swinging his weapon with practised ease, and Alvaro knew that Cuevas had been right; the prince had become expert in the art of duelling with an axe during his captivity in Granada.

Almanzora said a few final words to Roderigo, then both

returned to their horses, mounted and drew their swords, which they placed across their pommels, ready for use if any outsider tried to join the fight. The seconds had agreed that Juan would give the signal that would start the duel, and one of the gentlemen-at-arms tied a small square of white silk to the end of a lance.

In the meantime the two principals approached each other and stood on a patch of hard, level ground, about twenty feet apart. Don Pedro was arrogantly confident, and with good reason: he was six inches taller than his opponent, his arms were long and the muscles in his shoulders and back were sinewy. Lifting his axe, he twirled it over his head nonchalantly as though it were a Muslim scimitar, and he handled it with such easy grace that he appeared to be exerting no effort.

Alvaro, studying him carefully, took a deep breath, tried to smile and twirled his axe, precisely as the prince had done. He quickly discovered that the weapon was far heavier than the curved sword the Moors used; his wrist ached and he could feel the muscles in his forearm quivering. Realizing that he was weakening himself unnecessarily, he gripped the handle again and lowered the axe to the ground. He felt annoyed because he had indulged in a cheap gesture that had accomplished nothing, but a glance at his foe indicated that perhaps his instinct had been right.

Pedro, no longer relaxed and debonair, was scowling thoughtfully, his eyes clouded. He had expected his opponent to be totally unfamiliar with the kind of fight he had suggested, but it was obvious that Alvaro could handle an axe, and the prince didn't want to make the same mistake that had scarred his brother's face. He looked the shorter man up and down carefully, and paid him the compliment of respecting him as a duellist.

"Are you ready, Your Highness?" Almanzora called.

"Ready," Pedro replied, holding the axe before his face.

"Don Alvaro, are you ready?" Roderigo's voice was hoarse.

Bending down, Alvaro scooped up a handful of loose dirt, dusted his palms with it and sprinkled a liberal amount on the handle of his weapon. Common soldiers frequently took similar precautions before a battle to make certain their weapons didn't slip out of their hands, and Don Pedro's mouth twisted in a cynical, disgusted smile. But Alvaro didn't care what his opponent thought of him; it was more important to reduce risks to the minimum rather than ape the elegant manners of grandees and lose his life.

"I'm ready, Don Roderigo," he said, and belatedly wished he had tied Doña Teresa's handkerchief to his belt.

Cuevas said something to the king, and Juan nodded. "Gentlemen," he said, following the ancient code of the duel, "if either of you is willing to reconcile your differences, speak."

There was no sound but the metallic jingle of a horse's armor plating.

Juan was holding his lance vertically, and after a moment's pause he lowered the tip. The white square of silk touched the ground, and the duellists were free to start their combat.

Don Pedro advanced slowly, cautiously, and Alvaro, waiting for him, raised his axe, holding his right hand at the base of the handle and gripping the smooth oak about six inches closer to the head with his left. It was impossible to parry an opponent's swing, and virtually none of the principles of swordplay could be utilized; a man could defend himself only by leaping out of the path of his foe's weapon, and an attack also required perfect coordination, speed and balance.

Alvaro stood motionless, his feet close together. He thought it likely that the prince intended to strike first, and Alvaro was willing to give his enemy the initiative, then launch his own counterassault. He knew that, no matter which man won, the duel would not be prolonged. Unfortunately, heavy axes were not swords, and one or the other fighter would be either dead or maimed in a short time.

Pedro swung his axe with both hands, putting all of his strength into the blow as he aimed at his opponent's throat. Had he found his target, he would have decapitated his foe, but Alvaro leaped out of the path of the gleaming blade, and Pedro spun about, making a complete circle.

Before he had a chance to regain his balance, Alvaro closed in. Raising his axe only a few inches, he chopped at the prince's forearms. Pedro took two steps backward and barely managed to escape injury, for one edge of Alvaro's axe glanced off the handle of the prince's weapon. Taking advantage of the initiative he had gained, Alvaro attacked again, chopping repeatedly with short, hard strokes that made it difficult for Pedro to halt, plant his feet apart and swing again.

King Juan was cheering his favorite in a high-pitched voice, but Alvaro ignored the sound and, gaining confidence, chopped more sharply. The prince continued to give ground, and Alvaro, wanting only to injure his opponent sufficiently to halt the match, aimed all of his blows at his enemy's arms. He heard Pedro gasping for breath as he retreated, and the thought crossed Alvaro's mind that he was not duelling in the manner that the Moors had perfected. Instead he was a small boy again, fighting in the narrow, garbage-strewn streets of the *Mozarab* district of Toledo. Rules were non-existent, codes of honor were abstractions that hampered a combatant, and any trick, any act of cunning that could achieve victory was not only permitted but desirable.

Pedro was as courageous as he was arrogant, and moved backward slowly, shifting his arms constantly in order to avoid the sharp blades that threatened him. He had chosen the wrong form of duel, and in spite of his superior strength and greater size, he was facing an opponent who stubbornly refused to be intimidated. If anyone was suffering a handicap, it was the prince, who had spent his entire life in the restricted circles of the higher nobility, and he became confused when Alvaro pressed forward steadily, chopping with hard, rhythmic strokes and giving his tall enemy no chance to utilize the polished techniques he had learned from the Moors.

At last Pedro broke away, ran across the field and halted, panting. He had escaped without injury so far, he had no intention of subjecting himself to another ferocious attack, and he stood, the head of his axe resting on the ground, while he regained his breath.

Alvaro, however, had discovered a technique that would enable him to win the fight, and he was determined not to play the prince's game. He decided to wait until Pedro swung at him again, and then he would employ the same tactics he had used previously, close in, and start chopping. He waited, holding his axe close to his body with both hands, and tensed as his enemy slowly started toward him.

Juan shrieked in agony, but his warning came too late. Don Pedro raised his axe, twirled it and threw it with all of his strength and skill at his opponent's head. Alvaro, taken completely by surprise, flinched involuntarily but could not escape from the gleaming weapon. He caught a glimpse of burnished steel flashing in the sun; then a pain more excruciating than any other he had ever experienced numbed him. He felt himself falling to the ground, and a flame seemed to be spreading from the left side of his head through his entire body as he lost consciousness.

The bed stood beneath a canopy of blue damask, the mattress of feathers was incredibly soft, and the sheets, the pillows and even the bell-rope that hung near a small bedside table were made of shimmering silk. Heavy curtains of thicker silk, trimmed with cloth-of-silver, screened out the bright sunlight. Drapes of the most expensive velvet were suspended at either side of the window set high in the stone wall. Magnificent tapestries covered the area between the window and a hearth in which pine logs, sprinkled with incense, were burning.

Alvaro looked around in wonder after he opened his eyes, then slowly struggled to a sitting position. The room was strange, the crest embroidered in gold on the coverlet unfamiliar. He couldn't understand how he had come to this foreign place. A dull, throbbing ache on the left side of his head caused him to raise his hand involuntarily, and when his fingers touched a thick, soft bandage, he suddenly remembered what had happened to him. He moved his head cautiously, found that he could turn from side to side without additional discomfort. The feeling of relief made him weak. Lowering himself to the pillows again, he fingered a nightshirt of heavy silk, the most expensive garment he had ever worn, and when he felt a crest on the left side, near his heart, he tried to examine it. It was difficult for him to twist his neck in order to see it clearly, but as nearly as he could determine, it was the same insignia that was emblazoned on the coverlet.

Perhaps, he thought, he had been carried to Toledo and was in the royal palace, although that was unlikely. And he knew he was not the prisoner of Don Pedro, for he had no illusions about his fate under such circumstances; at best, he would have been thrown into a dungeon cell, and in all probability would have been chained to a prison wall.

The door opened, and a woman came into the room, her taffeta petticoats rustling beneath her gown of violet silk. She was carrying a tray laden with a decanter, several phials and a glass, and she almost dropped her burden when Alvaro exclaimed, "Doña Teresa!"

She stopped, stared at him and made no attempt to wipe away the tears that came to her eyes. "Thank you, Saint Teresa," she murmured, then turned to the young man in the bed and said joyously, incredulously, "You know me."

Alvaro felt a twinge of annoyance and wondered if she had forgotten she had given him her handkerchief as a token. "Of course I know you," he said testily.

Teresa placed the tray on the table and shook her head. "You've been out of your mind for two months. Most of these weeks you've thought I was your mother."

Alvaro was too stunned to reply.

She moved quickly to the far side of the room, picked up a silver-backed mirror of Venetian glass from the top of a chest of drawers and, after wiping her eyes and straightening her hair, carried the mirror to the bed. "Look at yourself."

Alvaro stared at his reflection and started to laugh. His face was long and thin, unusually pale, and his eyes were enormous. What startled him, however, was the pointed blond beard of a grandee on his chin.

"A barber has visited you every morning since you've begun to recover your strength." She poured a few drops from each of the phials into the drinking glass with the sure hand of an experienced nurse, added a quantity of wine and mixed the concoction with a spoon. "Drink this, and then I'll report to the physicians that you've recovered your wits, precisely as I knew you would."

There were many things Alvaro wanted to know, but he accepted the glass obediently, lifted it to his lips and shuddered. The bitter herbs in the medicine burned the roof of his mouth and scorched his throat. But when he saw that Teresa was frowning sternly, he took a deep breath and gulped down the concoction.

The girl laughed as she took the glass from him. "That's an improvement. How you've cursed at your tonic. You've even thrown glasses at the physicians."

He flushed, but forgot his embarrassment as she turned away. "Wait, please. If I've been—mad—for two months, the physicians can wait for a few moments longer to learn that I've become reasonable again. Where am I?"

"In your own house, milord," Teresa replied demurely.

Alvaro thought she was teasing him. "I own no house other than a small place in the *Mozarab* district of Toledo, and I'm not a lord."

"I'm sorry," she replied contritely, drawing up a chair and sitting beside him. "It's difficult for me to realize that you don't know any of the things that have happened. Have you no memory of these past weeks?"

He raised his hand to the bandage. "Prince Pedro threw his battle-axe at me, and I couldn't dodge it. That's the last thing I remember. Now, please, where am I, and what are you doing here, and how does it happen that I'm in this great bed, and—"

"One step at a time. You're in your own villa. You suffered from a graze, a head wound, when Pedro threw his axe at you. The Duke of Cuevas' half-brother was killed trying to escape after Pedro injured you, and King Juan made you Marquis of Almanzora."

"But the title and property should revert to the Duke of Cuevas—"

"The *Cortes* approved unanimously. My uncle says the nobles had no choice. And Domenico of Cuevas is proud to call himself your good friend. He has returned to his castle from Toledo, and he rides over every day to see you."

"I don't understand," Alvaro said, utterly bewildered.

Teresa patted his hand. "It's very simple," she replied soothingly. "Pedro's treachery aroused the whole country— you're a great hero to the people of Castile. Not many men would fight a duel against a prince of the blood with battle-axes." She smiled, but her eyes were hard, contemptuous. "Not many men would make Pedro's mistake, either. He escaped with his life because, in all the excitement, the soldiers were reluctant to attack the cousin of the king. But there's a price on his head now. He's sulking in Navarre, and Alfonso refuses to give him sanctuary in Aragon. Catalina

writes me that Enrique is furious, too. He had hoped to come
to Toledo himself, but public feeling is so intense and his
brother's effigy has been burned in so many cities and towns
that he's been forced to stay in Aragon. My uncle says that
your injury has saved Juan's throne, at least for the present."

Alvaro tried to assimilate all that he had been told, and
sighed.

"I'm tiring you," Teresa said, starting to rise.

He reached out and caught hold of her wrist. "Please, don't
leave. Tell me the rest."

"Well, the council ordered all regiments of the army
mobilized, but the troops have been sent home again. If
Pedro tried to come to Castile now, the people would drive
him out, and Enrique wouldn't fare much better."

"Then the king is truly safe." Alvaro grinned weakly and
relaxed.

"You have as strong a feeling of loyalty for Juan as he shows
toward you." Teresa looked at him curiously.

"Of course. He's the king," Alvaro replied simply, then
shifted his position so that he could see her more clearly.
"You still haven't told me how you happen to be here."

"Catalina and I came to Cuevas as soon as we heard of
your tragedy."

"Is Her Highness here, too?"

"No, the council insisted that Juan return to Toledo, and
she went with him."

"But you stayed, obviously."

Color rose in Teresa's face. "It was essential that someone
who—cared about you—look after you. Roderigo de Pinar is
still here, too," she added hastily.

Alvaro felt a stab of jealousy. Roderigo had displayed an
interest in Teresa, and there had been an opportunity for
him to pay court to her during the long weeks they had been
thrown into each other's company.

Teresa sensed Alvaro's reaction. "The people of Segovia have a saying that fits Roderigo."

Alvaro noted that she called his friend by his Christian name.

"*Bien sabe el sabio que no sabe, el necio piensa que sabe.* The wise man knows that he is not wise, but the fool imagines himself to be wise."

"Roderigo is no fool."

"He is just wise enough to know that if he remains close to you, he will rise with you."

Alvaro tried to laugh self-deprecatingly. "You have great faith in my untried talents."

"I agree with your brother, who spent a few days here last week. Father Ruminez says there's something in you that sets you apart from every other man in Castile, and he's right. I sensed it the first day we met."

"I hope I can fulfill your prophecy."

"When you return to Toledo," Teresa said with unexpected intensity, "you'll be made a member of the council."

Alvaro laughed aloud, and the side of his head ached.

"When you learn to curb your recklessness, you'll become a great man," she said fiercely. "You'll win all that you want."

Apparently she was aware of his ambition. "It would seem that I revealed many of my inner thoughts when there was no sentry to guard my tongue."

Teresa's manner changed, and her shrug of indifference was as pretty as it was artful. "You told me nothing I had not learned about you long ago, milord, from my own observations."

Alvaro glanced at her obliquely. "You say that I spoke of my mother."

She stood abruptly, forcing him to look straight at her. "You are ashamed of her."

"No!" Clenching his fists, he jerked himself to a sitting position.

"You feel shame for her and pity for yourself," Teresa declared bluntly, "but you're wrong. I've spent my whole life at the royal court, and I've seen all the great ladies. I've listened to their gossip, I've watched them open their doors late at night. Be proud of your mother. She was honest."

Alvaro stared at her. "Why are you being so sympathetic, so understanding?"

Teresa returned his gaze steadily. "Because I know how you feel. Because I've always watched others enjoy wealth and power. I've been tolerated because my uncle is a member of the council and the sister of the king has made me her friend. But who am I? What dowry can I bring to a husband, what influence can I offer a man? My uncle is old and wants to retire to a little estate he owns in the forests of Leon. Some day Catalina will be married to a king who asks for her hand, and then I'll stand alone. You aren't the only ambitious person in Castile, Don Alvaro de Luna."

Realizing she had said too much, Teresa gathered her skirts around her and left the room quickly.

Propping himself on the pillows, Alvaro ignored the ache in his head and stroked the crest on the coverlet, his insignia. A marquis could offer marriage to a lady of high birth, and Teresa had made it plain that she would accept his proposal. His mind functioning clearly in spite of the pain, he weighed the idea carefully. He was strongly attracted to her, just as she was drawn to him, and she would be a great asset to him in his career. She would be no mere decorative possession but a partner who who would work and scheme with him, fight at his side and help him to become master of Castile.

Until this moment he had never dared to admit his goal to himself, but he felt certain that he had revealed it to Teresa when he had been out of his mind. Smiling faintly, he reflected that he would climb more rapidly with her at his side. It was unfortunate that he didn't love her and he doubted that she loved him, but she could help his career immeasurably, and when he sired children, her lineage would increase the stature and importance of the new noble house of Don Alvaro de Luna, grandee of Castile.

"Cada uno case con su igual," he said aloud. "Let each marry with his equal."

3

The Infanta Catalina sat regally in a high-backed chair on a small dais near the windows of the living room of her private suite, but her quick smile, the rising color in her face and the happiness in her eyes were similar to the reactions of any girl who was pleased to see a young man.

Alvaro paused in the door and bowed low. "I am honored," he said formally, "that Your Highness has summoned me to an audience within a few hours of my return to Toledo."

"Had I done less, I would have failed in my duty," she replied primly. "I appreciate your efforts—and your suffering—for my family, Don Alvaro."

He could not resist staring at her as he closed the door behind him and, conscious of her effect on him, wished she were plain, dull and insipid.

Catalina started to speak, but changed her mind.

Alvaro fingered the hilt of his sword, nervously cleared his throat and became irritated because he was invariably tongue-tied in her presence.

"I trust that you've been restored to good health." Her words were banal, but she studied him, anxiety evident in her eyes.

"I'm completely recovered, Your Highness."

"I prayed for you, every day."

Too embarrassed to reply, Alvaro continued to stand near the door.

"Please come in and sit."

He walked slowly across the room, his footsteps echoing

on the tiled floor. There was another awkward silence, and he made a clumsy attempt to break it. "I expected to find you surrounded by your ladies and pages."

"I preferred to receive you alone. I sent them away," she said defiantly.

Alvaro was afraid to let himself read too much into her remark.

"Perhaps," Catalina said, her tone becoming impersonal, "you would have been happier if Teresa had remained."

"Doña Teresa was very kind to me." Alvaro spoke with care. "She nursed me back to health, and she showed me every consideration." He paused, then added delicately, "I saw her last only two weeks ago, but I have not had the joy of seeing Your Highness for many months."

"It has been a long time." The words slipped out, and Catalina raised a hand to her mouth.

"Very long," Alvaro said, averting his face.

The princess fingered the lace edge of a thin silk handkerchief, unable to hold her hands quietly in her lap. "Teresa tells me you became close friends during your convalescence."

"She was very generous with her time."

"Am I wrong," Catalina demanded suddenly, "to assume that the attachment may become more than that of two friends?"

Alvaro was startled by her candor, but replied honestly. "I try to think of my future, Your Highness. It is very new to me to look in my shaving mirror and say, 'Alvaro, you are a marquis.' I was a nonentity, Your Highness, but now I am in a position to found a new line. The portraits of *your* ancestors line the corridors," he added recklessly. "You don't know how much it means to someone like me to start a new house."

The princess stood and absently straightened her voluminous skirt. "I understand more than you realize. You've been in my mind—constantly."

He took a single step toward her, then halted. "I have no commitment to Doña Teresa, nor to anyone." It was wrong to shout, and he rebuked himself.

Catalina stepped down from the dais, her eyes glowing. "I'm glad," she murmured.

He clenched his fists, and his recently healed wound throbbed.

"Today," Catalina continued, sounding as though she had rehearsed the speech, "you are a marquis. There is no limit to the height you can reach."

Alvaro wanted to proclaim his love for her, to tell her that she had meant everything to him since he had first met her, but he knew he wanted the unattainable. Even if Catalina herself were willing to marry him, the grandees, the Church, even the common peope, would not permit such an alliance. But it was insane to dream: for the moment, perhaps, a princess was allowing sentiment to sway her because he had risked his life for her brother's cause, but she was too sensible to create a storm that would destroy both of them.

"Kings," he said hoarsely, "and the sons and daughters of kings fix their eyes on the stars. They need only reach out their hands, and anything they want is given to them. We who are ordinary people know there are peaks we cannot climb. We learn, early in life, to limit our ambitions to the feasible."

Catalina stood still, her arms at her sides, looking up at him.

Alvaro reached for her, touched her shoulders.

She made no attempt to resist him or pull away, and waited for his kiss.

A man was responsible for what he did, but a woman, even a princess, was only a woman. Alvaro thrust Catalina aside, turned and ran blindly into the corridor.

King Juan was admitted to the council chamber on his thirteenth birthday, and from that time forward sat at the head of the table. But the cautious Don Juan Hurtado de Mendoza, who still held the post of minister-in-chief, continued to preside over meetings, and Juan, who was bored by affairs of state, usually stared out of the nearest window or scribbled notes to one of the new members of the group, Alvaro and the Duke of Cuevas. The guards were being changed in the courtyard outside the council chamber one morning in April, 1418, and the king watched the ceremony for a few moments, then began to scribble some light verse on a sheet of thin, white parchment. Alvaro, who was listening to a financial report that the Duke of Lerma was making, sighed inwardly. Juan would ask him to set the words to music, and he would be forced to obey the royal request, although there were too few hours in the day.

"As I see it," Don Fernando de Robres remarked when Lerma had finished reading from a long column of figures, "we'll have too little money in the treasury to pay our obligations at the end of the month."

Cardinal Torello glanced around the table. "Are you surprised, gentlemen? You've seen your resources dwindling for the past six months, but you've taken no action."

"Well, we must act now," the minister-in-chief declared. "Do you have any thoughts on the subject, Your Majesty?" he asked as a matter of form.

Juan, not bothering to look up from his verses, shook his head.

Robres shuffled a stack of papers and smiled coldly. "I shall no doubt be opposed by my future nephew-in-law, but I believe the crisis can be ended overnight. Increase the tax on bread by one *penique,* raise the tax on red wine by one-half *penique* per liter, and the problem is solved."

Alvaro sat erect in his chair and as he frequently did when disturbed, ran the fingers of his left hand under his hair along the length of the scar on his head. "My esteemed future uncle-in-law is correct," he declared passionately. "The poor are always made to pay for the burdens of the government. A few coppers mean nothing to anyone in this room, but a shepherd whose sheep die because his grazing land is too dry or an artisan who can't find employment may be forced to watch his family starve to death because there aren't enough coppers in his purse."

"What do you suggest, Don Alvaro?" Mendoza asked, a hint of irony in his voice.

"Tax the grandees!"

The older members of the council exchanged wryly amused glances. "You realize, nephew," Robres said, "that you'd be taxed heavily."

Everyone in the chamber was conscious of the fact that Juan had heaped titles on Alvaro, who could now call himself a marquis three times, a count four times and a baron twice. "I'm willing to pay, uncle. I have the resources."

Robres chuckled. "If you'll permit the observation of one who knows, you'll have no funds to spare when Teresa becomes your financial responsibility instead of mine."

Lerma and Mendoza joined in the laughter.

"I agree with Don Alvaro," Don Domenico of Cuevas said. "We who own estates and vineyards and groves of fruit trees should pay for the cost of governing Castile. The army protects our property, and the wages of the soldiers should come from our pockets."

"Do you suppose the *Cortes* would approve a tax imposed on the grandees?" the minister-in-chief demanded.

"The *Cortes,*" Alvaro interrupted, "should be given no voice in the matter."

"No man is strong enough to impose his will on the nobles of Castile, nephew," Robres declared impatiently. "Milord, I request a vote on the issue."

The council split in a way that had become routine: a majority, composed of Mendoza, Robres and Lerma, favored an increase in the tax on wine and bread. Alvaro and Cuevas were opposed, the cardinal was present as an adviser and had no active voice in the proceedings, and Juan continued to write his verse.

"There is another matter to be discussed before we adjourn this morning," the minister-in-chief said. "His Majesty has just received a letter from Prince Enrique, requesting the hand of the Infanta Catalina."

Alvaro was startled. "I am absolutely opposed to such a marriage!"

"I assumed that you would be," Mendoza replied mildly. "Personally I can see nothing wrong with the idea. Alfonso has given his brother some rather extensive estates near Saragossa, and although Enrique has no voice in the government of Aragon, a marriage would keep him occupied."

"But why the Infanta Catalina, milord?" Alvaro demanded angrily. "It seems to me that he's trying to strengthen his claim to Castile."

"A tenuous claim," Don Miguel de Mateo of Lerma said. "As His Majesty enjoys the best of health, Prince Enrique may claim what he pleases. I agree with milord Mendoza. A marriage may give Enrique something to think about other than his plots and schemes against us."

The cardinal cleared his throat delicately. "You forget, gentlemen, that this body has no authority in such a matter. Theoretically, His Majesty has the right to dispose of his sister's hand—"

"I don't like Enrique," Juan said emphatically, raising his head for a moment.

"—but in practice," the cardinal continued, "Her Highness, who is an adult, will make her own decision. Where is the letter?"

The minister-in-chief handed him the communication, and it was passed around the table.

"Has the Infanta seen it?" Don Domenico asked.

Mendoza shook his head. "No, the courier arrived only this morning, and requests a reply before he returns to Saragossa." He tugged anxiously at his beard. "The situation is a complicated one, gentlemen. As His Eminence has said, the Infanta Catalina will make up her own mind, and as we know, she certainly has a mind of her own. My fear is that, if she rejects Enrique, he'll believe the council influenced her."

Alvaro laughed harshly and rubbed his scar. "I can solve that dilemma, milord. Let me take the letter to Her Highness. My feelings are no secret, and Enrique can't hate me more than he does at this moment."

The others agreed, and the meeting was adjourned. Juan hurried off to his own quarters to finish his poem, and as the men left the chamber Cardinal Torello caught Alvaro's arm. "A word with you."

"Yes, Your Eminence?" Alvaro carefully folded Enrique's letter and put it into the portfolio he was carrying.

"You make it your business to know everything that happens in Castile—I dare say you've heard that the post of vicar-general of my archdiocese is going to be vacated when Bishop de Guzman becomes Cardinal of Seville."

"So I've been informed, Your Eminence." Alvaro hesitated, wondering how to promote the candidacy of his brother without interfering in Church affairs, an offense the primate would be sure to resent.

Cardinal Torello smiled broadly. "I've already made my recommendation to His Holiness, and I've received his answer. I know you'll be pleased to hear that Father Ruminez will be promoted. I hope to consecrate him as a bishop before he performs your wedding ceremony."

"I'm delighted, Your Eminence."

"Of course you are, Don Alvaro, but I had a private reason for wanting to tell you the news. Your own rise has been extraordinarily rapid, and you have many enemies in the *Cortes*."

Alvaro shrugged.

"So it may be that I do you no favor. I'm afraid the uninformed will say you had a hand in your brother's selection. The grandees who resent you will become more fearful of your growing power and will try to pull you down."

They walked a few paces in silence. "May I ask an impertinent question, Your Eminence?"

"You've asked many since you became a member of the council."

"Why did you recommend Francisco?"

"Because he's a man of great ability."

Alvaro halted and grinned. "You've answered my enemies, Your Eminence. The poor cry for help, but their burden becomes greater. The brothers of Alfonso conspire against us and the Moors capture our merchant ships, raid our land and take innocent people into slavery. Castile needs competent men."

The cardinal refrained from telling him that Pope Benedict had written a brief personal note to the effect that if Father Francisco Ruminez showed half of his brother's promise, he would wear a red hat before he ended his career.

Alvaro respectfully took his leave of the older man, and returning the salutes of the sentries in the corridors, climbed the stairs to the ladies' apartments on the third floor. Armed guards who were stationed outside the entrance to the princess' quarters on his own orders admitted him to the suite, and he was surprised, when he entered an antechamber, to find Roderigo de Pinar, his boots dusty, chatting with Teresa.

Both stood, and after Alvaro had greeted his future wife decorously, kissing her on the cheek, he shook hands with his friend. "When did you arrive in Toledo?"

"Within the hour. I left Montalban as soon as I received

your message. I've been paying my respects to the ladies until you were free."

"Roderigo has been asking me why you sent for him," Teresa said.

"I've been developing a plan that you know nothing about, my dear." Alvaro reached into his portfolio, removed several charts and papers and gave them to Roderigo. "Study these and we'll discuss them at dinner."

"What are they?" Roderigo shuffled through the documents.

"I don't like the present method of raising troops. When there's trouble, we ask every grandee for help, and those who are inclined to give it, those who feel it suits their interests, send us some of their retainers. Only a small percentage of our army is made up of regiments paid by the crown. I want to develop a national corps that takes orders from no one except Juan."

Teresa, quick to realize that these men would owe their allegiance to Alvaro and obey his orders, smiled in approval.

Roderigo continued to ponder. "The *Cortes* won't like the idea," he said at last. "It limits the power of the grandees."

"That's why I'm hoping to change the system. Just in the past three weeks I've learned that a marquis and two barons are in the pay of Prince Pedro, the Duke of Avila has been corresponding with Juan of Navarre, and the Duke of Segovia is on very friendly terms with Prince Enrique. We need men who put the honor of Castile above everything else, men who will support the crown in an emergency."

"You think of everything," Roderigo said admiringly.

"I try."

"And he succeeds." Teresa linked her arm proudly through Alvaro's.

"My dear, I'm not here to see you," he told her, putting military problems out of his mind for the moment. "The council has sent me on official business to confer with Her Highness."

Teresa knew better than to ask him the nature of that business, realizing he would give her a full account later.

Roderigo took his plumed velvet hat from a chair. "I'll go to the room I've been assigned and meet you at dinner, Alvaro." He bent low over Teresa's hand and withdrew.

Alvaro and Teresa, alone for a moment, kissed again, and he would have prolonged the interlude, but she straightened her gown and went off to inform the princess that he requested an interview with her.

Catalina, who had been spending the morning in the garden, appeared in the white cotton blouse and full skirt of a peasant. Her hair was hanging loose. She wore no cosmetics and she looked so fresh and innocent that Alvaro stared at her for an instant before he dropped to one knee before her. "Your Highness," he said impulsively, "the spirit of Castile is embodied in you."

"How quickly you've acquired the tongue of a courtier, Don Alvaro," she replied reproachfully, trying to hide her embarrassment.

"I always tell you the truth, Your Highness." He stood and waited for formal permission to sit.

Catalina made herself comfortable on a padded stone bench, spread her skirts and indicated with a nod that he might join her. "Teresa says you're waiting on me at the orders of the council. What do their lordships want with me?"

Silently he took Enrique's letter from his portfolio and handed it to her.

Catalina read it carefully, then studied it a second time.

Alvaro, watching her obliquely, saw her eyes darken, but when she finally lifted her head and turned back to him, her expression was bland.

"What are my brother's wishes?" she asked, her tone a shade too light and carefree.

"His Majesty has no desire to dictate to you in a matter involving your happiness," he replied, choosing his words cautiously.

"And the lords of the council?"

"They leave the decision to you, Your Highness."

Catalina seemed determined to bait him. "What is your opinion, then? Surely you can advise me, Don Alvaro."

"That would be presumptuous." Unable to meet her gaze, he averted his eyes.

"Only a few moments ago you said you always tell me the truth."

She was bantering, but he sensed a deeper quality behind the façade, and could neither identify nor understand it. "Your Highness," he said earnestly, "my own estimate of Prince Enrique is well known to you—I won't dwell on it. Let me limit myself to the obvious. Most princesses are married at an early age. You've been more fortunate than most. Your mother rejected various suitors during the years of her regency, and more recently we've been trying to establish a stable regime. We've had little opportunity to think in terms of foreign alliances."

Her shrill laugh startled him. "I've been wondering about your opinion of me. Thank you."

The last subject he wanted to discuss was his own feeling for her, but he could not ignore the challenge. "I was referring to the collective views of His Majesty's ministers."

"And I'm talking about Don Alvaro de Luna, who regards me as a lifeless figure on a chess board, an inanimate object to be manipulated for the glory of Castile."

"I've never regarded you in that way, and you know it!" Alvaro shouted.

"Then what do you think of me?" She forced herself to ask the question.

"I don't have the right to express my feelings."

"I give you the right."

He stared at her, his fists clenched. "I'm afraid the privilege isn't in your power to bestow."

"Are you trying to deprive me of my prerogatives?" Catalina was becoming angry, too.

Alvaro knew the argument was as senseless as it was futile. "I have never allowed myself to forget that you're a princess," he said slowly.

"This isn't the first time you've hinted at things you haven't said."

"What would you have me do, Your Highness?"

Catalina's mouth tightened. "There is nothing you can do, Don Alvaro. You've become betrothed to Teresa."

"Is it so wrong for me to want to found a family?" he asked, and although he couldn't explain in detail, he silently pleaded with her for understanding.

She laughed scornfully. "Teresa isn't an heiress."

"I know that." His sense of frustration increased.

"Then you aren't marrying her only because of your ambitions."

Catalina looked like a girl who was making no attempt to control her jealousy, but Alvaro was afraid to let himself think about the possible depth and intensity of her feeling.

"You're attracted to her!" She sounded as though she were accusing him of committing a crime.

"Any man who failed to find her attractive would be blind." Alvaro longed to tell her that neither Teresa nor anyone else was as beautiful as the Infanta of Castile.

"Then there's no more to be said." Wooden-faced, she dismissed him with a sudden, imperious gesture.

He remained motionless. "You forget, Your Highness, that I didn't come here to talk about myself."

She glanced down at the letter she was holding, and the sheet of parchment trembled in her hand.

"It isn't my fault that you're one of the most eligible princesses in Europe." He refrained from adding that he would gladly admit his love for her if she were not the daughter of a king.

Catalina's bravado collapsed. "No, Alvaro, it isn't your fault any more than it's mine." She tried to smile, failed and looked very tired.

He reached out before he could check himself, and his hand closed over her wrist.

Catalina made no attempt to pull away, and looked up at him for a moment, desire and misery in her eyes.

Using all of his self-control, Alvaro released her.

She lowered her head and, in an attempt to hide, held the letter in front of her face. "Do I have a choice in this marriage?"

"Of course. If you didn't, I wouldn't have been sent to you."

"I have no desire to be married at present."

A wave of relief engulfed him.

"Therefore I choose to reject Enrique's offer." Suddenly she crumpled the letter and threw it to the floor in a gesture that indicated revulsion.

"His Highness' courier is waiting for your reply."

She looked up helplessly. "What can I say to him?"

"There are several ways of wording your reply tactfully."

"Will you write the letter for me?"

Alvaro knew she was capable of writing her own letters, and tried to understand her perversity. But he could not refuse a request from an Infanta, and bowed. "If that's your wish."

Catalina laughed, and there was a trace of hysteria in her voice. "Knowing your opinion of Enrique, I thought you'd enjoy writing him."

"I shall," Alvaro confessed.

Catalina laughed more stridently, then broke off abruptly

and raced from the room, a handkerchief pressed to her mouth.

Bishop Francisco Ruminez performed the ceremony that united his half-brother and Doña Teresa de Robres in marriage. The cathedral was lighted by thousands of candles, the red stained-glass windows which had been imported from Brussels and Antwerp at great expense cast a rosy glow over the high altar of alabaster, and the silver armor of the groom, who stood with King Juan, seemed to pick up the reflection of every taper. The bride, escorted by her uncle, wore a gown of pure white silk and a priceless lace mantilla that belonged to her friend, the Infanta Catalina. Members of the royal council sat in the front pews, Cardinal Torello occupied his throne and a large number of high-ranking clergymen were present, but surprisingly few grandees attended the event. Most of them had found it necessary to attend to urgent business at their country estates.

The cathedral was crowded, however, for Alvaro had insisted that the common people be admitted, and the pews were filled with merchants and artisans, steelworkers and wine sellers, Moors and Jews from the *Mozarab* district. A company of royal pikemen controlled an even larger crowd outside, and when the bride and groom appeared on the steps a spontaneous cheer frightened the pigeons that made their home on the roof of the church. The throngs were so dense that the wedding party, riding in open carriages, made its way back to the Alcazar with difficulty, and in the arcaded Zocodover, the main plaza of the city, a group of apprentices broke through the lines of soldiers and pelted the bride with rose petals.

The banquet that was served in the great hall of the castle was truly royal. Snow from the mountains had been carried to Toledo to chill the first course, *gazpacho,* a soup made of minced cucumbers, and the cooks had worked for three days blending the sauce that was poured over the *cigala,* a delicate Mediterranean shellfish. Each guest was served a whole partridge, baked in a crust of the finest wheat flour from the fields outside Toledo, and huge tureens of *pisto,* veal cooked with wine, cabbage and peppers, were carried to the tables by lackeys. Perhaps the greatest delicacy was *manchego,* a dry cheese of goat's milk, which the king had obtained by making a secret business arrangement with the Moors of Granada. Everyone loved *manchego,* and although it was obvious that the dish had been procured from the enemy, the guests asked no questions and consumed every crumb.

Only the bride and groom ate sparingly, drank small quantities of the many wines poured into golden goblets for them and sat, tensely quiet, at a table placed on a special dais that had been built for the occasion. Later, however, when a company of musicians appeared and the tables were cleared away, both became livelier. Alvaro serenaded Teresa with a song of his own composition, accompanying himself on the lute, and afterwards they danced together spiritedly. Every gentleman present insisted on claiming a dance with the bride; Alvaro danced with the Infanta Catalina and the wives of the council members. Innumerable toasts were drunk in grape brandy and in a liqueur made from crushed almonds and a double-distilled apple wine, and by sundown even the most staid ladies and gentlemen had become merry.

The bride and groom slipped away to change into traveling clothes, and when they came out into the main courtyard, where a carriage was waiting for them, they had to run a gauntlet of friends who threw ribbons of silk at them. Laughing and breathless, Alvaro and Teresa climbed into the carriage and rode out through the gates with a farewell salute from fifty royal trumpeters ringing in their ears.

Teresa was surprised when the coach circled around the outer wall of the Alcazar and halted in the shadows beside

a small, undistinguished black carriage. She blinked in bewilderment as two footmen transferred her leather clothing
boxes to the waiting vehicle and lashed them to the roof, but
she obeyed when Alvaro said, "Hurry!" and led her to the
drab coach.

He offered no explanation until they had resumed their
ride, and then he laughed. "It's lucky," he said, "that the king
can keep no secrets from me. Without realizing what he was
saying, he told me yesterday that he expects us to go to the
estate he gave us as a wedding gift near Algodor."

"Aren't we going there?"

"Tomorrow, not this evening. It's only an hour's ride from
the city, and Roderigo plans to lead the whole wedding party
there later tonight to serenade and annoy us."

"I might have guessed that you'd outwit everyone in
Castile," Teresa said and, sitting back against the hard, thin
cushion, leaned against his shoulder. "Where are we going
instead?"

"You'll see." The carriage was moving down into the
narrow streets of the city, and Alvaro took his bride's left
hand and stroked it. A ring that she wore on her little finger,
a square-cut emerald surrounded by small diamonds, picked
up the light of a watchman's torch as the man raised the burning brand, identified the passengers and waved the vehicle on
toward the Zocodover. "Some day," he said, "after we've
placed the country's finances on a sound basis, I'll be able to
afford something more expensive."

She smiled at him, then examined the ring critically. "It's
a lovely wedding gift, and I'll always be grateful to you for
it."

Many of the guests had worn more expensive jewels, but
Alvaro had emptied his strongbox in order to buy the gift,
and his wife's tact pleased him.

"I'd be criticized if I wore something more ostentatious
now," Teresa continued thoughtfully. "Later, when you re-

place Mendoza as minister-in-chief, it will be time enough for me to wear diamonds as large as Catalina's."

Alvaro refrained from saying that, in the event that he should succeed Mendoza, he would revise the tax structure so drastically that no grandee would be wealthy enough to indulge in such wild extravagance. But he didn't want to strike a sour note so early in his marriage, and he replied mildly, "It would be very costly to compete with an Infanta of Castile."

Teresa laughed, baring her teeth slightly. "She won't be a princess of the realm after she marries Enrique."

"That will never happen."

"I disagree. He can be very stubborn, almost as persistent as you. And he's wanted to marry Catalina for years. When he does, she can follow him in exile from one country to another. It will serve her right."

Alvaro was startled. "You sound as though you relish the idea."

"I do."

"But I've always thought you've been such good friends." He couldn't see her face clearly in the dark.

"I'd rather not begin our marriage by discussing another woman."

"Of course."

Teresa laughed quietly. "You and I aren't sentimental, but there are certain conventions we must observe. I'm sure you'll agree."

"To an extent." He shifted uncomfortably. "I'm not quite certain I know your definition of sentiment."

"We didn't marry," she said candidly, "because we fell madly in love with each other."

She had spoken the truth, but her unexpected bluntness was startling. "I've always thought you very lovely and desirable."

"I'm well aware of that, too, and I've been attracted to you

—in many ways. Not the least of them is my awareness of
your ambition. It's as consuming as mine, and I think we'll
make a good match." Teresa's smile became broader, and she
patted his hand.

Alvaro raised it to his lips and kissed her palm.

Teresa sighed gently, sat back and peered out of the window into the night. "Isn't this the *Mozarab* quarter?"

Alvaro nodded. "Be patient a few moments longer."

The carriage bounced over rough cobblestones, and the
sides scraped as the coachman drove down narrow streets.
Occasionally the odor of decaying garbage drifted into the
vehicle. Teresa said nothing, but glanced at her bridegroom
obliquely, seeming more surprised than annoyed. Finally the
carriage drew to a halt, and a watchman in civilian clothes
emerged from the shadows, opened the door and saluted.

"Has there been any trouble, sergeant?" Alvaro asked as
he handed Teresa to the ground.

"No, milord. The men and I have had a quiet evening."

"It's as I expected. You'll have no problems." Alvaro raised
the latch and stood aside to let Teresa precede him into the
candle-lit entrance hall. He wanted to carry her across the
threshold, but resisted the temptation because of the watchman, who was grinning at them.

"You called that man 'sergeant,' " Teresa said.

"Yes, I assigned a squad of royal household troops to duty
here. They're wearing civilian clothes because the people of
the district aren't friendly to soldiers."

"What is this place?" She looked curiously at the floors inlaid with new, gleaming tiles and the heavy drapes of raw silk
from which seamstresses' threads were still hanging.

"It's your house and mine," he replied, offering her his arm
and leading her up the stairs to a drawing room on the second
floor. "It belongs jointly to my brother and me, but Francisco
has agreed that we may live here as long as we wish. He ac-

tually signed a paper waiving his property rights, although that wasn't necessary."

Teresa paused and looked through the open door into a room simply but expensively furnished. The chairs were comfortable, an oak table gleamed beneath a lamp of polished silver, and porcelain containers of crushed pine needles kept the air fragrant. "Was this your mother's house?"

Alvaro was watching her anxiously. "Yes, she left it to Francisco and me. I've had it repaired and furnished for us."

"You intend to live here?"

"I spend enough time waiting on the king, and if we accept an apartment at the Alcazar we'll never have any privacy."

Teresa stared at him incredulously.

He urged her to enter the drawing room and, hiding his sudden fears, turned away from her for a moment to pour two small glasses of almond liqueur. "Other members of the council own their own homes. Why shouldn't I?"

She took the glass he gave her and twirled it. "I think," she said distinctly, "that you'd be wise to tear up the document your brother gave you and make out another, deeding the house to him."

"If you're afraid that my memories of my mother will disturb me, I assure you they won't. You've exorcised her ghost."

"Perhaps the vicar-general of the archdiocese will be content to live in the *Mozarab* quarter, but it isn't suitable for milord marquis, count, baron and knight."

Alvaro laughed uncomfortably. "I hold more titles than I've earned. Oh, I've served creditably enough on the council, but I've been given no chance to put any of my plans into effect. My one accomplishment was an act of bravado. Prince Pedro was stupid enough to cheat when we fought, and he's been eliminated as a danger to the throne for the present.

King Juan heaps honors on me because he knows I like him for himself, but I'm still a man of the common people."

Teresa drained her glass and handed it to him. "You're going to become the first grandee of Castile!"

"I'll drink to that with you, my dear." He refilled both glasses.

"The only thing that can prevent you from being made minister-in-chief of the council—and a duke—is your own foolishness. And it's the height of folly to live in slums with artisans and trollops and sausage-makers. You'll be laughed out of the *Cortes*."

Alvaro set his jaw stubbornly. "The gentlemen of the *Cortes* and I don't hold very good opinions of each other right now."

Teresa sipped her liqueur, sat down on a divan covered in tufted maroon velvet and tried a different approach. "How many houses do we own?"

"Four that I've visited in different parts of the country, and three others that I haven't yet seen. It's disgraceful, particularly when so many thousands of people are lucky to have mud roofs over their heads."

She looked into her glass for a moment, and when she gazed up at him her eyes were limpid and her voice caressing. "I'm sure we'll solve our problems, just as I know you'll be able to help the people who seem to be on your mind so much. You're going to be so powerful that you'll have everything you've ever wanted." She glanced around the room, hid her distaste for it and turned back to him again, confident of her own ability to influence him.

4

Gold supplied by King Juan of Navarre and Prince Pedro resulted in apprentices' riots in several cities, a refusal of farmers to send their wares to the markets and public demon-

strations by fishermen in a number of seaports. Prince Enrique renewed his bid for the Infanta Catalina's hand, and
the minister-in-chief, afraid there would be trouble on the
border of Aragon, urged her to accept, but she rejected the
proposal in a two-line letter. The council considered the possibility of sending troops on a march through the country to
intimidate the citizens, and the *Cortes* debated the idea of
increasing taxes again in order to make the people more sub-
missive to authority.

During this period, when every official was offering contradictory advice, Alvaro de Luna finally made his voice heard.
King Juan, he said, should travel through the realm accompanied only by a small detachment of household troops; he
should let himself be seen by his subjects, listen to their com-
plaints and win their loyalty. The king displayed unexpected
enthusiasm for the project and agreed to the expedition, provided Alvaro would accompany him.

They started out at once, with an escort of only fifty men,
and rode from city to city, journeying south to the Mediterranean, where they passed close to the borders of Muslim
Granada, riding north to the proudly independent Basque
provinces of Leon through the western mountain passes.
They completed the circle by turning east, won the respect
of their enemies by traveling within a half-day's ride of the
Navarre frontier and finally started south again, sometimes
sighting the border of Aragon. For the present, Alvaro rea-
soned, Castile had nothing to fear from the most powerful of
her Iberian neighbors, for King Alfonso, following the policies established by his father, was busily engaged in expand-
ing his nation's trade with the Italian states. The most competent of Juan's cousins appeared to realize that a war with
Castile would be a tragedy for both countries, and it was
rumored that he was making plans to conquer a number of
Mediterranean islands, the Balearics, Sardinia and Sicily,

which he believed necessary to insure the security and promote the economy of his subjects.

Gambling on his theory that Alfonso was a man of honor, Alvaro frequently led Juan and the small escort within sight of mounted patrols on the far side of the border. His daring disturbed the older members of the council, who received regular reports on the progress of the tour, and the minister-in-chief wrote him several letters cautioning him against behaving recklessly, but his faith in Alfonso's chivalry and common sense was justified, and after spending three months on the roads of the kingdom, the king and his chamberlain arrived safely at the royal lodge outside the town of Tordesillas.

Juan ordered a double ration of grape brandy served to the troops and, accompanied by Alvaro, went to the great hall, where a fire was burning in the hearth. Piles of letters awaited them, and they read the first correspondence of any consequence they had received in many weeks, sipping spiced wine and warming themselves before the fire.

"I thought Catalina and Teresa would join us here," the king said, glancing quickly through a letter from his sister, "but there's no word here about the possibility."

Alvaro was studying official communications before turning to his personal mail, but he nodded. "I haven't expected Teresa. She's too busy decorating our new palace near the Duke of Lerma's in the Toledo hills."

Juan's friendship with his favorite had deepened during the months they had spent together, but there were some subjects that Alvaro rarely mentioned, and the king hesitated for a moment. "Is it true that you went into debt to the bankers to buy the palace?"

"No, Juan," Alvaro replied truthfully. "I sold various properties so that I could pay the bankers their fee, but I've accumulated no debts."

"I'd make you a gift if you needed more money."

Alvaro smiled at the earnest boy. "You've given me more than enough. My enemies say I don't deserve your favors."

"I don't care what people say."

"You must be above criticism, or you'll be attacked through me. Wait until I've accomplished something tangible before you give me any more rewards."

"The king may do as he pleases," Juan said, his temper flaring.

"No, he must do only that which is good for the people."

"Now you sound like my tutors." The king changed the subject. "I don't blame Teresa for wanting a big palace."

Alvaro stared at the logs burning in the hearth. "Neither do I," he replied in a clipped tone that, he hoped, would indicate he didn't want to discuss his wife.

Juan was gazing at him curiously. "Was that house in the *Mozarab* district one of the properties you sold?"

"Nothing would induce me to part with it."

There was an uncomfortable silence, and the king knew there was a barrier his friend would permit no one to penetrate. "Here, do you want to read Catalina's letter?"

"I don't think that would be proper."

"She says quite a bit that concerns you."

Alvaro tried to curb his curiosity; as a matter of principle, he believed, it was wrong for any outsider to read correspondence between members of the royal family. "Tell me what you think I ought to hear."

"She says the council is annoyed because our journey has been a triumph for you. Mendoza and Robres are annoyed because the crowds have paid very little attention to me."

It was true, Alvaro knew, that he had been the center of attention in almost every city and town. The people had learned of his attempts to shift the tax burden to the nobles who could afford to pay large sums, and he had been cheered everywhere, although the grandees who had been their hosts had virtually ignored him. "What is Her Highness' opinion?"

"Oh, Catalina feels just as I do, that you're right. But all the nobles we've seen have told me the *Cortes* will veto the proposal if it should ever be proposed by the council."

For the immediate future the problem seemed insoluble and Alvaro shrugged as he reached for the next letter on the stack that awaited him. The seal was that of the council secretariat, he noted, and breaking it hastily, he read the brief communication. "Mendoza and Robres are going to join us here and ride back to Toledo with us."

Juan became petulant. "I wanted to go hunting for a few days before I start spending all of my time studying and being examined by tutors!"

It was useless to explain that the two old men, who had held power for so long, were reluctant to permit the favorite who had become so popular with the people to repeat his triumph in the capital. Obviously the ministers would be accompanied by a large entourage and would assign an obscure place to Alvaro when the party rode into Toledo. However, he missed Teresa, and he preferred to suffer the jealousy of his senior colleagues than waste several days hunting deer with Juan, who could handle neither a lance nor a bow and arrow. "As they should arrive late tomorrow, I'm afraid we have no choice," he said diplomatically.

"When am I going to be allowed to do as I please?"

Alvaro tried to pretend the question was rhetorical, and sliding the letters from Teresa into his belt to read later, he stood, smiling. "If you're as hungry as I am after a long day's ride, I hope it will please you to eat dinner."

The boy's mood changed immediately, and they went together into the dining hall, where a roast of lamb, a suckling pig and a smoking joint of beef were placed before them. Alvaro thought, as he did frequently, that the waste in the royal kitchens was prodigal. There was enough set before two people to feed twenty, but as Juan had never known any other way of life, he said nothing. It was impossible to describe poverty to someone who had never starved.

The king, eating heartily, began to discuss the possibility of going hunting the following day in the pine forest south of Tordesillas. Alvaro, trying to humor him, planned the details with him. They heard loud voices at the gates of the lodge, but thought the guard was being changed and paid no attention to the brief commotion.

Alvaro was caught completely by surprise when a group of a dozen or more men carrying heavy swords pushed into the room, led by a tall figure in silver armor.

Leaping to his feet, Alvaro reached for his sword, but realizing that he could not fight so many, he did not draw the blade. Instead he held his hand on the hilt and stepped between the king and the intruders.

The leader of the party removed his helmet, and Alvaro recognized him only because of the long, crossed scars on one leathery cheek.

"Cousin, it's good to see you," Prince Enrique said, bowing, then turned to Alvaro with a faint, ironic smile. "We meet again, de Luna."

"We do, Your Highness, and under circumstances that force me to inform you that His Majesty admits no armed men except members of his own household guard to appear before him."

"Of course." Enrique's smile broadened, emphasizing his twin scars. "You may retire," he told his retainers, and they withdrew immediately.

Juan was furious. "What are you doing here, Enrique? How dare you burst in on us this way?"

"A man who holds power can dare many things." The prince glanced at the table. "I have not eaten yet this evening. May I join you?"

Alvaro waved the angry Juan back to his chair and resumed

his own seat. "It will be interesting to learn whether you're here as a guest, Your Highness."

Enrique looked at him appreciatively, chuckled and helped himself to a cut of beef, which he placed on a thick slab of bread. "You've grown since our last meeting, de Luna. I'm not surprised to find that the stories I've heard about you are true." He sliced a piece of meat deftly, speared it with his knife and ate it with relish. "Anyone who accepts the hospitality of the king of Castile is His Majesty's guest. Don't let me disturb your conversation."

Juan started to retort angrily, but Alvaro silenced him with a warning look. "We were talking about going hunting tomorrow, Your Highness, but it appears that you've been stalking bigger game."

The prince touched the scars on his cheek. "If it were possible to forget the past, I could almost take a liking to you, de Luna."

Alvaro picked up his own knife and, simulating a calmness he did not feel, began to eat again. "Precisely what is our situation?"

"I've come to pay my respects to my cousin—"

"Spare us your humor, Your Highness," Alvaro said sharply.

"Very well. You made a mistake, de Luna, riding around Castile with such a small escort. I'm surprised at you. I crossed the border with three hundred followers and disarmed the royal guard. I don't ask you to take my word, either. You may investigate the situation for yourself."

"Enrique," Juan said furiously, "you're guilty of treason!"

"Softly, cousin. I mean you no harm."

There were many things Alvaro wanted to know, and he felt his way cautiously. "Has Aragon declared war against Castile?"

"Certainly not." Enrique poured himself a goblet of wine. "Alfonso is the only one of my brothers who clings to the outmoded concept of honor. He doesn't know I've crossed the border, and as I want no interference from him, none of his subjects are in my suite. Every one of my followers is Castilian."

"Very clever," Alvaro said, approving grudgingly.

"Even more clever than you realize. Pedro is marching south with a column from Navarre. I was afraid he might reach our cousin first and claim the right to set himself up as protector of the crown." The prince grinned smugly, then glanced again at Alvaro. "Pedro, I'm afraid, is a crude bungler. I see that your scar doesn't show through your hair."

Juan became alarmed. "If you hurt Don Alvaro—"

"Have no fear, cousin," Enrique interrupted soothingly. "I admire men of ability." He paused and added dryly, "I have even greater respect for popular opinion, and don't want to alienate the people of Castile."

Alvaro saw no need to temporize. "What are your intentions?"

The prince returned his gaze without blinking. "At the moment, the government is in a state of transition. Don Juan Hurtado de Mendoza and Don Fernando Alonso de Robres retired from public office late this afternoon."

Juan gasped.

"It's true, cousin. I met them on the road, and after a short discussion they agreed they've spent enough years in the service of the country. Robres has left for a lodge he owns in Leon, and some of my best men are escorting Mendoza to a charming villa at Seville."

Alvaro's tone remained matter-of-fact. "You plan to replace Mendoza as minister-in-chief."

"No, I'm going to disband the council after I've been officially proclaimed regent. Lerma will agree, I'm sure, and I have no doubt that you can persuade Cuevas to go back to his own province, de Luna."

"What makes you think I'll try, Your Highness?"

Enrique's eyes narrowed. "You'll follow orders because you want to keep your post as royal chamberlain—and your life."

The household troops were stripped of their arms and sent back to Toledo, and Enrique escorted the king and Alvaro to the town of Huete, where he owned a small, heavily fortified castle. A suite of three rooms was assigned to Juan and his friend, armed men were stationed outside the entrance, and a squad of pikemen patrolled the barren plateau beyond the rock-filled moat. Enrique did not visit the apartment for two days, and the king, who was despondent, spent most of his time stretched out on a four-poster bed, his face buried in pillows. But Alvaro, keeping watch at a window set high in the stone wall, saw a steady stream of messengers arriving and leaving, and knew that eventually the prince would come to them.

"Remember, Juan," Alvaro told the boy, "Enrique can do nothing without your consent."

"He can do anything he pleases," was the muffled reply from the bed. "We're his prisoners."

"Let me deal with him."

"What can you do?"

"Anything in my power to thwart him."

"Well, don't draw your sword in his presence, or he'll have you executed. I think he allowed you to keep it so you'd be tempted."

"Perhaps, or it may be that he remembers this is the sword I took from him and is ashamed to redeem it."

Their conversation was interrupted by a tap at the door, and a burly guard saluted courteously. "His Highness requests an interview with His Majesty."

Juan made no move.

"His Majesty is fatigued," Alvaro said quickly, "and has deputized me to conduct all business for him." He turned and winked at the king as he left the chamber, but Juan did not look up from the pillows.

Enrique was waiting in the sparsely furnished drawing room of the suite, and the two men bowed stiffly to each other.

"I regret to inform you that His Majesty is indisposed," Alvaro said, "but I am authorized to act in his name."

"That will be more convenient for both of us." Enrique took the one comfortable chair in the room. "A blond beard," he said suddenly, "looks like no beard at all."

"My wife likes it." Teresa had never commented one way or the other.

"I defer to her judgment," the prince replied politely, then stood abruptly and began to pace up and down the room. "It's odd that I should be negotiating with you."

"Odd to you, Your Highness, but not to me."

"I should have recognized your ambition long ago." Enrique touched his scar. "I can use it now. I gambled and won, de Luna, but two of my brothers are greedy. I've sent out a call summoning the *Cortes* to a meeting here next week to confirm me as regent, and I expect Juan to appear before the grandees and announce that he's offered me the post voluntarily. But Pedro, supported by gold and troops from Navarre, is challenging me. Look at this." He took a folded sheet of parchment from an inner pocket.

Alvaro read it quickly, and was not surprised to learn that Prince Pedro was summoning the nobles to a meeting of the *Cortes* at Avila, where he owned property, to confirm him as regent. "As I have good reason to know, your brother is an impetuous man who lacks good sense, Your Highness."

Enrique became suspicious when Alvaro laughed.

"I know how the king feels. Under no circumstances will he agree to a regency under Prince Pedro."

"But he'll accept me and appear before the grandees at my request?"

Sheer vanity, Alvaro thought contemptuously, prevented

Enrique from realizing that the king hated him as much as
he hated Pedro, that it was necessary to act cautiously only
because they were Enrique's prisoners at the moment. "I believe," he said carefully, "that it will be possible to make
satisfactory arrangements. First, of course, the danger from
Don Pedro must be eliminated, or Castile might be plunged
into civil war."

"Precisely my thinking." Enrique snatched the parchment
and stood, his feet planted apart, scowling at it.

"It should be very simple to dispose of Don Pedro's claim.
A plain statement by the king, rejecting him as regent, will
be sufficient."

"Will he write such a statement?"

Alvaro smiled, walked to a chest of drawers on the far side
of the room, and taking a quill, a jar of ink and a sheet of
parchment from one of them, wrote industriously for a few
moments. "I'm sure you'll find this a flat and unequivocal
statement. I'll persuade Juan to sign it this afternoon, and if
you'll send someone for a stick of wax, he'll put his official
seal on it with his signet ring."

Enrique studied the lines. "I couldn't have written anything stronger myself."

"I'm prepared to add a statement of my own to it, saying
that His Majesty is refusing Don Pedro's offer himself, freely,
and that you have exerted no pressure of any kind on him.
I've acquired a following of sorts, and people will know I
speak the truth."

The prince's eyes were searching. "You and I have no
liking for each other, de Luna. Why are you cooperating
with me?"

Alvaro faced him squarely. "I'm a practical man, Your
Highness, and if I've enjoyed any small success, it's because
I'm a realist. As you have reason to know, my beginnings
were humble, but I own a handsome estate outside Toledo
and I'm married to a beautiful young noblewoman. I don't

want to lose my wife, my property or, as you mentioned the other evening, my life. I know what will happen to me after you've become regent if I oppose you."

"You're more sensible than I had imagined." Enrique sounded mollified. "But I hope you realize that Juan is too friendly toward you. When I become regent I want him to depend only on me. I'll have only a few years to consolidate my position before he's eighteen and the regency will be dissolved."

"I'll be content to retire to my new estate and live there with my wife." Alvaro made a supreme effort to lie blandly.

The prince smiled coolly. "We've reached an understanding," he said, and extended his hand.

Alvaro shook it firmly, but remained tense, afraid that an insignificant gesture might reveal his true feelings.

"You may be able to help me in another matter, too. Perhaps you can persuade the Infanta Catalina to accept my proposal. If force can be avoided, the first year or two of marriage will be less stormy."

It was difficult for Alvaro to hide his jealousy. "I'm afraid I have no influence over the princess. My wife was her lady-in-waiting before our marriage, but you must know that the Infanta Catalina takes no advice except her own."

"I had been led to believe otherwise, but I see no reason why you should balk in this matter when you're working with me in others." Enrique dismissed the subject with a shrug and started toward the door. "How soon can I expect the king's signature on that statement rejecting Pedro's claim?"

"I can persuade him to sign it at once if you'll grant a simple request, Your Highness."

The prince paused, one hand on the latch, and his mouth became a thin line.

"Your men have undoubtedly told you that Juan is grieving, but I'm sure they don't know why he's been so disturbed.

Just before you arrived at Tordesillas, he was looking forward to going hunting with me the next day. If you'll permit
us to go out later today, he'll prove amenable in everything."

Enrique was silent for a moment. "His mother didn't raise
him to be a king," he said at last scornfully.

Alvaro was able to agree without reservation. "Naturally
you'll want to assign a few men to keep watch over him from
a discreet distance."

"I'd be taking a risk. As long as Juan is in my hands, I'm
master of Castile. If he escapes, I'm a political pauper."

"Juan," Alvaro said, letting a note of disdain creep into
his voice, "isn't the sort who'd take chances."

"No, but you are." Enrique laughed harshly. "You're as
great a gambler as I am, de Luna."

The comparison was distasteful, but Alvaro smiled. "I
gamble only when I think there's a reasonable chance I'll
succeed. In this instance, it would be mad to try to run away.
If Juan were ten years older and had a fighting instinct, I
wouldn't hesitate. But he'd be more of a hindrance than a
help."

"Why is this outing important to you, then? I can't accept
your argument that Juan is sulking and would be easier to
handle if I grant him this favor. I'm sure you can find other
ways to persuade him to name me regent."

"No doubt." Alvaro continued to smile blandly. "But the
circumstances of his present position won't be lost on the
grandees or the people. I'm thinking of my own future, and
it just happens that your interests and mine coincide. It will
be claimed that you've held Juan as your prisoner, but you'll
have the perfect reply if you let him spend a few hours in the
open."

"I can see how I'd benefit," Enrique said thoughtfully,
"but how would an afternoon of hunting help you?"

"As you undoubtedly know, Your Highness, I'm not popular with many of the nobles. I'll be accused of conspiring

with you, but if I can say that the king freely invited me to share his pleasure—and Juan will substantiate my account, because it will be true—I'll be in a better position to resist the pressures of those who might want my patents of nobility taken from me."

An expression of grudging admiration appeared on Enrique's dark face. "You're clever, I'll say that for you. But as it happens, there are few woods in this area."

"It doesn't matter. And, if you will, Your Highness, so much the better for you. Your guards will be able to keep a closer watch on Juan."

Enrique shrugged, half-convinced. "You'll find no game other than hare."

Alvaro hoped his laugh sounded sufficiently condescending. "The results would be the same if the woods were teeming with wild boar. Juan's aim is so poor he can't hit anything."

Enrique joined in the laugh. "If the past didn't stand between us, de Luna, I could find a place on my staff for you."

The five members of the escort fell back as the party approached a patch of woods, and Juan leaned out of his saddle and looked anxiously at Alvaro. "Now will you tell me why you wanted me to sign that statement about Pedro?"

"Later." Alvaro looked up at the sky and estimated that night would fall in approximately an hour.

"Have you made a compact with Enrique? Is that why he's permitted us to go on this outing?"

"He thinks I've made a compact with him." The woods were directly ahead now, and Alvaro spoke quickly. "Do you trust me, Juan?"

"Of course."

"Then follow my orders, without discussion or argument. And don't forget the riding lessons I gave you last year."

"You taught me to crouch low in the saddle when I gallop. But we aren't going to gallop through the woods—"

"Softly, please." Alvaro glanced over his shoulder and was relieved when he saw that the men, who were riding about fifty paces behind them, were paying no attention to the boy's talk. "Stay close to me," he directed and, taking the lead, moved into the woods that extended for three or four miles on both sides of a small stream.

He rode toward higher ground, where the underbrush was thinner, and, increasing his pace almost imperceptibly, began to leave the escort farther behind. Juan, who carried a leather case filled with light-weight lances suitable for spearing small game, drew one of his weapons and peered intently through the bushes.

"Don't ride so fast," he complained. "You'll scare off the hare."

Alvaro ignored the protest and, swerving suddenly, rode down to the bank of the river, followed it for a distance and then called quietly over his shoulder, "We're crossing to the other side. Keep your gelding under control, and try to avoid splashing."

The king finally realized that his companion was executing a carefully planned escape and, his face flushed, he nodded eagerly.

They guided their horses through the water, then started up through the trees on the far side. When Alvaro reached a path, he spurred his mount to a slow canter. Juan followed his example, and they rode swiftly, silently for several minutes. Enrique's men were at least one hundred and fifty paces behind them now, but still had no idea they were being tricked, and, following the rules of the hunt, avoided all conversation. The rays of the sun filtered through the tops of the cedars and pines at an angle and Alvaro, half-standing in his saddle for a moment, pointed toward the south.

Juan nodded excitedly, and they pushed through under-

brush, their horses stepping gingerly around bramble patches
and fallen trees. They could see open country through the
screen of pines, and when they emerged from the woods Alvaro said sharply, "Gallop!"

They raced several hundred yards before the guards realized what was happening. The commander of the squad
shouted in anger and dismay. But Alvaro, riding across open
fields, turned in his saddle to make certain Juan remained
close behind him and, smiling to encourage the boy, rode still
faster. A dirt road cut across the plateau to their left, but
Alvaro, gratefully watching the sun sink lower, preferred the
unmarked pasture land. His mount thundered past thatch-
roofed mud huts, dilapidated barns and small herds of cattle
and sheep. Startled peasants stared in amazement at the fleeing pair, realized they were being pursued and hastily retreated across the high ground. The common people had
learned through long, bitter experience that it was unwise to
see or know too much when members of the nobility became
involved in a dispute.

Alvaro achieved a lead of at least a quarter of a mile, and
Enrique's men were unable to close the gap. The sun was
setting now, making it more difficult to keep the fugitives
in sight. As the daylight faded, Alvaro skirted around the
edge of a small stand of hardwood trees, galloped past an
astonished girl who was throwing feed to some chickens behind a house and, taking his bearings for the last time before
the stars came out, continued to ride due south.

So far, he thought, his plan was working perfectly. He had
placed Juan in the rear deliberately, reasoning that the
guards, who carried long spears and powerful bows and arrows, would be reluctant to shoot at the king. What was
more, he enjoyed the advantage of knowing where he was
going. If his luck held, he might be able to lose the pursuers
before the moon rose. Increasing his pace again, he continued

to race across the countryside, the shouts of the guards echoing faintly in his ears.

It was dark, as only Castile could become dark at nightfall,
and for a few anxious moments Alvaro was afraid he had lost
his way, but he saw the lights of a village off to his right, the
shadow of a church spire loomed above the tops of a grove
of poplars and he breathed more easily. The long, grueling
hours he had spent at the Sanctuary of Santo Domingo studying the geography of Castile had not been wasted; he had become familiar with every hill, every sloping valley, and could
almost see the creased charts and maps of the priests over
which he had pored by candlelight. He silently thanked
Father Sebastian for forcing him to concentrate so hard on
every topographical feature of his native land. Patting his
horse, he laughed aloud.

By the time the first bright stars appeared in the cloudless
sky, he could no longer hear the hoofbeats of the guards'
mounts, and when a yellow half-moon rose slowly over the
horizon, he looked back over his shoulder but could not see
them. Juan, still wildly excited, called out to him exuber-
antly, "I've been watching, Alvaro. I think we've lost them!"

But it was too early to rejoice. Alvaro continued to ride
rapidly toward the south, avoiding villages and towns, crossing rivers at shallow points and, in order to spare the horses
as best he could, making detours around hills. After riding
steadily for several hours he felt his mount falter slightly and
knew it was imperative to rest. He drew up then before a two-
room mud house in which a candle was still burning. Dismounting, he beckoned to Juan to follow him. As he approached the entrance, the door opened and a man dressed
in rough work clothes and holding a heavy club in his right
hand peered out into the night. A woman and a younger man,
similarly armed, stood close behind the peasant, who waved
the intruders away.

"Get off my land!" he shouted.

"We come in peace," Alvaro replied quietly. "We want to rest our horses for a little while, and if you can sell us some bread and wine and fodder for our animals, we'll pay you well." He carried a few gold *dolars* and several silver pieces-of-eight in his purse; and, wanting to prove his good intentions, he reached for the leather thongs.

"Don't come any closer," the man warned. "And if you try to draw a weapon, I'll kill you."

Juan stiffened. "I'll have them put to death for this," he said, his teeth clenched.

There was no opportunity for Alvaro to explain that frightened people became violent when they thought their lives and property were being threatened. Halting, he raised his hands over his head. "As you can see," he answered in the rough dialect of the poor, "we mean you no harm."

The woman sniffed. "Decent folk don't ride around the countryside at this time of night."

The younger man, obviously the son of the peasant, joined his father. "You talk like us, but you're dressed like members of the gentry."

"They're probably bandits," the older man declared. "A band was caught last week near Madrid, Josep told me."

"We're friends," Alvaro said, carefully modulating his voice, "and I hope you'll give us the chance to prove it." He continued to stand motionless, his hands raised, while Juan glared imperiously at the trio.

"Margarita, light the lamp and bring it out here," the man directed.

There was a tense, silent wait while the woman obeyed, and her husband inspected the strangers, holding his club ready for instant use if either attacked.

"The older one wears a sword," he announced, "and the boy carries a quiver of spears."

"They're lances, and they're used for hunting small game," Alvaro said patiently.

The woman brushed her long, grey hair away from her face with an impatient gesture. "You won't find any game around here," she replied tartly.

The peasant's son was staring hard at Juan, then at Alvaro. "You look familiar," he muttered.

Alvaro remained silent.

"I've seen you, both of you." Taking a fresh grip on his club, he stepped a pace closer. "I know! It was in Toledo!" Dropping his club, he fell to his knees.

His parents looked at him in astonishment.

"It's King Juan and the Marquis de Luna!"

The woman crossed herself and her husband, bowing his head, followed his son's example.

Alvaro gave Juan no chance to speak. "Please rise," he said gently. "We stand on no ceremony, and we need your help."

The awed trio were unable to reply.

"Not all of His Majesty's subjects share your sense of loyalty. He has enemies who would make him their prisoner if they could. We want to buy food from you, and then we'll be on our way again."

The peasant opened his mouth and closed it several times before he finally said, "Great lord, if you and His Majesty would enter my poor house—"

"If our enemies should find us here, it might go badly for you," Alvaro said, interrupting.

The man's attitude changed, and he threw back his shoulders proudly. "Luis, take the horses to the barn. Give them food and water, and make certain you keep the door closed. Keep your ears open, and blow out your candle if you hear anyone riding this way."

"Feed and water them sparingly," Alvaro cautioned. "Our night's ride isn't finished." Taking Juan's arm, he guided the reluctant boy into the hut.

Alvaro had seen many such cramped homes, but the king blinked at the unpainted pine stools, the single mattress spread out on the floor of the tiny inner room, and the crude wooden rakes and spades that were piled against the near wall. The single window was a square hole cut in the far wall, and above it was a roll of cloth, which was lowered when it was cold or on the rare occasions when rain fell. A hearth dominated the room, used for the dual purpose of cooking and providing heat. A kettle was balanced on two pronged sticks of green wood above the glowing coals and the woman stirred the embers, threw several chips of wood onto the fire and stirred the contents of the blackened, greasy pot.

Juan continued to stand in the middle of the room until Alvaro, pressing gently on his shoulder, nodded in the direction of a stool. The king sat on it tentatively, perching uncomfortably on the edge, but Alvaro took another stool and promptly hooked his feet around the legs and sat back, at his ease. Aware that the peasant was still gaping at them, he deliberately spat on the hard earth floor. "Good luck to all who live in this house," he said.

The peasant laughed and spat, too. "Good luck to all who visit this house. You've heard of our customs, great lord."

"I wasn't always a great lord," Alvaro replied. "I'm a man of Castile as you are. So is His Majesty," he added vigorously.

The man went to a corner, picked up an earthenware jug and removed a long cork from the stopper. "This is the best I can offer you, great king," he said, and handed the jug to Juan.

The boy accepted it, then looked blankly at Alvaro, who urged him in pantomime to drink. Juan lifted the jug to his lips, swallowed and coughed.

Alvaro jumped to his feet, wiped the mouth of the jug on his sleeve and drank heartily. "Last year's grape crop was good," he said.

The peasant, following his example, grinned. "God was kind to us last year."

Out of the corner of his eye Alvaro saw that Juan, who was wiping his eyes, had caught his breath.

The woman took a stack of wooden bowls from the corner and, after dabbing at each with her apron, handed them to the men. Her husband and Alvaro followed her to the fire and the king, after a moment's hesitation, did the same. She ladled quantities of a highly seasoned lamb stew into the dishes. Alvaro returned to his stool, picked chunks of meat out of the bowl with his knife and drank the thick juice. Juan, who continued to watch him carefully, copied him.

"That was a good meal," Alvaro said, and glanced meaningfully at the young monarch.

"I liked it, too," Juan said, trying to sound enthusiastic.

The peasant and his wife exchanged proud smiles, but the man's expression changed when Alvaro reached into his purse. "No, great lord. We will accept no money. Luis, our son, is going to be married next month, and it will be our joy to tell our grandchildren some day that Juan II of Castile honored us above all people of the district by sharing a pot of our *zacho* with us."

Alvaro bowed gravely. "I would not insult you by trying to pay for our food. We came to you as strangers, and offered you money. But you welcomed us as friends. It is as a friend that His Majesty wants to make you a gift." He took a gold coin and forced it into the man's hand. "Buy some new sheep and a spade of iron. When your son marries, give him a strong plow with the thanks of his king."

The man made an inadequate attempt to express his gratitude. "If enemies are threatening the king," he said, "I'll gladly go to my neighbors and we'll fight them for you."

"Farmers who have no weapons except wooden rakes are no match for knights in armor who carry swords." Alvaro gripped the peasant's shoulder. "But the time will come, soon, when your son and the other young men of the nation will be called to serve their king. We'll give them real weapons and teach them how to fight our enemies." He turned to the silent Juan. "Your Majesty, we have a long ride before sunrise."

The peasant and his wife followed them into the open, the young man brought their horses from the stable, and after a final round of farewells, Alvaro started south again.

Juan, riding close beside him, was puzzled. "Why were they so hospitable, Alvaro?"

"Because you're their king."

"But the woman scraped the bottom of the pot. They have nothing to eat in the morning."

"They won't care."

"Do you suppose there are many people in Castile who feel as they do?"

"I'm sure there are only a few of your subjects who don't feel that way, Juan."

"I see." The boy's voice sounded strained. "Now I begin to understand why you believe so much in the common people."

"It's because they believe in you, Juan. You have an obligation to help them."

"I will." There was a new note of determination in the boy's voice. "As soon as we reach Toledo, draw up your tax plan in a decree, and I'll sign it. We won't even ask the *Cortes* to approve."

Alvaro peered ahead in the darkness. "We aren't going to Toledo. It's too far, and Enrique will think we're riding that way. He'll try to block the roads to the city." He could sense a jumble of questions, and smiled faintly. "Save your breath, Juan. We'll know by morning whether I deserve your confidence or whether I'm a fool."

The first streaks of dawn were showing in the sky when the weary riders approached a small, thick-turreted castle that stood on the crest of a bare hill. No lights showed in the old fort, and the small town, nestled in a valley beyond it, was dark and silent, too. Alvaro dismounted and led his tired horse across a small drawbridge to the unguarded gate of the castle, and as Juan followed him, yawning and stumbling, he pounded on the heavy oak door. After a long wait a sleepy man-at-arms appeared, dressed in an undershirt and breeches.

"Tell your master that King Juan and Don Alvaro de Luna are here!"

The man stared at the pair for a moment, then turned and ran up a flight of circular stone stairs. There was an excited babble, and Roderigo de Pinar appeared in a silk dressing gown, his eyes puffy and his hair tousled. "Saint Cristoforo!" he exclaimed. "It's really you." Looking slightly ridiculous, he bowed to Juan. "Your Majesty, I'm overwhelmed."

"You'll be even more overwhelmed when you learn why we're here," Alvaro replied dryly, and explained the situation.

Roderigo, wide awake, became agitated. "Do you plan to send to Toledo for reinforcements?"

"Enrique would find us before any royal troops could reach us, I'm afraid." Alvaro thoughtfully watched the man-at-arms lead the two horses around to the stables at the rear of the castle. "How large a staff do you keep here, Roderigo?"

"There are only seven of us."

"Are the citizens of Montalban loyal?"

"Completely! I swear it on my life!"

"That's exactly what you're doing, my friend, whether you know it or not. Send your retainers into the town quickly, and tell them to round up every able-bodied man who is willing to fight for his king. Then give His Majesty some breakfast and a bed, and we'll look to our defenses."

By noon the castle was ready to withstand a siege. Sixty-four men, twenty of them veterans with military experience, had responded to the call to arms and were crowded into the castle. Every household in the town had contributed bread and wine, cheese and meat, so that there was enough food on hand to enable the little garrison to hold out, and three couriers had been dispatched, each taking a different route, to Don Domenico of Cuevas in Toledo, asking him to assemble the entire household guard and lead it to Montalban. The drawbridge had been raised, and the moat had been filled with water by removing several stones that diverted the flow of a brook that ran behind it. Alvaro, accompanied by Roderigo, made a thorough tour of inspection.

Cauldrons of oil had been hauled to the roof, kindling had been stacked under each, and teams of three men had been assigned to keep watch over each kettle and to boil the oil when ordered. Armor and pikes had been distributed from the castle's small arsenal, and the veterans with battle experience were stationed in each of the three turrets. They had been given the only battle-axes and long-bows that Roderigo owned, and were under strict instructions to report any movement of large bodies of men immediately. Alvaro ate some bread and cheese as he went through the castle, his first food since his meal in the peasant's hut, and when he finally satisfied himself that he had taken every precaution, he went off to Roderigo's bedchamber. Removing only his boots, he threw himself down on the feather bed and fell asleep at once.

The sun was dropping behind the hills of Montalban when his host came into the room and shook him. "They're here."

Alvaro sat up and pulled on his boots.

"A column of at least two hundred and fifty men is approaching from the north. I went up to the turrets myself, and I recognized Don Enrique's banner. And I counted eleven other pennants in his entourage."

Alvaro buckled on his sword belt.

"My friend, I don't mean to make light of your courage, but I wish you'd let me deal with them. You have no armor, and mine is too big for you."

Shrugging, Alvaro picked up his soft velvet hat and put it on his head at a jaunty angle. "Where's Juan?"

"Still sleeping behind the barred door of the main guest chamber."

"That's the best place for him. You've ordered the men to light the fires under the cauldrons of oil?"

"I have. Now about this matter of dealing with Enrique—"

"Roderigo, listen to me and answer me honestly."

"We've always been honest with each other."

"Then you realize this is a desperate situation. If they overwhelm us, you'll lose your life as well as your property."

Roderigo grinned.

"I brought the king here without consulting you, without asking your consent. If you want to betray us to Enrique in order to save yourself, I won't be able to blame you."

"My honor," Roderigo replied stiffly, pulling on his steel helmet, "means more to me than my property, my title or my life."

They shook hands and climbed the stairs to the roof.

The vanguard of the approaching column was no more than a half-mile from the castle, and Alvaro, looking out through a slit in the stones of the main turret, saw Enrique, his armor dusty, leading the procession at a canter. The men in the castle followed the careful instructions they had received, and none showed themselves. Except for smoke rising from the fires under the cauldrons, the old fort looked deserted.

Enrique gave a command, and his troops split into two wings; one surrounded the castle, the other followed him to the edge of the moat and a herald blew a trumpet. Enrique raised his visor and called loudly, "Don Roderigo de Pinar."

"I hope Father Sebastian will have cause to be proud of his pupils," Roderigo said, and stepped out onto the narrow walk between the turret and the outer, shoulder-high wall, "Who calls me?" he shouted arrogantly.

"The Infante Enrique, Regent of Castile! I demand that you release the person of King Juan and hand over to me the traitor, Alvaro de Luna."

Laughing softly, Alvaro took a long-bow and a quiver of arrows from a retired sergeant who was Montalban's cobbler. Fitting an arrow into the notch of the bow and holding the weapon low so that it couldn't be seen by men below the wall, he moved out into the open beside Roderigo.

A hoarse shout greeted him, and Enrique glared up at him.

"There is no regent of Castile," Alvaro said in a loud, clear voice. "His Majesty rules in the land, and has assigned his prerogatives to no one."

An arrow whistled past him and struck the heavy stone turret to his left.

He saw the man who had fired at him and, raising his own bow quickly, aimed at the figure on horseback and returned the shot. The squire, who was wearing only a suit of light mail, fell to the ground, gasping and clutching his throat, from which the arrow protruded.

"Any man who attacks this castle," Alvaro said calmly, "is a rebel, and will be punished by execution. Don Enrique, I advise you to restrain your rabble."

The prince's face was pale, and the scar stood out on his cheek. "You tricked me, de Luna. I trusted you, and you played me false."

"You played the king false, Don Enrique." Alvaro ignored the frantic Roderigo, who was urging him in an undertone to stop exposing himself to enemy fire.

"I accuse you of kidnaping King Juan and of holding him here against his will," Enrique shouted, losing his temper. "Release him immediately!"

The charge was so absurd that Alvaro laughed.

The prince made a short, chopping motion with his right hand. Roderigo caught hold of Alvaro and dragged him to his knees behind the wall as arrows whistled past them and a

spear struck the turret behind them. Indignant and humiliated, Alvaro crawled back to the safety of the tower while
Roderigo, hampered by his heavy armor, pulled himself
slowly to his feet.

The men below were forming a triple battle line of horsemen, and several squires in the rear were unfolding scaling
ladders of hemp, to which they tied thick hooks of rough oak.
Watching the preparations, Alvaro was forced to admire Enrique's efficiency; men who knew no better used iron grap-
pling hooks to assault a fortress, but the prince obviously
had learned that metal clamps frequently slipped on the
stones and that carved, notched oak gripped the ramparts
more securely.

The volunteers from Montalban were watching Alvaro
anxiously. "We'll treat them to an oil bath, and they'll ride
straight for the border of Aragon," he said.

"Don Roderigo de Pinar!" Enrique called. "Do you surrender?"

Not deigning to reply, Roderigo pulled down his visor,
drew his sword and walked calmly back to the tower, ignoring
a spear that sailed past his head. "We need a bigger garrison,"
he muttered gloomily to Alvaro.

"Hold your fire," Alvaro told the men who were standing
at the slits overlooking the field below.

Someone cried out in alarm from the far side of the ramparts, and his voice was anguished. "They're attacking the
south wall!"

Alvaro started toward the entrance, but Roderigo pulled
him back. "You can't wander around in the open without
protection. All armored men, rally to me!"

Alvaro watched his friend hurry away, followed by two
volunteers in loose-fitting suits of chain mail. Others joined
them, and in a few moments the sounds of blows, hoarse
shouts and curses drifted back to the tower. Enrique had not
moved, however, and Alvaro felt certain that the main assault

would be made against his bastion. Aware that he could not assume responsibility for Roderigo's sector, he concentrated on the prince.

The moat was a formidable barrier, but a score of riders in heavy armor, accompanied by foot soldiers who were stripping to the waist, moved to the water's edge. It was plain that the knights, who were carrying quivers of light lances, intended to drive away the defenders from the wall opposite them while the infantrymen swam across the moat and lowered the drawbridge. The enemy's tactics were sound, but could be countered, Alvaro thought, and became annoyed when a middle-aged wine-seller, a former corporal, fired an arrow at the group. "Wait!" he said sharply and, bending low, moved out to the roof.

Thick, black smoke was rising from the nearest cauldron, and the men who were tending the fire responded eagerly when Alvaro waved them toward the wall. They removed the kettle from the fire with long-handled iron hooks and, crouching to avoid being struck by stray arrows or lances, dragged the cauldron to a spot directly above the drawbridge. They would have dumped the contents over the wall at once, but Alvaro restrained them.

"Flatten yourselves against the wall," he said and, abandoning the kettle for the moment, set the example.

Enrique's knights were throwing their lances now whenever they saw anyone moving on the roof. Alvaro waited patiently until five of the enemy foot soldiers managed to swim across the moat, climbed out of the water, and began to hack at the ropes of the raised drawbridge with knives they carried in their belts.

"Now," Alvaro said, and his men, still using the iron hooks, picked up the cauldron.

A lance pierced the leather doublet of one man, who staggered and dropped his iron rod. He fell to one knee, clutching his shoulder, and Alvaro leaped forward to take his place.

The rain of lances became heavier, but Alvaro paid no attention to a steel-tipped shaft that grazed his right cheek. Working in unison with the volunteers, he lifted the cauldron to
the edge of the wall. They tipped it slowly, and a stream of
bubbling, smoking oil splashed onto the group below.

One of the attackers screamed, stood rigid for a moment
and fell into the moat. The others, nursing lesser burns,
plunged into the water and swam back to safety.

Alvaro wiped the grime from his face with the back of a
blistered hand. "Don't waste oil," he said. "We'll take the
cauldron back to the fire. And you, there, help the man who
was wounded."

The invaders were repulsed four times, but on their fifth
attempt they managed to cut the ropes and the drawbridge
fell with a crash. Heavily armored knights rode across the
span to the castle, three abreast, and men in lighter armor
began the laborious task of trying to raise the scaling ladders.
Alvaro ordered his followers to fire at will, and when the
volunteers had used their own supply of spears, they collected lances that had fallen on the roof and hurled them
back back at their attackers.

Enrique, having created an opening, directed his entire
force to concentrate at the drawbridge. Roderigo and his
armored men, who had held off the enemy on the south wall,
were now free to join Alvaro and the main body of defenders.
The volunteers were courageous, but the majority of them
were inexperienced, and in spite of their valor and energy
they were no match for the prince's battle-hardened mercenaries. Alvaro directed the archers and spearmen, who held
their ground firmly, although several members of the unit
were injured by the more accurate fire of their opponents,
who were supporting the attackers from the far side of the
moat.

Roderigo and his followers were less fortunate and, as twi-
light shrouded the roof of the castle in a haze, they were

driven back from the wall. The attackers hooked a scaling ladder over the stones, and several warriors appeared over the edge of the wall, following each other rapidly, their heavy swords drawn and ready for use. Roderigo fought valiantly, but the citizens of Montalban knew nothing of the art of duelling, which was never taught to commoners, and it was clear to Alvaro that the garrison would be overwhelmed as soon as enough of the invaders climbed the wall.

Recklessly he threw himself at a knight in chain mail, a towering man armed with a two-edged sword. Unable to afford the luxury of wasting precious seconds on the etiquette of personal combat, he aimed his blade at the opening between the man's helmet and his collar of iron mesh. The point penetrated deeply, and as the nobleman collapsed, Alvaro leaped to his side, snatched his battle-axe from his belt and turned to the wall. Realizing intuitively that it was essential to destroy the ladder at all costs, Alvaro struck desperately at the nearer of the notched oak hooks. He missed, struck again and in his frenzy succeeded in driving the axe through the hard wood. The ladder hung by only one hook now, and a knight who was climbing over the wall lost his balance and clung to the roof.

Alvaro chopped grimly at the gloves of iron mesh, and they disappeared suddenly as the man fell backward and toppled into the moat. Two final blows broke the second wooden hook, and the ladder dropped out of sight. There were seven of the prince's men on the roof now, but Roderigo disposed of two of the invaders, his men killed a third and the others, surrounded by the aroused citizens, surrendered.

One cauldron of oil was still boiling. Alvaro, aided by more men than he needed, dragged it to the wall above the drawbridge and poured the scalding contents on the invaders milling about beneath them. Horses neighed in terror, men screamed and a sudden panic swept through the ranks of the mercenaries. The able-bodied retreated hastily across the battered drawbridge, leaving their dead and wounded behind them, and the men massed outside the moat broke ranks and rode away at a gallop, followed by the pikemen, who discarded their weapons as they ran.

A trumpeter sounded a retreat, and the few knights who had held their places drew off. Prince Enrique sat alone for a few moments, staring up at the walls, and when he saw Alvaro looking down at him, he pulled up his visor and, his face solemn, raised his sword in salute. Then, wheeling abruptly, he rode off into the gathering night.

Don Domenico, Duke of Cuevas, arrived at the castle with five hundred members of the royal cavalry shortly before noon on the day following the battle, and King Juan was placed under a guard of trained men who were sworn to protect him. The five citizens of Montalban who had lost their lives in the fight were buried with honors, and at Alvaro's suggestion, Juan granted their families pensions from the royal treasury. The wounded were rewarded, too, and while the newly arrived cavalrymen repaired the damage to the castle, Alvaro wrote a decree for the king's signature, relieving Montalban of all tax obligations for twenty-five years.

The next morning the king and his escort set out for Toledo. Roderigo, who had been made a count by the grateful Juan, rode at the king's left, but Alvaro and Cuevas lagged behind, deep in discussion. Castile faced a major crisis. Although a battle had been won, the monarchy might collapse if they failed to act quickly and decisively. As Enrique had sent Mendoza and Robres into retirement, the council had been disbanded and, for all practical purposes, the king had no government.

Alvaro proposed that the *Cortes* be summoned to an emergency meeting in the capital the following day, and when Juan readily agreed, several officers were sent ahead of the column to announce the royal decision. "It would appear," Cuevas said thoughtfully, "that you, Don Roderigo and I will make up the new council, Don Alvaro."

"Do you think the *Cortes* would confirm us?" Alvaro's muscles ached, and he shifted uncomfortably in the saddle.

"They're frightened by the threat of civil war. I don't think they'll have much choice."

"They'll insist on electing some of their friends to serve with us, and virtually every grandee in the country is friendly to either Enrique or Pedro."

Don Domenico shrugged. "It's true that when Don Miguel of Lerma heard about the siege at Montalban he made a speech in favor of Enrique, and I myself saw seventeen names on the petition demanding that the prince be appointed regent. We have to find some way to control the nobles elected by the *Cortes* to a new council."

Alvaro's chin itched, and he decided to shave off his beard. Teresa would be unhappy and claim he looked like a peasant, but he would try to explain to her that he had no desire to copy the styles and customs of the grandees. "When a man has been given power," he said slowly, "it's too late to control him."

"It's too late to call Mendoza and Robres out of retirement, too," Cuevas replied tartly. "They've been discredited."

"It didn't occur to me that the old council could be formed again. But we'll be asking for a revolution if we give places to either Enrique's supporters or Pedro's. First they'll find some way to get rid of Roderigo, which won't be difficult. He's a great help in a fight on a castle roof, but he has no understanding of political warfare. Then they'll play your interests against mine, and if they ever succeed in dividing us, they'll send us either to prison or into exile while they take over the country."

"Unfortunately, Don Alvaro, we can't govern Castile with

royal guards and my few retainers. If we could, I'd suggest that we try. But no one supports us."

"No one," Alvaro said softly, "except the king and the people."

"What do you have in mind?" The duke looked at him curiously.

They spurred toward the crest of a hill, and Toledo loomed in the distance, the Alcazar dominating the city. Alvaro halted and searched the area directly ahead. Finally he caught a glimpse of what he was seeking, a carriage that was waiting near a grove of pear trees. "I have many ideas, Don Domenico. We must fight fire with our own fire, ruthlessly. I'll be obliged if you'll halt the column and wait here for a short time until I return."

"Of course, but what—"

"Enrique once called me a gambler, and he was right. I'm gambling right now for the highest of stakes, the future of Castile." Alvaro rode down the hill to the orchard, and several men in uniform who were guarding the carriage saluted him respectfully as he approached.

He dismounted, the door opened and he hesitated outside for a moment.

"Will you join me?" Catalina asked.

The sound of her voice aroused him, as it always had, but he took care to speak respectfully. "Thank you, Your Highness." He climbed into the carriage, closed the door and tried to see her in the dark.

"May I open the blinds?" she asked.

"I think it better if you don't."

"As you wish. I've followed your instructions to the letter, Don Alvaro. I've ridden out here privately to meet you, the windows are covered and I've told no one of your request." Catalina sounded bitter.

"I sent you a message asking you to meet me, Your Highness. I didn't send you instructions." The meeting was starting badly, and Alvaro wondered why she seemed irritated. "Have I offended you?"

"No, but you've made me feel as though you'd invited me to—to an assignation. I've compromised myself by meeting a married man privately, under circumstances that are mysterious, to say the least."

"Your honor is safe, I assure you. This coach is surrounded by loyal men, and I've been accompanied by an esort of hundreds of troops. They're waiting for me a short distance from here."

Catalina was not satisfied by his reply. "What was so urgent? Why couldn't you have ridden into the city and waited on me in my suite in the usual manner?"

"Because these aren't usual times. As you've undoubtedly heard, there was a battle in which the king's life was in jeopardy—"

"I've heard conflicting reports. I've been told that my brother's life was not endangered at any time."

"May I ask your source of information?" It was obvious to him that she had heard a biased account from one of Enrique's supporters.

"I don't think it important. What does matter is that, for the sake of your loyalty to—to my family, I've followed your bidding. However, I must return to the Alcazar before evening. I'd like to know, now, why you wanted to meet me."

"Castile is in danger. Prince Enrique wanted to make himself regent, but he's lost his chance. We must act quickly, before he can recover."

"We, Don Alvaro?" she asked coolly.

"The king's party," he retorted.

Catalina was silent.

"The grandees look out for their own interests. They care nothing about Juan or the country."

"I've never taken an active part in political affairs."

"I understand your situation, Your Highness. Let me explain in another way. I'm trying to move quickly, to rally the king's supporters in order to shield him before his enemies can strike again."

"I find it hard to believe," she said, twisting a ring on the little finger of her right hand, "that any Castilian would want to harm Juan."

"There are men who want to use him to promote their own selfish ends." Enrique's emissary, he thought unhappily, had done his work thoroughly. It was not easy for a woman to visualize the fierce struggle for power that drove men to commit desperate acts, and Catalina was confused and uncertain.

"I want to help my brother, Don Alvaro," she said, forcing herself to clasp her hands and hold them quietly in her lap. "But what can I do?"

"I have no right to ask you to make a sacrifice." Alvaro's mouth and throat were painfully dry. "But a formal alliance with a powerful neighbor would cool the ardor of the men who plot against Castile. France is such a neighbor."

Catalina stiffened.

He had to finish what he had started. "Prince Philip of Orleans, the heir to the French throne and the commander of the army of Paris, has asked for your hand. If you accept him, France will come to our aid in time of need."

"Are you proposing to barter me, Alvaro?" she demanded angrily.

"You've always known that some day you'd marry a prince or a king," he replied bleakly. "I'm thinking of Castile."

"At my expense. How convenient for you." She was working herself into a rage. "Once I believed you were sincere when you hinted that I—meant something to you—"

"More than I've ever had the right to tell you."

"—and I was even stupid enough to tell myself that your marriage meant very little to you. I actually believed you married Teresa so that you could found a family."

This was not the right moment to discuss his disappointment, his growing fear that Teresa was incapable of bearing children.

"You accuse Enrique of being unscrupulous, but it's you who are ambitious. You're so clever! You've pretended to care for me, but you'd send me off to marry a foreigner and live in an alien land. You're deceitful and vile."

"Please, Catalina—"

"Get out!" She was weeping now, and could no longer control her anger.

"I beg you to be reasonable. If I had been a prince, I would have declared myself to you long ago." He realized that he was admitting his love for her, but it was too late to retract what he had said.

Catalina sobbed, reached out and struck him across the face. "If you won't leave, I'll have you thrown out!" she cried.

Alvaro held one hand to his cheek, opened the carriage door and stepped down. The princess called an order to her coachman and slammed the door. Her escort formed around the carriage. Heartsick, Alvaro continued to stand, watching her drive off. He had failed to help the king, he thought miserably, and far worse, he had alienated the girl who meant more to him than anyone else in the world.

Teresa was pacing up and down the small living room of the suite that Alvaro maintained at the Alcazar, and when he entered the chamber she wasted no time on greetings, even though they hadn't seen each other in a long time. "You'll have to act quickly," she said, "or you and I will follow my uncle into permanent retirement."

Alvaro pulled off his dusty gauntlet gloves. "Perhaps you haven't heard of our complete victory at Roderigo's castle. Don Domenico has rounded up enough loyal troops to guarantee the safety of the king—there's no immediate danger."

Teresa bit her lower lip. "Obviously you don't know that Enrique is here."

Alvaro looked at his wife in astonishment.

"He rode here straight from Montalban."

"Then he's hoping to win over the household regiments and have me arrested."

"I don't know what he's planning. But I can tell you this much, that he went straight to Catalina when he arrived, and he's with her again right now. He joined her after she returned a short while ago from a ride into the country. She looked very upset, as though she had been weeping. Enrique was waiting for her, and they went together to her apartment."

With a sinking heart, Alvaro realized he had inadvertently pushed Catalina into the camp of his enemy.

"Enrique has been busy talking to everyone who'll listen to him. He insists that the battle was a tragic mistake due to a misunderstanding. That's the story he's already told Catalina and Cardinal Torello, and he's going to repeat it to the *Cortes* tomorrow."

Alvaro made a desperate attempt to think coherently.

"What will you do?" Teresa was tense, but spoke quietly.

"Only a few hours ago, Enrique and I were trying to kill each other in battle. Now we're spending the night under the same roof. The situation is mad." He moved toward the door.

"Where are you going?"

"I have a few errands to perform." He paused and smiled wryly. "There's an old saying that your uncle forgot, and that's why he was sent off to Leon before he was ready to leave. *En invierno no hay amigo como una capa.* In winter there is no friend like a good cloak."

Teresa came to him, put her arms around his neck and kissed him. "I have every confidence in you."

His mind was racing. "If I win this time, you'll be one of the first ladies of Castile."

"The first, above all the others." The door closed behind him.

The significance of her remark didn't occur to Alvaro until much later. Deeply engrossed, he sent pages for the two friends he knew he could trust, Cuevas and Roderigo, and they met him in the king's private apartment, where he explained the situation to them. Juan listened gravely, and added a word of his own. "Enrique came to pay his respects to me after I changed into fresh clothes, but I refused to see him. Catalina was angry with me."

Alvaro knew his blunder in trying to persuade Catalina to marry Philip of France was bearing bitter fruit. She had turned against him, and Enrique was undoubtedly exploiting the situation. "What did she say?"

Juan's slow smile was haughty. "I gave her no chance to say anything. When I reminded her that I'm her king, she curtsied to me silently and joined Enrique again in the corridor."

Roderigo scratched his head. *"El melon y la mujer malos son de conocer,"* he muttered. "A melon and a woman are difficult to know."

His indelicate remark broke the tension, and the others laughed. "True," Alvaro replied. "Only an expert knows a good melon from its exterior, and the same applies to a woman." Sobering, he turned to the duke. "Don Domenico, I shall be obliged if you will assign two hundred of your best men to guard His Majesty all night. Station some in the corridor, others in the garden below, others where you think necessary to insure his safety. Take command of the company yourself, and escort His Majesty to the meeting of the *Cortes* tomorrow."

Cuevas apparently saw nothing unusual in taking orders from someone who had no legal right to give him commands. Saluting Juan, he said simply, "You may depend on me."

Roderigo, assuming that he would assist the duke, started

to leave the apartment with Cuevas, but Alvaro detained him. "I have another task in mind for you, my friend," he said. "Wait for me in your room."

Roderigo had consumed the better part of a jar of wine when Alvaro finally tapped at his door, walked into the chamber and frowned when he saw the wine. "Are you sober?"

"Certainly," was the indignant reply. "It takes more than a few drops of Madeira to make me drunk, just as it takes more than a few hired knights to subdue me in battle."

"Stop boasting and sit down." Alvaro spread several sheets of parchment on a table beneath an oil lamp.

Roderigo examined the documents. "I see nothing remarkable in these papers. This is an order for a new suit of armor, this one is a complaint about the price of a stallion—"

"They're in Enrique's handwriting." Alvaro saw no need to explain that, after a long, earnest conversation with the king, he had broken into Enrique's quarters and stolen the papers.

In personal matters Roderigo displayed an ability to think clearly and swiftly. "Weren't you taking a chance?"

"I made certain first that he wasn't there. He and Catalina were taking the air on the ramparts."

"All the same, if you had been seen, you might have been accused of petty robbery."

Alvaro curbed his impatience. "It was necessary to take the risk."

"These papers are worthless."

"I think not. They're in his own hand." Alvaro hesitated for an instant, then said carefully, "Do you remember how you amused yourself at the Sanctuary, copying the penmanship of others?"

A gleam of appreciation appeared in Roderigo's eyes, and he leaned forward in his seat.

"Father Sebastian wouldn't approve of what I have in

mind. He always taught us that evil is evil, that there can be no compromise with Satan. He's right, of course. But it's far easier to behave like a saint in a monastery than it is in the world where men fight for power."

"You sound as though you were arguing with your own conscience," Roderigo said.

"That's precisely what I'm doing. There must be wickedness in me, or I wouldn't think of perpetrating an evil act."

Roderigo laughed casually. "I'm lucky. My conscience never bothers me."

"Yes, you're very fortunate." Alvaro stared at him soberly. "But regardless of conscience, regardless of what one may think is right or wrong, there are situations that require desperate acts. It would be a catastrophe for Castile if Enrique ever became regent."

"We can't let that happen!"

"It won't. I've convinced myself that it's better to do an evil deed in order to preserve good than it is to turn the other cheek and let the wicked flourish."

Roderigo agreed heartily.

"Enrique is a clever man," Alvaro continued. "He's capable of persuading the *Cortes,* as he seems to have persuaded the Infanta Catalina, that an unpleasant and unnecessary accident took place at your castle. Most of the nobles are sympathetic to him, and they'll be inclined to let him take up residence here again."

"We can't permit it!" Roderigo's fist smashed on the table, sending some of the papers flying and rattling the lamp.

Alvaro bent down and picked up the sheets of stolen parchment. "Then, in a few weeks, perhaps a few months, he'll gather all of the powers of the kingdom in his hands. If that should happen, you and I will have to flee to Portugal. I'm afraid that not even the monastery of Santo Domingo would dare to give us refuge."

"I've known you for too long to be frightened, Alvaro. You

aren't the sort who'll sit back meekly and wait for someone else to strike first."

Alvaro poured himself a small glass of wine. "I wonder how the members of the *Cortes* would react if they learned that Enrique was conspiring secretly with King Mohammed-ibn-Azar of Granada?"

Startled, Roderigo shoved his chair backward so violently as he jumped to his feet that it toppled.

"Even the grandees who support him would be shocked, I think, if they discovered that he had made a pact with the Moors, agreeing to give them some of our southern provinces if they'll help him gain the throne of Castile."

Roderigo, red-faced, cursed under his breath.

"Of course," Alvaro added mildly, "it will be necessary to produce the evidence, in Enrique's own handwriting."

His friend understood and, grinning, picked up his chair and straddled it.

"Two or three brief letters should be enough. I'll word them for you after you've had a chance to practice."

Roderigo took a jar of ink and another of sand from a chest of drawers, held one of the samples of the prince's handwriting before him, upside down, and began to copy the strokes with a fine crow's quill. His hand moved slowly at first, then the sweep of his wrist became bolder, and he laughed. "His Highness' writing is distinctive because it's so bad. He had a timid tutor, I imagine, and he was more interested in brawling than in learning to write." The pen was moving back and forth very rapidly, but suddenly it stopped. "If you present the letters, you'll be accused of having prepared forgeries."

Alvaro didn't want to hurt his friend's feelings by saying he had thought of the obvious. "The letters will be presented to the *Cortes* by a churchman. The old archbishop of Segovia would be the best for the purpose, I believe. He hates the

Moors and is always trying to persuade anyone who'll listen to him to start a new campaign against them."

"But how will he get the letters?"

"Have you forgotten that my brother is vicar-general of Toledo?"

"But a bishop won't lend himself to a deception, Alvaro, not even for a purpose as honorable and righteous as ours!"

"I don't intend to tell Francisco that the letters are forgeries, Roderigo. You and I are the only people on earth who'll ever know the truth."

They worked steadily, without interruption, for several hours, and it was very late when Alvaro finally made his way back to the small suite on the second floor. Teresa, her hair hanging loose, was reading a leather-bound book of poetry in bed when her husband entered the inner chamber, and she glanced at him quickly, then relaxed against the pillows.

"I'm afraid this has been a sorry reunion after our weeks of separation," he said.

Her smile broadened. "I'm sure we'll enjoy the benefits of this night for the rest of our lives."

She knew nothing about his scheme or his hard labors, and he looked at her in bewilderment.

Teresa laughed and stretched sinuously. "I knew when I saw your expression just now that we're going to win." She watched him undress, waiting for him to join her. "I made no mistake when I married you," she murmured, blowing out the candle and turning to him.

Every member of the *Cortes* who had been able to reach Toledo in time for the meeting was in attendance as King Juan adjusted his ermine-trimmed robes of state and, his face and bearing surprisingly mature, looked from his throne at the peers of his realm. Don Domenico of Cuevas stood on the dais at the king's left, and the presence of the troops of the household guard who were stationed behind the throne, in the aisles and at each entrance emphasized the gravity of the situation.

Alvaro, whose rank entitled him to a place on one of the front benches, had chosen a seat off to one side, and in spite of Teresa's urging, he had refused to wear either brightly colored clothes or armor. He was inconspicuous in a suit of deep maroon velvet, and although he knew that many of the grandees were looking at him, nudging each other and whispering about it, he sat quietly, his arms crossed. Guillen Cardinal de Veque, the archbishop of Segovia, was several rows away to his left, surrounded by his staff, and their excitement was so intense that Alvaro knew the forged letters had been placed in the right hands. His work was done, and he was content to let the drama spin itself out.

Juan lifted his golden mace, and the grandees became silent. "As we rule at present without a council," the young king said, carefully repeating what Alvaro had taught him the preceding evening, "we will conduct this meeting without the aid of ministers of state. We have summoned our lords to hear charges against our cousin, Don Enrique, but we do not see him here. Does any man know where he may be found, or has he fled from his native land?"

"I'm here, Your Majesty!" Enrique, bold and confident, spoke from the rear of the hall, and heads twisted as the grandees turned to stare at him. "I submit that I have committed no fault, and I can offer supreme proof of my contention."

Enrique was defending himself before formal charges had been lodged against him, and Alvaro wished Juan would silence him. But the king, incapable of dealing with the unexpected, merely stared at his cousin.

"Those who accuse me of trying to harm the person of His Majesty are liars," Enrique continued, his voice becoming stronger. "You, my colleagues and friends, are aware of the devotion and love of the Infanta Catalina for her brother. If it were true that I attacked His Majesty, his beloved sister would be my enemy." Pausing theatrically, Enrique turned to the entrance.

Catalina, wearing a gown of white silk and a mantilla of white lace, moved into the hall, took his arm and walked slowly down the center aisle with him to the dias. She curtsied low before her brother, and Enrique bowed to the king, then helped Catalina to her feet.

"It gives me great joy," the prince declared triumphantly, "to announce that the Infanta became my wife at a ceremony held this morning in the Alcazar chapel."

Alvaro was stunned, and heard neither the surprised murmurs nor the sudden burst of applause. He stared at Catalina, and for an instant their eyes met, but she seemed to be looking through him, beyond him.

When the grandees became quiet again, Cardinal de Veque stood solemnly, a striking figure in his red robes. "No man," he said, "may separate those who have been united in matrimony at the altar of the Lord. Yet I cannot believe that Her Highness would have married Don Enrique had she known he is a traitor." He took the letters from the vicar-general of his archdiocese, and read them slowly.

The grandees listened in hushed silence. Catalina was so pale and limp that she looked as though she might faint, and Enrique, his temper soaring, tried repeatedly to interrupt, but the cardinal gave him no chance and continued to read steadily, his veined hands shaking as he held the sheets of parchment before him. Alvaro clenched his fists, and as he watched Catalina, he knew that he had paid a high price for his victory.

"Those letters are forgeries!" the outraged Enrique shouted when the old man had finished reading the last one.

"They are genuine," Cardinal de Veque replied austerely. "You conspired with Mohammed-ibn-Azar, the heathen of

Granada, against Castile. Your Majesty," he added, "if there is any doubt about the authenticity of these documents, let them be examined by a committee of lords appointed by you."

"If Your Eminence is satisfied, we do not question your judgment," the thoroughly rehearsed Juan replied.

The old man gazed around the hall. "If any lord is in doubt, let him come forward."

Don Domenico of Cuevas, still standing at the king's left, raised his voice. "Your Eminence!"

"Your Grace of Cuevas?"

"I saw those letters this morning, when Your Eminence asked me to join you at breakfast. In my opinion, they are authentic." Cuevas spoke with hoarse indignation.

Waves of shame seemed to engulf Alvaro, but he could not halt what he had started.

Juan pointed his mace at his cousin. "Traitor, were you not a kinsman, we would have you put to death. But because we share a common blood, you will be judged by our lords." Rising, the king faced the members of the *Cortes*. "All who agree that Don Enrique, prince of Castile, should be banished from the land of his birth, shall rise."

Only one grandee remained seated. Alvaro, his head bowed, realized that Catalina would be forced to share Enrique's exile.

Cuevas gave a sharp order, and a squad of troops escorted the prince from the hall. He continued to protest vehemently, but Catalina, who walked beside him, remained silent, her lips compressed and her eyes glazed.

"Our business is not yet finished," Juan announced, looked down at Alvaro and smiled. "We have decided not to appoint a new council."

The grandees, who had not yet recovered from the scene they had just witnessed, were shocked.

"It is is our desire to appoint one man who will act as minister-in-chief, and all authority will be vested in him." The king sounded like a happy boy now, and unable to maintain his solemn air, he grinned broadly at Alvaro. "We are establishing a custom employed by our ancestors, and it gives us great joy to designate Don Alvaro de Luna as Constable of Castile, a position he will hold as long as he lives."

Alvaro rose and, his legs heavy, walked to the dais, where he dropped to his knees before the king.

Juan handed him the mace. "Stand, Constable, and take your place beside us."

Gripping the mace tightly, Alvaro moved to the king's right. Looking at the grandees, he saw precisely what he had expected, envy and hatred. The cardinals and bishops looked pleased, Roderigo was smiling and a few of the younger nobles seemed pleased, but most of the lords were unable to conceal their hostility.

Alvaro put Catalina and Enrique out of his mind for the moment. "I will devote my life to the service of Your Majesty and of Castile," he said firmly. "Gentlemen, I ask you to help me. In the days ahead I will appoint ministers of state who will serve under me." He paused, saw that most of the audience was still staring at him resentfully and spoke more emphatically. "I shall always want your assistance, and I hope you will give it to me, for the glory of Castile. But any man who refuses will oppose me at his peril." He stared at the grandees until Roderigo brought the silent duel to an abrupt end.

"Long live Juan II and his Constable!" The deep voice was so powerful that the delicate glass of the chandeliers tinkled.

The nobles had no choice, and following Roderigo's example, they stood and repeated his cry. But Alvaro knew as he followed Juan out of the hall that he had not reached the end of a road, but was starting out on a climb that would be treacherous and difficult.

Alvaro conferred with Don Domenico of Cuevas and Cardinal Torello for the better part of the morning; and after appointing officials to key posts that had to be filled at once so that the government could begin to function again, he left the council chamber and started toward the suite where he and Teresa had spent the night. His portfolio was filled with proposed royal decrees, financial reports and a sheaf of unanswered diplomatic correspondence, and he was so engrossed in the problems of state that he was only vaguely aware of his escort, a symbol of his new position and responsibility. Eight cavalry officers, all armed with swords and knives, accompanied him, and when he reached the staircase it finally dawned on him that two were preceding him, another pair flanked him and the others were bringing up the rear.

Suddenly the officers who were leading the procession stood aside, their hands on the hilts of their swords, and Alvaro was embarrassed when he saw Catalina and Enrique, dressed in traveling clothes, descending toward the courtyard under heavy guard. They halted at the landing, and he tried to smile as he approached them. "My felicitations, Your Highness," he said to Enrique.

The prince's face was wooden. "I've underestimated your talents too frequently, de Luna. I won't make the same mistake again. I must admit those false letters were ingenious. I couldn't have devised a more clever trick myself." He started off down the stairs, but Catalina, still pale, lagged a step behind him.

"Castile will miss you," Alvaro said to her.

"I wish great joy to you, Don Alvaro, and to your family." Catalina rejoined Enrique and took his arm.

Since it was beneath the dignity of the most powerful man

in the kingdom to gaze after her, Alvaro resumed his climb, and his officers took up sentry posts outside the suite. Teresa, radiant in a cloth-of-silver gown, was waiting for him, and after he kissed her, she curtsied to him. "Castile is at your feet, Lord Constable."

He caught her hands and helped her to rise. "Castile, perhaps, but not you."

"All of my dreams have come true, Alvaro. Roderigo came to see me while you were at your meeting, and told me everything."

His eyes narrowed. "I plan to give Roderigo considerable responsibility—I hope he doesn't waste time gossiping."

"How stern you can sound." She laughed and touched the small necklace of diamonds that encircled her throat. "He gave me an account of what happened at the meeting of the *Cortes*. I could scarcely wait to hear the details after I learned you had been made constable."

He relaxed and smiled.

"I've had your new suit laid out for you—you'll have to change quickly. I've notified the stewards that we're dining in state with Juan."

Alvaro glanced ruefully at his portfolio. Royal banquets were ceremonial affairs that lasted several hours, and he couldn't afford to waste the afternoon at a dinner, but didn't want to hurt Teresa's feelings.

She saw him hesitate. "Juan was very pleased."

"Of course. He can afford pageantry." Sighing, he left the portfolio on a table and went into the bedchamber to change.

Teresa, still ecstatic, followed him. "I hope you decided at your meeting that Juan should make you a duke."

"Frankly, the idea didn't cross my mind." He pulled off his stockings and picked up a fresh pair, made of white silk.

Exasperated and amused, Teresa shook her head. "You've become the first lord of the realm in political affairs, but others will still rank above us until you're given a duchy.

Now that we've managed to get rid of Catalina, I intend to move into her shoes—in every way. We'll take over that lovely apartment she's had on the third floor, and as Juan is too young to marry, I'm not going to allow any woman in Castile to rank ahead of me." She inspected herself in a long mirror, preened and adjusted an earring.

Alvaro, who was changing his shirt, glanced at her obliquely. "What do you mean by getting rid of Catalina?"

Teresa gestured casually. "You've had Enrique sent into exile, and she's gone with him. How she'll hate living in Aragon! Alfonso's wife is related to her, you know, and has always despised her."

He fastened the pearl buttons of his shirt and struggled to overcome his guilt. He was responsible for Catalina's marriage and exile, and knew he would carry the burden as long as he lived. "I can't pretend I like her choice of a husband," he said, "but I hope she'll find happiness in her new life."

"She won't," Teresa said impatiently. "This is the most glorious day of our lives, so let's not spoil it talking about Catalina. The whole court will be watching for us to make our entrance. I've been waiting a long time for this occasion."

He combed his hair quickly and pulled on a doublet of cream-colored silk. "I didn't realize you hated Catalina."

"Why shouldn't I have hated her?" Teresa walked to a mirror, studied her reflection and smiled contentedly. "She had all the things I wanted. They're mine now."

Alvaro stared at her.

"This is just the beginning," she continued, unaware of his scrutiny. "We're going to own castles in every part of Castile. We'll keep a huge stable, and I'll have so many gowns that two serving maids will spend all of their time taking care of my wardrobe." She laughed, then broke off as she saw her husband watching her. "Why do you look at me with such contempt?"

"I'm surprised, not contemptuous."

"Is it odd that I share your ambitions?"

"No, but—"

"We're going to have everything we've ever wanted," she said sharply. "But you aren't acting like a man who has just won a great victory. Stop mourning for your precious Catalina. She's gone. Forget her."

"Your callousness," Alvaro said angrily, "astonishes me."

"You mean that you're uncomfortable because I'm speaking honestly. Let's enjoy our reward instead of bickering." Teresa started toward the door. "You aren't soft and romantic. Neither am I. I knew you'd fight your way to the top. That's why I married you, and I'm not going to let anyone forget I'm the wife of the constable."

Alvaro caught hold of her arm. "Why do you think I married you?" he demanded.

She shrugged. "I'm aware of my attractions. I also happen to be of noble birth, and there weren't many of my station who would have married a man who had neither a name nor a fortune. Now," she added with a pleased smile, "you have both."

"I wanted a family," he said in a low, intense voice. "Honors mean nothing to me unless I can pass them to my sons."

"The doctors have told me I'll never bear children," Teresa said carelessly. "But I'll help you in your career, which is more than most wives could do." Not waiting for a reply, she walked out of the room.

Alvaro followed her into the corridor, indifferent to the acclaim that awaited him, feeling crushed and desolate. Justice, Father Sebastian had said, was a two-edged sword, and the priest was right. No matter how much glory and power Alvaro accumulated, he would never achieve his greatest ambition, and he knew he would spend the rest of his life living with a sense of frustration that would be a constant reminder of his chicanery.

3. The Constable

1

The atmosphere was tense in the central hall of the hunting lodge that the king had built in the hills outside Toledo near the country estate of his friend, Alvaro de Luna. Twenty grandees, all of them wearing the sash of the Military Order of Santiago, an exclusive society of high-ranking officers, were in complete agreement with the Grand Master of the Order, Diego Gomes de Sandoual, Count of Castro Xeris, who was making an impassioned speech.

"I am totally opposed to an invasion of Granada," the count cried. "We have fought the Moors for centuries, and the heathens still flourish. An expedition would be expensive, the costliest enterprise we have ever undertaken, and who would pay the price? You and I! No, a war against Mohammed-ibn-Azar isn't worth the effort."

King Juan, still looking boyish at twenty-five, twisted a curl of his dark hair in his fingers and idly studied a tapestry on the wall adjacent to the huge, open hearth. The picture woven on the fabric, depicting a young shepherd playing a lute as he courted a shy maiden who sat beneath an olive tree, was one of the king's favorite works of art, and although he was familiar with every detail, he gazed at it fondly.

Francisco Cardinal Ruminez, who had recently succeeded the late Cardinal Torello as archbishop of Toledo and primate of Castile, was the only man present who was not a member of the order. He had been invited to the meeting as a courtesy, and as it was customary for one in his position to express no opinion except when asked, he carefully watched the fire that helped to dispel the December chill.

Alvaro was not indifferent, however. Running a hand through his hair, which was heavily sprinkled with grey although he was not yet thirty-five, he glanced at the count contemptuously. "The weight of milord Sandoual's purse is more important to him than the fate of his country. He prefers to count his *dolars,* and is so busy hiding them beneath his mattress that he can't hear the cries of Castilians who have been ravaged by the Moors. The heathens have made eighty-three raids on our territory in just this current year, and 1430 hasn't yet come to an end. But milord count cares more about his gold than he does for the suffering of those whose homes have been burned, whose sons have been sold into slavery and whose daughters have been condemned to spend their miserable lives in the harems of Islam."

"I applaud the patriotism of the lord constable," Sandoual retorted heavily. "Perhaps, if I were Duke of Truxillo, of Segovia and Cordoba, if I were a marquis eleven times and a count seventeen, I might be careless about money matters, too."

Alvaro realized he was vulnerable, and silently blamed Teresa, who persisted in persuading Juan to grant him new titles. "You forget that I pay heavier taxes than any man in Castile." It was a tactical error to mention taxation. More than ten years had passed since he had relieved the poor of their tax obligations and had forced the grandees to pay, according to their means, yet they would never stop hating him.

"If my wife could afford to wear a collar of diamonds and rubies or an emerald pendant the size of a cider mug, I wouldn't object to paying high taxes." The count had lost his temper and was shouting.

Most of Teresa's jewels had been gifts she had coaxed Juan to give her, and Alvaro looked at the king, hoping a royal explanation would clear the air. But he should have known better, and sighed when he saw that Juan was smiling fatuously as he examined the tapestry. Not even the constable could expect consistent support from an irresponsible monarch who, as he grew older, was beginning to behave like his pleasure-seeking mother.

"May I suggest," Francisco asked mildly, "that you confine yourselves to the subject under discussion, gentlemen. Recriminations accomplish no useful purpose."

"We know where Your Eminence stands," Sandoual replied heavily.

Francisco put a hand on his brother's arm to prevent Alvaro from leaping to his defense.

Pero Maurique, Adelantado de Leon, one of the younger members of the group and a son-in-law of Don Domenico of Cuevas, pushed back his chair. "I agree with the cardinal. Let's be reasonable."

He was considered one of Alvaro's supporters, and his colleagues looked at him cynically.

"Technically, at least, Castile is peaceful and prosperous," Adelantado continued, fingering his deep lace cuffs. "Of course, some of you will claim that as all troops now serve the crown, we can't quarrel among ourselves. And I must admit that it isn't easy to fight with a neighbor when no noble is allowed more than fifty retainers. No one except the constable, who employs more than two thousand men-at-arms under his own banner."

The surprised grandees realized he was attacking Alvaro, and brightened.

"We pay a high price for our so-called peace, gentlemen." Adelantado was warming to his theme. "How many troops do we keep on the borders of Navarre and Aragon to make certain that King Juan and King Alfonso don't invade us, how many spies keep watch on Prince Pedro in Pamplona and

Prince Enrique in Saragossa to warn the constable if either tries to cross our frontiers?"

Alvaro had heard rumors that the young grandee disliked his father-in-law, but Adelantado had always maintained a discreet silence. Now, however, Cuevas was confined to his bed after a hunting accident, and the lord of Leon apparently felt free to express his own views. It would do no good to explain that the king's cousins had never abandoned their schemes to gain control of Castile, so Alvaro remained silent. Young men who had never dealt with Pedro and Enrique couldn't imagine the danger they represented.

King Juan stirred for the first time. "Enrique and Pedro would steal the throne if they could."

"Are you certain, Your Majesty, that they don't merely share the desire of so many of your lords, and want you to appoint a constable whose views are sympathetic with those of the nobility?"

Juan was outraged. "That's treason!" he said shrilly.

"Is it treasonable to accuse a state minister of favoring the common people at the expense of the grandees?"

"Adelantado," Alvaro said wearily, "you may consider yourself under arrest." He signalled to two armed guards at the door, then looked away as they escorted the indiscreet lord of Leon from the room. So many of his opponents had been sent to prison, Alvaro reflected, that he should have become callous, but he couldn't force himself to condemn a member of Cuevas' family to a term in a dungeon. As Don Domenico and Roderigo were his only true friends, he would merely place Adelantado under house arrest for a few weeks and hope his father-in-law could soften his antagonism.

"Are there other traitors here?" Juan demanded angrily.

"There are none," Alvaro said, his tone firm but soothing. "Their lordships are loyal to you and to Castile. Unfortunately, they don't like me, and I'm afraid they don't share my vision." He glanced slowly around the table at dark, hostile eyes and bristling, pointed beards. "The day must come when Iberians, who share a common heritage, will stop scheming and fighting against each other, when they'll unite under one king for our common good."

Diego de Sandoual gestured contemptuously. "Are you actually suggesting, Constable, that Alfonso of Aragon and Juan of Navarre bend their knees to Castile?"

"No, but I can look forward to the day when their sons or perhaps their grandsons will become our partners in a common cause. Leon hasn't suffered by merging with Castile. Neither will Aragon and Navarre."

"Perhaps," the elderly Don Fadrique of Casarruvias said politely, "the constable hears voices, like that French peasant girl the English have captured and are placing on trial."

Alvaro controlled his temper. "I have followed the exploits of the maid called Joan with great interest, milord. She may be odd, but she rescued Orleans from her country's enemies last year with only four thousand troops, she crowned her king at Reims and she united France. Would that I could hear the voices that guide her!"

There was an uneasy silence, and several of the grandees looked obliquely at Francisco, who had made no attempt to reprove his brother. "I am not competent to judge whether the acts of the French girl are miraculous, as she claims," the cardinal said.

"I don't care what happens in France," Sandoual declared flatly. "But I do know that only a miracle will unite the Spanish countries. The constable may dream, if that's how he likes to amuse himself, but I'll be damned if I'm going to pay for his hallucinations."

"I don't ask for an immediate union with Aragon and Navarre." Alvaro spoke quietly, patiently; after years of dealing with impetuous grandees he had learned that their lack of self-discipline rendered them incapable of dealing logically with a problem. They preferred to indulge in emotional out-

bursts and to shirk responsibilities, but they could be maneuvered into facing situations squarely. "You're right, milord.
My dreams are my own concern. All I request is that the
Grand Master of the Military Order of Santiago lead an expedition against the Moors, whose raids are turning the
southern provinces into a wasteland."

There was an expression of vicious triumph in Sandoual's
eyes as he looked at his colleagues. "Like my brother generals
and colonels, I know how to lead armored knights into battle,
Constable. I don't understand this new army of archers you've
organized, and I don't like the new form of drill you've in-
stituted. Roman legions marched into battle in a phalanx,
but modern Castilians don't!"

It was clear that the others agreed with him.

Alvaro wanted to shout that they were all old-fashioned,
short-sighted fools, but instead he smiled calmly. "You read
the reports and diagrams of the victory that Henry of England
won in his war against the French?"

"I glanced through them."

"I trust you listened to the accounts of the veterans of
Agincourt whom I brought to Castile at great expense."

"Needless expense," Sandoual retorted. "I still don't see
why my taxes should have been squandered on English and
French officers who had nothing better to do than reminisce
about a battle they fought."

Not one of the nobles was willing to admit that Henry of
England had revolutionized warfare, and Alvaro's temper
soared.

"The armored knight," Sandoual continued, "has been the
rock on which successful armies have been built for more
than three hundred years. But members of the gentry aren't
welcome in the constable's legions of commoners. He prefers
to take peasants and artisans, train them as crossbowmen and
call them soldiers." Turning to the king, the count removed
his sash, on which the diamond emblem of the Grand Master

of the Order was pinned. "Your Majesty, it would be beneath my dignity to lead such a rabble. Should you want me to command a real army, I shall be at your disposal."

Juan was unperturbed, and a brief smile of sly pleasure crossed his face. "Don Diego, you have solved a problem that has vexed us for some time. It would have been graceless, in view of your past services, to ask for your retirement, but you have saved us the necessity." Taking the sash, he looped it over Alvaro's head. "From this time forward, our Constable shall be the Grand Master of Santiago. He will lead our army against the heathens, and we will accompany him into the field in order to see him win a glorious victory."

Alvaro and Francisco rode together down the road, the members of their respective escorts following at a respectful distance. The diamonds of the Grand Master's emblem picked up the light of the winter sun, and Alvaro couldn't resist glancing down at his chest, but his brother failed to share his elation. "Juan," the cardinal said, frowning, "does you no favor when he heaps so many honors on you."

Alvaro was in no mood to listen to a sermon. "Sandoual is an idiot. As Henry of England proved, the nature of warfare has changed."

"Perhaps, but the nature of human beings hasn't. You're the only man in the history of Castile who has ever been Constable and Grand Master of the Order of Santiago. Never has any one person held so much power."

Laughing unconcernedly, Alvaro waved to a pair of shepherds warming themselves at a small fire they had built in a field.

"The grandees see you becoming stronger, and they're afraid of you. That's why they band together against you."

"Let them. I've smashed a dozen or more petty conspiracies. They'll change their thinking when they see how easily I can beat the Moors with my English type of army."

"You're wrong," Francisco replied vehemently. "Every success you win makes them all the more envious and fearful. And it's unfortunate that you and I are related. Your new appointment will make life more difficult for me."

The wind was blowing steadily from the north, and Alvaro reluctantly closed his cape. "You're too sensitive to criticism."

"Am I?" Francisco smiled sardonically. "Do you know what's being said about us? Have you heard the accusation that Castile is being ruled, spiritually and temporally, by the sons of a whore?"

Alvaro turned in his saddle. "Tell me the name of the man who made that statement, and I'll send him to prison before the day ends."

The cardinal remained calm. "As I have no doubt that you'd carry out the threat, I have no intention of telling you." He laughed dryly. "And you tell me that I'm sensitive to criticism. Don't you see that you've risen too high in the world? There's only one direction you can go now." A hand encased in a scarlet-dyed kidskin glove pointed toward the ground.

"Apparently you choose to forget all I've done for Castile," Alvaro said irritably. "When I became constable, the nation was almost bankrupt. We're entering 1431 with more gold than the vaults of the treasury have ever held. The towns-people are prosperous, and our ships are carrying more of our goods to foreign lands than ever before. If you think I've done harm rather than good, ask those shepherds we just passed whether they approve of my rule. Or go to the house of some peasant down the road from my castle."

Francisco sighed. "I'm aware of all that you've accomplished, and there's no need for me to interview peasants or shepherds. Can't you understand that I'm trying to warn you, Alvaro?"

Staring straight ahead down the hard-packed road, Alvaro wondered whether his brother had turned against him. They had worked together without friction, but perhaps the Church was jealous of Alvaro's power, as Teresa had intimated.

The cardinal seemed to read his thoughts. "I won't pretend that I like Teresa any more than she likes me. All I ask is that you remember I've always been loyal to you, and I'm sorry the time has come when I must speak against the influence your wife is exerting in the wrong direction."

"Teresa doesn't influence me in anything." Alvaro was annoyed. "I've been so busy that we rarely see each other, except at dinner." He couldn't force himself to reveal, even to his brother, that he found it convenient to sleep in a bedchamber adjacent to his office rather than share Teresa's apartment.

"Your spurs are made of gold, your cloak is lined with furs imported from the northern German states and you dine on a service of silver," Francisco said relentlessly. "That ruby on your left thumb is worth a king's ransom. Your private stable is the largest in Europe."

"Don't you think I'm entitled to a few luxuries in return for my efforts?"

The cardinal ignored the question. "You heard what was said at the meeting today. You're the lord of three duchies, you're a marquis ten times—"

"Eleven."

"—and although you've forced the grandees to disband their private armies, you have so many retainers you've had to make Roderigo de Pinar your personal seneschal."

"Roderigo is loyal. He commands my troops and manages my estates. I have no time for such matters, and he's the perfect assistant. He isn't capable of holding a ministry of state, but he follows directions, and I never have to question him."

"You're being evasive." Francisco caught his brother's arm. "Forget that you're the constable and that I'm archbishop of Toledo. I'm just a simple priest, and we're both the sons of a woman who allowed her greed to warp her life. I don't want to see you walk in her footsteps. Hate me, if you will, but there's no one else who would dare to say this to you. You're master of Castile, but you'll have to assert yourself as master of your own household or your wife's insatiable ambition will ruin you."

Alvaro felt warm, and opened his cloak. "It's true, Francisco, that Teresa is ambitious. I need no more titles or estates, yet she collects them as she collects her jewels. I suppose I've humored her because she's never had children. But surely my indulgence has done no harm."

Francisco thought it remarkable that an able administrator whose work required an understanding of human nature could display such ingenuousness in his own personal relationships. "Your enemies attack you with any weapons they can find, and they never stop condemning Teresa's extravagance. She's the weakest link in your armor, and the campaign against her has been so effective that even the townspeople and shepherds hate her."

"I've done more for the commoners than anyone else since Alfonso XI, who died nearly one hundred years ago."

The cardinal's hands were cold beneath his thin gloves, and he flexed his fingers. "Have you been so isolated you've never discovered that hatred is neither reasonable nor necessarily just? You've reduced the burdens of the poor, but men continue to work until they're exhausted to earn enough so they can buy food and clothing for their families. How do you think they feel when they see your wife riding from one of her palaces to another, covered with jewels more magnificent than any queen has ever worn?"

"She does them no harm."

"That's irrelevant. She's doing you great harm, and some of the stories that are being whispered about her undermine your position and your authority."

"What stories?"

Francisco hesitated for a moment. "Why does Roderigo de Pinar go everywhere with her?" he asked reluctantly.

Alvaro was as stunned as he was angry. "When I'm busy, as I am so often, Roderigo acts as Teresa's escort. He's my friend."

"I repeat the gossip to you so that you'll be warned and can deal with it. Your enemies never stop working for the day when they can force you out of office and recall Enrique and Pedro from exile. They were heartened when the king's bride died, and there is talk that Enrique would like to dispose of Juan and claim the crown for himself, through his wife's name."

"I never discuss Catalina." Alvaro spurred to the summit of a hill and stared at the turrets of his own castle, which stood on a rise beyond a patch of woods.

Francisco, not changing his pace, rode up the slope more slowly. "Alvaro," he said earnestly, drawing to a halt beside his angry brother, "I'm not your confessor, and I don't intend to pry into your inner feelings. I can only beg you to guard against loose talk that hurts you. Send Don Roderigo back to his own estate, dismiss Beatriz de Pimente from your wife's service and force Teresa to live more modestly. Your enemies will become even more active now that you've been made Grand Master of Santiago, and if they can be rid of you, all that you've accomplished for Castile will be reversed overnight."

Alvaro was as perplexed as he was annoyed, and failed to see how Teresa's attractive lady-in-waiting, Beatriz de Pimente, threatened his security. "Doña Beatriz," he said with a smile, "is a decorative member of my household, but to the best of knowledge she knows nothing about diplomacy, politics or the schemes of disgruntled nobles. Are you trying to tell me that she's in league with my enemies?"

"You're so far removed from the world below you that you no longer hear what's being said in the streets." Francisco raised his collar of thick wool. "It's believed everywhere, even in foreign lands, that Beatriz de Pimente is your mistress, that you allow Teresa to go her own way and that, in return, she closes her eyes to your affair."

"What nonsense!"

"You'll know better than I how to lay the rumors." The cardinal removed his right glove and extended his hand. "We'll meet in the city next week?"

"I'll dine with you even sooner. I'll have to start planning the expedition against Granada immediately." Alvaro tried to hide a surge of embarrassment. "I wish you'd come with me for a cup of wine to warm you on your ride."

"Your house is more peaceful when I don't intrude." Francisco turned away and rode off toward Toledo, his entourage closing in around him.

Alvaro galloped toward his castle, leaving his escort far behind, and when he arrived in the courtyard he flung himself from the saddle, threw his reins to a groom and stalked into the great hall, still disturbed. This was one of the most important days in his life, but the knowledge that he was the most powerful man in the history of Castile gave him neither pleasure nor satisfaction. Francisco had succeeded in making him thoroughly dissatisfied with himself, although his conscience was clear. He knew that gossip could hurt him, and decided to discuss the problem frankly with Teresa. She disliked serious conversation and would accuse Francisco of meddling, but if it was true that the people were criticizing her ostentation, she would have to live more discreetly. It was certain that the cardinal disliked her, but he had no reason to lie to his brother.

A handsome woman with a jeweled comb in her black hair was sitting before the hearth, embroidering, and when Alvaro noted her gown of dark-green velvet he thought he had found Teresa alone. He wanted to talk about the situation at once, and was disappointed when she heard his footsteps and turned; he had never realized that Beatriz de Pimente bore such a strong resemblance to his wife.

"Your Grace!" she exclaimed, flustered, rising and curtsying. "I didn't hear the men-at-arms arrive."

"They dawdled on the road." Alvaro removed his cape and threw it over a chair.

It slid onto the floor, and Beatriz retrieved it. "Your meeting ended earlier than Her Grace expected," she said, her manner betraying a trace of nervousness.

"Is she here?" Alvaro started toward the stone staircase that led to the private apartments on the second and third floors.

"No, sir. She thought you'd be delayed, and went into the city." Beatriz carefully folded the cape.

"Without you?"

"Don Roderigo escorted her. They took the small coach. There isn't room in it for more than two."

Alvaro was sorry that Francisco had told him the ugly rumor about Teresa and his friend. Teresa made frequent trips into Toledo, and until now the thought that she might be unfaithful to him had never crossed his mind.

"You've been made Grand Master of Santiago, Your Grace!"

The lady-in-waiting's breathless ecstasy brought Alvaro back to the present, and he touched the diamond emblem on his sash. "You surprise me. I didn't know that ladies were familiar with military insignia."

Beatriz's full lips parted in a smile. "I've made anything that concerns Your Grace my business. May I drink a toast to your success?"

"Thank you." He watched her as she moved to a table and poured generous quantities of French brandy into two goblets. No man could live under the same roof with her and remain unaware of her appeal, yet Alvaro was able to tell himself honestly that he had never contemplated trying to make her his mistress.

Beatriz was conscious of his scrutiny and flirted with him subtly as she crossed the hall, handed him one of the goblets and raised the other. "Death to your enemies, Your Grace!"

It was childish to feel annoyed because Teresa wasn't celebrating with him. He had won so many triumphs that he could scarcely expect her to become excited about each one, and he had to admit, in all fairness, that his new appointment had been unexpected. However, he found the enthusiasm of a pretty and sophisticated girl refreshing. Sipping his brandy, he drifted toward the hearth, paused and gazed into the flames. "What is your ambition, Doña Beatriz?" he asked suddenly, imagining she would reply that she hoped to marry a nobleman of stature and raise a family.

"Why do you ask, Your Grace?" she parried.

He glanced at her casually over the rim of his goblet, then faced her squarely when he saw that she was studying him intently. "I can't command you to answer me, but I have valid reasons."

"I'd like to be wealthy and powerful, Your Grace," Beatriz said bluntly, her dark eyes meeting his.

"Your father owned several estates—"

"And my brother inherited them."

"How long have you been a member of my household?" Changing the subject abruptly, he drained his drink.

"Almost two years, Your Grace." Beatriz took his goblet and refilled it.

"It's odd, you know. In all this time, you and I have never had a private talk until today."

"The fault isn't mine." Although her tone was demure, her expression was challenging.

Alvaro retreated gracefully. "As I remember, you wrote a letter to my wife, asking if she could place you in her service."

"Our families had known each other, and Doña Teresa offered me a chance to escape."

"What was threatening you?"

"A life of boredom. A marriage with some dull-witted local grandee who could talk about nothing except the wheat and grape yield of his peasants, the price of wool in the Toledo market and his latest adventures on a wild boar hunt."

Alvaro chuckled indulgently. "You have a sharp wit."

"It would be difficult for anyone to spend two years in your house without growing more worldly, Your Grace."

He looked at her again, saw that she was regarding him steadily and noted that, in her high heels, her eyes were on a level with his. "I never say or do anything without a purpose."

"So I've been told." Beatriz was poised but alert.

"You may not want to remain in my wife's employ," Alvaro said curtly.

The girl was surprised and hurt. "Have I done something that displeases you, Your Grace?"

He shook his head. "You're spoiling your chances of finding a husband who can offer you wealth and power."

She lowered her head as she drank, and he couldn't see her expression.

"I'm afraid this is painful and embarrassing, but I've just heard something that is certain to influence you. My enemies have been spreading a nasty rumor—many people, both in Castile and abroad, believe that you are my mistress." He found the heat of the fire suffocating and moved away from the hearth.

"I've known of the stories for months," Beatriz said calmly.

Alvaro blinked in astonishment and absently rubbed the old scar on his head. "You don't sound upset."

Her half-smile gave him no clue to her feelings. "I've thought it ironic, Your Grace, that you should be the only man in Castile unaware of whatever charms I may possess."

"What leads you to believe I've been blind?" he demanded.

Beatriz had always treated him with careful respect, but

suddenly her manner changed and she looked at him defiantly. "You've given me no cause to assume otherwise."

Alvaro knew she was goading him, and her tactics were so obvious that he grinned. "Does Doña Teresa know of these rumors?"

"Of course."

His smile faded. "What does she think of them?"

She shrugged. "Her Grace is amused."

"Well, I'm not," he replied harshly. "I advise you to leave before you lose what may be left of your good name."

"As my reputation is ruined, I'd gain nothing by going." Beatriz drifted closer to him. "I suffer all the disadvantages of being your mistress, but I enjoy none of the benefits."

Alvaro curbed an urge to take her in his arms. "I'll see to it that you'll lose nothing." Finishing his drink, he picked up his cape and walked quickly up the stairs to his office on the second floor.

Perhaps, he thought as he spread a large map of Granada out before him on his desk, he was stupid to reject beauty when it was offered to him, and he felt no satisfaction because he had remained faithful to his wife. It was hard to admit to himself that Teresa probably wouldn't care if he indulged in an affair, but it was even more difficult to concede that he hadn't been thinking of her, but of Catalina, when he had left Beatriz in the hall.

2

"The peasant rabble," as the grandees called Alvaro's army, marched south from Toledo to Ciudad Real, where Don Domenico of Cuevas, his left arm still in a sling after his accident, joined the column with reinforcements from Estremadura. The legion, twenty-five thousand strong, skirted around the foothills of the Sierra Morena range and headed toward the formidable peaks of the Sierra Nevada, the natural barrier that the Moors used as a shield. King Juan traveled with the main body of the army, but Alvaro, who had been detained by affairs of state, remained in Toledo until he had received word that the entire army had massed at the town of Jaen, near the border of the Moslem state.

He knew his enemies were saying that he was a coward and unworthy of wearing the star of the Grand Master of Santiago, but he ignored the slurs while he concluded a new trade treaty with France and opened intricate negotiations with the ambassador from Lisbon that would, he hoped, unite Juan and Princess Isabella of Portugal in marriage. Permanent peace with Portugal in the west and Granada in the south would allow him to concentrate on Navarre and Aragon, and when he finally set out to join the army, he was determined to render Mohammed-ibn-Azar incapable of waging war again.

Accompanied by five thousand horsemen under the command of Roderigo de Pinar, he rode south to Jaen, where the king and his army of professional soldiers greeted him enthusiastically. Juan insisted that Alvaro dine with him, and it was late in the evening before the constable and his old friend, Cuevas, were able to retire for a private talk. They made themselves comfortable in Alvaro's tent, an equerry brought them cups of watered calavados, and sentries were posted around the pavilion of silk and canvas to insure privacy.

"I'm grateful to you for joining the expedition," Alvaro said. "It's strange, after all these years, that you and Roderigo are still the only men I can trust. Most of my officers, even General Huerrara, are minor grandees who have made a career out of army life. Are you sure your physicians say you're ready for a campaign?"

Cuevas laughed carelessly. "I don't listen to physicians. The very least I could do to repay your kindness to me was to take command of the foot soldiers for you."

"What kindness?"

"You could have had my son-in-law executed for his impertinence. You treated him honorably, which was a mistake."

"It's no mistake to honor a friend."

"Adelantado has been receiving considerable quantities of mail from Aragon lately." Don Domenico stared into his cup. "You've spoken for years of your dream. You want a united Iberia, but it may be a marriage of a sort you won't like. If we fail to beat the Moors decisively, I'm afraid Alfonso of Aragon is going to lead an expedition against us. Adelantado talks too freely when he drinks, and he's hinted that Alfonso has finally given in to the pleas of his brothers."

"I've been expecting him to threaten us."

"We can't blame him, I suppose. Castile is a ripe plum. The king is incompetent. He's a widower, there's no heir to the throne, and Alfonso would be one of the most powerful kings in Europe if he could add Castile to his realm."

Alvaro laughed wryly. "He'd have to fight Enrique and Pedro for it." Leaning forward on his stool, he lowered his voice. "I have a surprise in store for Alfonso. The king won't remain a widower much longer. If we can make a good showing against the Moors, Portugal has promised to send us Princess Isabella as our queen. I've seen her miniatures, and she's an attractive girl who will give us an heir. She'll be more of an asset to Castile than that frigid French wench who made the king so miserable for a year. I'm afraid I did him no favor when I arranged that marriage, but I'll more than make it up to him."

"Does Juan know of your plans?"

"Certainly not! It will be time enough to tell him when final arrangements have been settled."

Cuevas chuckled and tugged at his greying beard. "It's no wonder you've made so many enemies, Alvaro. You treat people as though they were figures on a chess board."

"I try to do what's best for Castile."

"If I didn't know that, I'd have gone over to the other side long ago." Cuevas finished his drink and stood. "You're aware of the risks you're taking in this campaign?"

"Teresa asked me the same question the night I left Toledo. As I told her, if I stand still, I'll be destroyed, and the new Castile I've created will die with me. I have no choice, and I want none."

The army of Castile paused at the border of Granada while Alvaro sent a messenger into the land of the heathen to challenge King Mohammed-ibn-Azar to a personal duel. Even though he believed that the English had devised a new type of warfare at Agincourt, he meticulously observed the ceremonial requirements of the code of chivalry. But the Moor was a realist, too, and his army retreated into high-walled towns that were virtually impregnable. There the Moslems could withstand long sieges, and no catapults or other artillery had yet been invented that was strong enough to batter down the turrets of stone.

Alvaro was prepared for such a maneuver and countered it by sending Roderigo on a series of raids that devastated the countryside. The cavalry captured the livestock of farmers and shepherds, wrecked the houses of peasants and destroyed their mosques. Three fast-moving columns penetrated the enemy countryside so deeply that they reached the Mediterranean, where the Moors' fishing boats were set on fire, and at last Mohammed-ibn-Azar realized that he was the victim of his own strategy. While his army waited in vain for conventional attacks against the garrisons, Granada was being transformed into an uninhabitable desert.

Forced to give Alvaro the battle he demanded, the king of Granada secretly evacuated his garrisons one by one and united his troops under his own command on the highland plateau north of his capital. When Alvaro learned from his scouts that strong cavalry detachments from Malaga and

Almeria were riding to join Mohammed-ibn-Azar, he sent to Castile for the ten thousand men he had left to maintain order at home. Until they could join him he lived off the countryside, continued his harassing raids, and when the enemy occupied heights they could defend with ease, he threatened the city of Granada itself and forced the Moslems to abandon their natural stronghold.

Mohammed-ibn-Azar established his headquarters at a village called Higuercula, and after eight thousand Castilian reinforcements had joined Alvaro, he decided the time had come to strike. He rode out with a strong patrol to inspect the enemy position, saw that a flat expanse of tableland extended for more than a mile and a half to the east of Higuercula beyond a grove of pomegranate trees, and concluded that the site was perfect for the type of battle he intended to fight. However, his army would be forced to move through narrow mountain passes in order to reach the position, and he realized the Moslems could spoil his plan and scatter his men by firing on them from above if they learned of his intentions.

Therefore he sent a detachment of cavalry to the west of the village, ordering the commander of the unit to make no attempt at concealment. In the meantime he marched with the main body of forty thousand men by an indirect route toward his destination, completing his maneuver in a long night march that brought the Castilians onto the plateau shortly before dawn on July 1, 1431. Knowing that the enemy would discover his presence soon after daybreak, he ordered the men to eat a hearty meal and snatch a few hours of sleep.

Trumpets inside the camp of the Moors aroused the legions of Mohammed-ibn-Azar, and Higuercula came to life. Moslem lords, assisted by their slaves, hastily donned armor, and the *janissaries,* a corps of fast-moving, professional cavalry, rode out to the edge of the grove of fruit trees and took a stand to prevent the Castilians from attacking before the defenders were ready. Officers shouted commands in guttural

Arabic, pikemen ran to join their units and great nobles mounted on pure white stallions imported from the deserts of Libya wielded long rawhide whips relentlessly, spurring the slow and the reluctant.

Meanwhile Alvaro formed his bowmen in lines three deep. Those in the front rank, who were equipped with short, heavy crossbows, rested on the ground, but remained alert and were ready to rise to their knees. Behind them were crossbowmen armed with longer-range weapons, who stood erect, and in the rear were the troops who had received the most intensive training, the longbowmen, who could hit any moving object at a distance of three hundred yards. General Ernesto Huerrara sat with the cavalry on the right flank, and Don Domenico of Cuevas took command of the reserves on the left, crossbowmen supported by two thousand conventional infantrymen, who wore chain mail and were armed with pikes.

Roderigo, who had made a wide semicircle around the enemy position with a small band of horsemen, returned to the Castilian lines and was dismayed to find Alvaro riding up and down in front of the army, letting himself be seen by the enemy, who might shoot him down if he failed to take cover. "The infidels have assembled at least sixty thousand men," Roderigo said, pushing up his visor and wiping sweat from his face.

"Our earlier estimates were accurate then," Alvaro replied cheerfully. "They must be deployed in depth behind the village."

"I counted seventeen squadrons of armored knights, and there may be others, but the *janissaries* sent out a strong patrol to capture us, and we had to come back. But I saw enough to convince me they have half again as many men as we've mustered."

Alvaro was unimpressed. "Captain," he called to an officer, "form your line of longbowmen at least four paces to the rear of your second rank. Don't crowd your rows too close to each other, or the men won't be free to move."

Roderigo removed his helmet and mopped his head with a square of linen. "I'm ready to attack right now if you'll give the word."

"Relieve General Huerrara and send him back to the bowmen, but you're not attacking yet," Alvaro told him firmly.

"If we wait until they're ready, they'll send us into a full-scale retreat." Roderigo was angry.

"You should have spent a few hours after dinner last night studying the tactics that Henry of England used at Agincourt," Alvaro declared, tempering his rebuke with a smile. "Writing letters on the evening before a battle is a waste of time."

Roderigo flushed and stared down at the ground.

"Look behind us. We'd have to cross broken ground to reach three narrow passes. The heathens would destroy us if we tried to retreat. We've got to make a stand here, and we're fortunate that the field is narrow. We've built our position in depth, as the Moslems can't move against us on a broad front."

"You aren't going to let them attack?"

Alvaro patted his friend's armor-plated shoulder. "Mohammed-ibn-Azar's knights are carrying at least fifty pounds more on their backs than you are. They aren't going to enjoy riding across the plain in this heat."

"I wish you'd listen to reason, Alvaro!"

"I've spent years planning for this day. Follow orders, Roderigo. That's all I ask of you."

Savagely pulling his helmet onto his head, Roderigo saluted stiffly.

"I swear to you that you'll see action before the day ends."

"It isn't my place to criticize the Grand Master of Santiago." Roderigo's eyes were dark and sullen.

Alvaro removed his right glove and extended his hand.

"We've been friends for too many years to quarrel now. Trust me, as I trust you."

Shifting uneasily in his saddle, Roderigo reddened again, accepted the hand that was held out to him and then rode off quickly to join the cavalry.

The thin, high wail of the rams' horns in the camp of the Moslems grew louder, more insistent, and priests moved through the ranks of the Castilians, blessing the men. A *janissary* commander, two green plumes protruding from his leather helmet, reviewed his squadrons, and at his command they rode into battle formation, two deep. Moslem knights in heavy armor formed a solid mass behind them, and thousands of pikemen marched into positions on the flanks. It was too late now for Alvaro to change his tactics, but he showed none of the tension he felt as he half-stood in his stirrups and surveyed his ranks of waiting soldiers.

"Where is His Majesty?" he asked the adjutant who sat beside him.

"In his tent, Your Grace, as you commanded. His horse is saddled and waiting for him, and fifty men who have taken oaths to give their lives for him are waiting to escort him to safety if we seem to be in danger of losing."

It was fortunate, Alvaro reflected, that Juan had agreed to take no part in the battle. If the English victory at Agincourt had been an accident and his own gamble ended in disaster, at least the king would escape. The nobles would be pleased if he lost, but he could not afford to think of them now; it was imperative to devote his full attention to the enemy. He ignored the diplomatic suggestion of the adjutant that he lower his visor. "Pass the word to hold steady," he said.

Unit commanders repeated the order, and his standard bearer raised his pennant, the pale blue flag of the duchy of Truxillo. Cuevas, Huerrara and Roderigo followed his example, and scores of Moslem banners waved in the air near the pomegranate grove. Again the rams' horns sounded, and Alvaro expected the Moslems to launch their assault, but they seemed to be waiting for something. Finally the ranks of the *janissaries* parted to allow a man in cloth-of-gold, wearing a turban of the same material, to ride out alone onto the field. Behind him was his standard bearer, but a single glance at the magnificent figure was sufficient to identify King Mohammed-ibn-Azar, the warrior-monarch of Granada.

It was difficult to read his expression clearly at a distance, but he seemed puzzled as he peered at the unorthodox formation of Castilians. The plumed *janissary* commander joined him, as did several other bearded Moslem lords, and a brief conference was held. Then Mohammed-ibn-Azar waved his subordinates away, and after they had rejoined their respective commands, he drew a scimitar of pure gold and raised it over his head.

"God preserve King Juan and Castile," Alvaro shouted, and his men repeated his cry.

The lightly armored *janissaries* started across the plain, three thousand strong. They moved in unison, first at a trot, then at a canter and finally at a gallop, and they were so well trained they needed no commands to coordinate their efforts. When the riders in the first rank were about four hundred yards from the Castilians they drew their scimitars, twirled the blades over their heads and shouted hoarsely. It was easy to understand why they had succeeded in frightening so many foes, and a ripple of uneasiness passed through the ranks of the defenders. But Alvaro remained motionless in his saddle, aware only of the tumultuous *janissary* tide.

When the front rank was no more than two hundred and fifty yards from his lines, he felt a sense of relief as he called, "Longbowmen, fire."

Huerrara repeated the order, and a shower of arrows descended on the riders.

"Rear crossbowmen, fire!"

The heavy shafts struck horses and riders, and the advance of the *janissaries* was checked. The men in the front rank faltered, those behind them hesitated, and the green-plumed commander, who had been wounded but still retained his seat, signaled a retreat. The light cavalry drew back, leaving its dead and wounded, and after hastily forming a second time, launched a fresh assault. The Castilians waited with greater confidence, and Alvaro allowed the enemy to draw still closer before he gave the command to fire.

The bowmen laid down a deadly barrage, and the *janissaries,* who boasted that they had never suffered a defeat, were shattered. No longer a cohesive unit, they fled in disorder, the survivors riding wildly through the ranks of the waiting knights and pikemen. But Mohammed-ibn-Azar knew he had lost a skirmish rather than a battle, and sent his main body forward. His knights, mounted on heavily armored chargers, advanced at a stately pace across the plain, their squires and slaves trotting behind each rider. More than forty thousand men were in motion, and they raised thick clouds of dust that obscured the sun and forced the vultures circling overhead to rise higher.

Alvaro, reacting instinctively, drew his own sword for the first time when he saw the enemy host drawing nearer. Moslem lancers would not discharge their weapons until they came within one hundred and fifty paces of their targets, and he waited coolly, certain now that Henry of England's victory at Agincourt had been no capricious event. His own reasoning had been sound, and when he saw the Moslem knights reach for the lances in their quivers, he smiled as he called, "All bowmen, fire."

The Castilian archers in the front rank, who had been given no chance to demonstrate their skill, were determined to make a better showing than their comrades who had routed the *janissaries,* and sent a stream of arrows at the enemy. The crossbowmen in the second rank fired at the horses, at the squires and slaves and at the thick mass of knights who were rolling across the field behind the lords who led the attack. The longbowmen, proud of their skill, picked off men of importance, those who rode beneath banners or carried heavily ornamented shields. The Moslems were forced to halt.

But they were not cowards, and those who were not struck down hurled their lances at the Castilians. Here and there a man was wounded and cried out in pain, but the three lines of defenders held firmly, and the bowmen continued to lay down their seemingly endless barrage. In desperation Mohammed-ibn-Azar brought his pikemen forward; it was the only move he could make, but it was a mistake, for the Moslem foot soldiers had seen the carnage and had no heart for battle. They moved forward slowly, and the arrows of the Castilians routed them. They were the first to panic, but the infection spread rapidly through the ranks of the knights and their retainers, too, and soon the disorganized remnant of the Moors' army was in flight.

Alvaro signaled to Roderigo, and the eager Castilian cavalry spurred after the stumbling, retreating foe, cutting down the few who still resisted, splitting the ranks of the Moslem units that managed to retire in some semblance of formation and taking prisoners by the hundreds. The king of Granada and members of his personal staff used the flats of their scimitars in a vain attempt to force their troops forward again, but Roderigo and his vanguard reached the pomegranate grove without meeting any real opposition, and the Moslems were finally forced to raise a white flag of surrender.

The sun was directly overhead as the battle ended, and the buzzards circled lower.

King Juan was sulky because he had not been allowed to take part in the battle, but he recovered his good humor when a herald from enemy headquarters brought word that Mohammed-ibn-Azar requested permission to visit the Castilian camp, submit his formal surrender and sue for peace terms. Alvaro agreed, and arranged to receive the Moor at sundown; in the interval both armies would have time to bury their dead and remove their wounded from the field. Strong outposts were established to prevent sudden treachery, and while the wounded were carried off to the rear, King Juan's cooks prepared a banquet for the vanquished ruler of Granada.

The jubilant Castilians drank wine freely, and Alvaro permitted a relaxation of his standing orders, which limited the quantity of spirits consumed in the camp. He himself abstained as he wanted to be clear-headed when negotiating with Mohammed-ibn-Azar, but he watched indulgently as Cuevas, Huerrara, Roderigo and even Juan drank cup after cup as they sat in the shade of a silken canopy erected outside the king's tent. Alert and aware of all that was happening around him, he was the first to see a courier in dusty royal livery pushing his tired mount past the bivouacs of the celebrating troops.

The messenger brought a dispatch from Toledo, and although it was addressed to the king, Alvaro broke the seal and read it. He was so stunned that he could only stare at the sheet of parchment, and his companions, aware of his consternation, sobered and clustered around him. He waved them back to their seats around the table that had been erected under the canopy and, his voice thick, he looked at each in turn.

"Today," he said, "Castilians have won the greatest victory against the Moors of Granada in our history. Therefore the news from Toledo is ironic. The *Cortes* has held a meeting during our absence from the capital, and their lordships have seen fit to form a new government. Their minister-in-chief,

Diego de Sandoual, demands that I must be dismissed from all of my posts, and he requests the king to send me into retirement at the hunting lodge I own near Madrid."

The others were on their feet. "No," Juan shouted shrilly.

The tired courier removed his hat and stepped forward. "There's talk in the city that the members of the Church protested, but the nobles wouldn't listen to them. Eventually Cardinal Ruminez walked out of the meeting, and all of the other archbishops went with him."

Alvaro, recovering, was the calmest member of the group. "What measures have the rebels taken to enforce their demands?"

"They've called up their old retainers, Your Grace, and they're preparing for a battle if you insist on fighting them. Every grandee in Toledo is wearing full armor. The cardinals and bishops have been pleading with them for the past few days, begging them to behave reasonably, but they won't listen."

Juan became hysterical. "There are ways to force them to listen to reason. Our army is stronger than any they may have gathered. We'll beat them in battle. Then we'll hang every last one of the conspirators."

The courier was no more than twenty, but he looked like an old man. "The vote in the *Cortes* was unanimous after the representatives of the Church withdrew, Your Majesty."

"If necessary," Juan said wildly, "we'll hang every grandee in the country."

The Duke of Cuevas rose, peered over Alvaro's shoulder at the ultimatum and became pale when, as he had suspected, he saw the signature of his son-in-law beneath that of Sandoual.

"Castilians must not be permitted to fight each other," Alvaro declared firmly. "We'll weaken ourselves if we wage a civil war, and we'll be prey to the buzzards who have been lingering for years in Aragon and Navarre."

Roderigo gaped at him. "You don't intend to give in to these demands?"

"Certainly not." Alvaro became increasingly confident, smiled at his tall companion and after telling the courier to go off for a rest, resumed his seat. "Gentlemen," he said emphatically, "the authority of the king is still absolute. And if any of you are inclined to forget it, we won a major victory this morning."

General Huerrara, a grizzled professional soldier who, like Alvaro, wore no beard, grinned and drained his cup of wine.

"So far," Alvaro continued, his tone becoming scornful, "what have their lordships done? Some nobles who are jealous of me have prepared a foolish document and act like little boys who pretend they're very fierce warriors. This paper is filled with assurances that the grandees are loyal to the crown. They know their own fortunes depend on that loyalty. If they reject the authority of King Juan as their overlord, they'll be regarded as traitors in every civilized nation, and they can expect that sooner or later their estates will be confiscated and their titles revoked."

"That's what will happen to them," Juan cried. "We'll make an example of Sandoual, and—"

"No, Juan," Alvaro said, interrupting gently. "We can't afford to weaken ourselves by driving your grandees into the camp of your cousins. And at the same time we can't permit the fruits of the victory we've won today to slip out of our hands."

Cuevas was studying him. "Obviously, you have a plan of action."

"I'm beginning to form one." Alvaro spread the sheet of parchment on the table and read it again carefully. "Don Ernesto," he asked suddenly, "how soon can the army be prepared for a long march?"

"The men will be ready at any time you give the order, Your Grace," Huerrara replied quietly.

"Then prepare for an immediate withdrawal, and start moving through the mountain passes at dusk, when the Moors can't see your movements. Leave a token force of five hundred men here. I won't need more."

The king started to protest, but Alvaro silenced him with an impatient gesture.

"Juan, your crown and country depend on our ability to maneuver quickly and deftly. Listen to what I have in mind before you reject it."

The king subsided, looking hurt.

"Roderigo, I charge you with responsibility for His Majesty's safety. Show no belligerence toward anyone, but let no man raise a hand against him."

Roderigo sat back in his chair, smiled and poured himself another cup of wine.

"Domenico," Alvaro continued, "you'll take command of the army."

Cuevas frowned.

"You'll march as rapidly as possible to Toledo, and you'll send word ahead that you're coming with the king."

"I don't understand what you think we'll accomplish."

"Think of the situation. King Juan, to whom every grandee pledges loyalty, arrives at his capital at the head of an army of almost forty thousand men who have just beaten the Moors of Granada. The man the lords resent, the man who is responsible for their rebellion, isn't with you. They don't want civil war any more than you and I want it. They'll welcome the king—and his army—with cheers."

"What will you be doing?" Juan asked.

"I plan to spend the evening here, arranging Mohammed-ibn-Azar's surrender terms." Alvaro felt tired, but shook off his fatigue. "The five hundred men who will remain with me will take up sentry posts at strategic points, and campfires will be lighted throughout the whole present camp area. There is no reason the Moslems should even suspect that the bulk of our force has withdrawn. The risk I'll be taking will be very slight."

Roderigo, admiring his old friend's cunning, slapped his thigh and laughed.

"I'll entertain the Moor, I'll accept his formal surrender and I'll sign a treaty of peace with him. By tomorrow, when he discovers that the bulk of our force has withdrawn, it won't matter. He's a man of honor, and he'll keep his word."

"You're disposing of the Moor admirably," Cuevas said, still looking unhappy, "but you forget that your deadlier enemies are in Toledo. You've already beaten the Moslems."

"By performing a necessary function here, I'll defeat my enemies at home," Alvaro said, "yet it won't be necessary for me to use force against them, and no blood will be shed. Don't you see, Domenico, the grandees will think the king has accepted their terms when you arrive in Toledo without me? Our troops will take charge of the city, and the nobles won't try to interfere."

Cuevas stroked his beard. "Then you'll follow us, I presume?"

"I'll break camp here tomorrow, and will arrive at Toledo the day after you've been received and order has been restored." Alvaro's eyes became bleak. "It may be necessary for me to send a few of the leaders of this conspiracy to prison for a time."

"My son-in-law deserves any punishment you think just."

Alvaro stood and swept the ultimatum from the grandees to the ground. "If I take personal revenge against those who believe they hate me, all that we've gained in today's battle will be lost. I believe that a lenient policy will win me friends."

Juan was confused. "Why do you want their friendship?"

"You take me too literally. They'll always think of me as an outsider, they'll always condescend to me. But if I can win their support by treating them as misguided patriots rather

than as insurrectionists, your crown will be safe as long as
you live and your heirs will sit on the throne for generations
to come. We've broken the power of the Moors, and this
blunder of the grandees should clear the air internally.
Castile is going to be more secure, more prosperous than
ever before."

3

The capitulation of Granada was complete, and although
Mohammed-ibn-Azar spent the better part of his evening
with Alvaro trying to haggle over details, he finally signed a
treaty favorable to Castile in every respect. Granada promised
to respect her neighbor's borders, return all Castilians who
had been captured and sold into slavery, pay the entire cost
of the campaign in gold, and cede fifty ships including mer-
chantmen, war galleys and fishing craft to the victors.

The Moors had suffered the most severe defeat in the long
history of warfare between Castile and Granada, and Alvaro
was in high spirits as he set out for Toledo the following
afternoon. He had slept unexpectedly late, since the negotiations with Mohammed-ibn-Azar had proved more exhausting
than he had anticipated, but he had good cause to rejoice and
sent a messenger ahead with the news. Perhaps, if the courier
rode rapidly, he might overtake the main body of the army
on the road, and the peace terms imposed on Granada would
make it easier to subdue the dissatisfied grandees, who had
good reason to be grateful to him.

Alvaro rode at the head of the body of troops who had
remained with him, and the people of every town and village
cheered him on his journey north. The citizens of Porcuna
expressed their gratitude by giving him a white cape, edged
with silver, and the guild of merchants in Ciudad Real presented him with a magnificent silver helmet. Even the people
of the tiny community of Consuegra insisted that he accept

a pair of golden spurs which, by accident, matched the scimitar of gold that Mohammed-ibn-Azar had given him as a parting token of friendship.

Ceremonies and speeches, banquets and parades were time-consuming, but Alvaro felt he could not reject the spontaneous expressions of appreciation from people who had lived in dread of the Moors all of their lives and were finally secure in the knowledge that they would never again be terrorized by the infidels. But the festivities delayed Alvaro's progress and, two days behind schedule, he kept watch for a messenger who might bring him word from the capital. But he received no letter from Don Domenico, and although he assured himself repeatedly that the scheme to replace him had failed, he grew increasingly uneasy.

The archers who comprised the major part of his small force grew tired after a fifteen-mile march, and Alvaro became so impatient that one morning, when he had reached a point only thirty-six miles from Toledo, he decided to place the column under the command of a colonel while he hurried ahead with a small escort of mounted men. He started out at daybreak, and late in the afternoon saw the familiar outlines of the Alcazar in the distance. He was tempted to race into the city, but his mount was tired and he resisted the urge. At the same time, although he was passing within a few miles of his own estate, he saw no reason to pause there, for he felt certain that Teresa would be waiting for him in Toledo.

Clouds of dust were being kicked up on the road ahead, and a member of the escort spurred ahead to the crest of a small hill. "A cavalry column is riding toward us, Your Grace!" he called.

Alvaro smiled and relaxed, certain that the plots against him had failed. When he reached the peak and saw Don Domenico of Cuevas leading the troop he knew that a guard of honor had been sent from the Alcazar to lead him in a triumphal procession through the streets of the city. Pleased, he halted and waited for his old friend to approach.

Cuevas drew his sword, saluted and sheathed his blade again. Alvaro returned the gesture, and was surprised when he saw the solemn expression on Cuevas' face. Perhaps the late afternoon light was deceptive, but Don Domenico looked old and tired, as though he had not slept in several nights. Reaching the crest of the hill, he dismounted and beckoned to Alvaro.

"Join me," he said without preamble, and walked toward a pair of stunted pines that stood on the rocky slope some distance from the road.

Following him, Alvaro sensed disaster. "Don't you greet friends after a separation of some days?" he asked, trying to force a jovial smile.

Cuevas' face remained wooden. "I was sent to intercept you, Alvaro. I don't know how to tell you this. You'd better read the king's letter yourself." He took a folded sheet of parchment from his belt.

Alvaro glanced at the seal, saw that it was Juan's and broke it. The message was brief and succinct, signed by the king; but Alvaro had to read it several times before he could believe the formal communication. Juan II, the statement declared, had relieved Don Alvaro de Luna of all offices and titles except his rank of knight, which no man could take from him. His property was confiscated, but in view of his past services to the crown, he would be permitted to keep one of three residences, his small lodge near Madrid, a tiny estate in Leon or a house outside Badajos, near the Portuguese border.

He stared at Cuevas. "Did my messenger arrive with the copy of the peace treaty that Mohammed-ibn-Azar signed?"

"He did, and because of your victory, the new council of state has graciously agreed not to place you under arrest. But Sandoual, the minister-in-chief, ordered me to inform you that his generosity is limited." Don Domenico swallowed painfully. "My valiant son-in-law is waiting outside the gates for you with a large body of men-at-arms. If you try to ride into Toledo, they'll take you prisoner and throw you into a dungeon."

"What happened?" Alvaro demanded, gripping his friend's arm.

Cuevas shrugged dispiritedly. "Juan has been near you for years, and you've been able to influence him. Now others have interceded, and you weren't there to protect yourself. The grandees argued that Castile would disintegrate if you weren't dismissed. I wasn't there, but I'm told they painted a frightful picture. Aragon, Navarre and Portugal would hack off sections of the country, and even the Moors of Granada would attack again. Sandoual is a convincing speaker, and so is Adelantado, though I wouldn't have believed it. At any rate, Juan listened to them."

Aware that the mounted men in the road were watching them, Alvaro held himself erect and tried to hide his feeling of horror. "Surely the army is loyal?"

"We gave our enemies too little credit. An order was issued under Juan's signature, instructing the troops to obey new leaders. The men grumbled, but did as they were told. You were the only person on earth who could have counter-manded the order, and you weren't in Toledo." Cuevas passed a hand across his eyes. "Now it's too late."

"If my army has been disbanded, I'll unite it again!"

"Sandoual has been too clever. By the way, he's calling himself Grand Master of Santiago again."

"I don't care about titles! What's happened to my army?"

"Regiments have been disbanded, and men have been assigned, two or three to a company, to the household troops of various grandees." Don Domenico gestured in the direction of the squadron that had accompanied him. "There's one of our cavalrymen in that unit, I believe. But only one. The rest are my son-in-law's retainers, and they've been ordered to escort me to my own estate, where they'll keep me under guard. I assume that our one veteran of the Granada campaign isn't too happy, but what can he do against so many?"

Alvaro's helmet felt oppressively heavy.

"Huerrara has been sent off to Leon, and Roderigo has been banished to his estate after escorting Doña Teresa to your castle. She's waiting for you there. All of the men whom you appointed to office have either sworn loyalty to the new regime or been dismissed."

"What does my brother say?" A searing headache blinded Alvaro.

"A strong guard commanded by young Lerma has been stationed around the cardinal's house, allegedly for his protection. Neither he nor any other member of the Church dares to speak out in your favor. If Pope Benedict were still alive, not even Sandoual would act so brashly. But he's taking advantage of the attempts of the Church to heal the wounds caused by the schism. Pope Eugenius has ordered the cardinals and bishops to cooperate with governments in every country, and as Sandoual is now minister-in-chief, not even Cardinal Ruminez will be able to raise his voice in a sermon condemning the plotters."

Alvaro remained silent for a long moment. "For the moment, it would seem, we're helpless."

"No, my friend. You've survived schemes of all sorts, but this time you've lost. Go to one of your lodges, and when we're permitted to travel again, we'll visit each other and talk about the old days." Don Domenico looked and sounded like a broken man.

"I refuse to give up without a fight!"

"Quietly, please." Cuevas was alarmed. "Adelantado's personal steward is second-in-command of that squadron, and he'll use any excuse to arrest both of us. My son-in-law would like nothing better than to seize my property and have himself made a duke."

Alvaro noted out of the corner of his eye that an officer at the side of the road was watching them closely, straining to hear the conversation.

"I have few satisfactions in store," Cuevas continued with a dry laugh, "but there's one prospect I relish. I'm going to live for many years and deprive my daughter's husband of my estates."

"You surrender too easily."

"I've lived through the events of the past two days in Toledo, Alvaro."

"I'm sorry. I was casting no reflection on your personal integrity." Alvaro's frenzy mounted. "Don't Sandoual and all the rest realize they're inviting an attack from Alfonso? If I know Enrique and Pedro, they're already hard at work, drawing up invasion schedules."

"Our new minister-in-chief is so intoxicated with the power he's enjoying that he can think of nothing except the present." Cuevas saw that the men of the squadron were becoming restless. "You're under instructions to ride on alone from here. The men who've come with you are to attach themselves to my escort. And this evening a delegation will call on you to learn which place of exile you prefer."

Alvaro gripped the handle of the scimitar that Mohammed-ibn-Azar had given him, and a familiar, determined look came into his eyes.

"One final word, my friend. The grandees know that Juan will always listen to you, so they've taken extraordinary measures to prevent you from seeing him. If you try, they'll kill you. Adelantado actually boasted to me that they hope you'll do something rash. He said it would be far more convenient for Castile if Alvaro de Luna were dead."

"We'll see each other again, under happier circumstances,"

Alvaro replied uncompromisingly and, removing his gauntlet, held out his hand.

Tears appeared in Don Domenico's eyes, but he brushed them away angrily and walked, stiff-backed, to his mount.

Alvaro, motionless, watched the commander of the squadron order his ten veterans to join the unit. His men turned to him for confirmation, and knowing they would be killed or wounded by a larger force if they resisted, he nodded. They were assigned places in the line, Don Domenico was surrounded and the squadron cantered off. Alvaro stared at the clouds of dust kicked up by the horses, too angry to feel dismayed. Then, aware of approaching nightfall, he walked slowly to his horse, mounted and started off toward his castle.

The first stars had appeared and the moon was rising when he rode across the drawbridge. No guards were standing sentry duty at the gate, which surprised him, and he became annoyed when he found the inner courtyard deserted, too. A few lights were burning in windows on the upper floors of the castle, but it was obvious to Alvaro that most of his servants had gone. He made no attempt to rouse a groom or footman, and instead led his tired horse to the stable at the rear end of the courtyard. There another unpleasant shock awaited him. Teresa's mare was in her stall, a saddled stallion that looked vaguely familiar was drinking water from a trough, and a grey gelding stood sleepily in an enclosure on the far side of the barn. But more than fifty stalls were vacant.

Too angry to unsaddle his own mount, Alvaro took a candle from a bin and hurried across the courtyard. His enemies, he thought bitterly, had lost no time confiscating his property, but they were badly mistaken if they thought he would submit meekly to theft and degradation. The common people had demonstrated their affection for him, and if necessary he would ride from one end of the country to the other, arouse popular support and force the grandees to submit to his authority.

The great hall of the castle was deserted, but Alvaro noted absently that a small fire was burning in the hearth and that scraps of meat and bread, several platters and a decanter of wine had been left on a table of polished oak. Apparently someone had eaten a meal in the hall only a short time previously, but he was in no mood to worry about minor matters and climbed the stairs to the private apartments.

His own office and bedchamber were dark, but he saw lights burning in Teresa's suite at the far end of the main corridor, and he started toward the apartment. His footsteps sounded loudly on the tile floor, a door on the left side of the corridor was thrown open and Beatriz de Pimente peered out. She was dressed in a low-cut velvet gown, but was wearing a feathered hat, too, and it was evident that she was planning to travel somewhere. Behind her several leather boxes were piled high, making it unnecessary for Alvaro to question her. She, like the other members of the household, was leaving.

Beatriz stared at him for an instant, then laughed softly, maliciously, and withdrew into her room again.

Her viciousness nettled Alvaro, but he refused to let himself think about the hatred of a young woman whom he had never harmed. Teresa was his first concern now, and he tried to plan for her safety. She would have to leave with him at once, before the delegation of grandees arrived, and he would find a refuge for her in a convent. She would protest, he feared, but there was no alternative, as she could not accompany him on his travels through Castile. He steeled himself for an argument as he drew near the entrance to the suite, and hoped that she understood the gravity of the crisis. There would be no time to wheedle, coax and explain.

The door to the sitting room of the suite was ajar, and when Alvaro saw that the chamber was empty, he hurried to the adjoining bedroom, raised the latch and stepped across the threshold.

Teresa, wearing a clinging silk gown, stood in the center of the room, returning the fervent embrace of Roderigo de Pinar.

The guilty couple sprang apart, and Alvaro, too startled to think, reached instinctively for the scimitar that was a symbol of his greatest victory.

Roderigo, his face flushed and his eyes reflecting deep shame, came forward slowly, his hands at his sides. "Do what you will," he muttered.

Alvaro realized that he had been holding his breath and, exhaling slowly, slid the curved sword back into his belt. "I can't kill a man who has been my friend and has saved my life."

Roderigo tried to speak, but choked.

"Get out," Alvaro said.

The man who had been his friend since boyhood stumbled as he made his way out of the suite, his head low.

Husband and wife were alone, staring at each other, and Alvaro saw that Teresa was drunk. She weaved unsteadily on her high-heeled slippers, her hair was disarrayed and her eyes were glazed, but she was aware of what had happened. Turning suddenly to a chest of drawers, she took a dagger from the top drawer. "If you touch me," she said thickly, "I'll use this."

Alvaro stared at her, disgusted.

"I hate you," Teresa said. "Once, long ago, I thought you were clever, so wise and strong that I could reach heights of glory through you. But I've been bored. And now you've fallen into the dust again."

Rousing himself, Alvaro turned and started to walk out of the room.

The dagger buried itself in the wall several feet to his left, but he paid no attention to the unsuccessful attac   nd, holding himself erect, quickened his pace so that he   uld not hear Teresa's screams and curses.

Scarcely aware of what he was doing, he made his way toward the central staircase, but halted when he saw Beatriz de Pimente blocking the corridor.

"If you had paid attention to me," she said in a low, intense voice, "if you had returned the affection I offered you, I would have told you the truth long ago. They've been lovers for years, and the whole country has been laughing at you. Do you know why your enemies have succeeded? Because your wife has made it impossible for anyone to respect you. Yes, you've allowed her to make you a cuckold, and you've let her spend huge fortunes as though she were a great queen."

Alvaro moved forward again, wearily, but Beatriz did not stand aside.

"If you'd taken me as your mistress," she continued, "you'd still be Constable and Grand Master of Santiago. Together we could have ruled Castile, perhaps all of Iberia. But you've earned your disgrace. You're no better now than a miserable beggar!"

He could tolerate no more and, shoving her aside, ran down the dark stairs. Beatriz' mocking laugh followed him, and in the distance he could hear Teresa, who was still shouting drunkenly.

Numb, he hurried out into the courtyard, crossed it and opened the stable door. Roderigo's stallion was gone, and Alvaro started toward his own mount. He knew his horse was tired and that he should saddle the gelding instead, but he could not remain at the castle one instant longer than was necessary. Hurrying, he led his war horse into the open and, holding the reins in fingers that felt anaesthetized, walked across the drawbridge.

So much had happened in such a short time that he could not grasp its enormity, but the sound of approaching hoofbeats awakened him to a fresh danger. Hastily he led his stallion into a patch of woods on a hillside and followed a narrow path that led to the summit.

There he tied the reins to the branch of a stunted pine, then shuddered involuntarily as he watched a large party of grandees riding toward his castle. The nobles, who were joking in loud voices, had been drinking, and it was obvious that they were planning mischief. All were heavily armed, and a number carried burning torches, as did the squires who followed them. Had Alvaro remained at the castle, it was possible, even probable, that they would have murdered him.

He knew he would be wise to leave the area at once, but he was too exhausted to start out on a fresh journey and, screened by the trees at the crest of the hill, he stared in fascination and dread at the proud establishment that had been his home. Lights appeared everywhere as the grandees ran through the building, and Alvaro was sufficiently close to hear their hoarse shouts of triumph. Leaning against a tree, he closed his eyes for a moment and held a trembling hand over them. Members of the nobility, proud lords whose ancestors had made Castile great, were looting his home, stealing the tapestries, the paintings and the tiny, graceful marble statuettes that had been his special pride.

When he forced himself to raise his head again, he saw that lights were burning very brightly in the castle, and suddenly he realized that the grandees were setting fire to things they didn't want, drapes of heavy silk and furniture too heavy to carry away. He had seen enough and reached for the reins, but paused when several figures appeared on the battlements; several of the men were carrying torches, so that every detail of the scene was clear to him, and he felt ill when he saw Teresa, still clad in her flimsy silk gown, weaving and lurching as she tried to escape from the nobles who were pursuing her.

There was a brief scuffle as two of the men caught her, but she broke away again, and Alvaro, hearing her voice faintly, was uncertain whether she was laughing or crying. She climbed up onto the wall overlooking the moat, the men still close behind her, but they halted when she screamed in terror. One of the torches had set her gown on fire. For a brief instant Teresa stood, enveloped in flames; then she either fell or plunged to her death in the waters of the moat below.

A long time seemed to pass before the grandees rode out across the drawbridge again. A drunken baron was waving a tapestry that had been imported from France at great expense, a young knight was clutching a glazed Venetian vase and every member of the party apparently had acquired some memento of his night's sport.

Bringing up the rear was Don Domenico's son-in-law, Pero Maurique, Adelantado of Leon, and he had won the greatest prize. Seated in front of him on his saddle, her arms curled lovingly around his neck, was Beatriz de Pimente, who was laughing flirtatiously at some comment he had made. At last she had found the man who, she believed, would give her wealth and position, and she neither regretted the death of the woman she had served nor, it was evident, had she learned a lesson from the tragedy.

Alvaro remained at the top of the hill until the flares disappeared in the distance on the road to Toledo and the sound of hoofbeats faded. Then, moving slowly, he walked down the slope and made his way back to the castle, where fires were still burning in at least four or five rooms. But he paid no attention to the damage. He headed straight for the spot where he had seen Teresa fall and looked down into the moat.

The flames created a glare on the surface, but the water was too muddy for him to see beneath the sheen, and he finally concluded that Teresa's body, tangled in the charred shreds of her gown, was resting at the bottom of the rock-lined moat. Unmindful of the destruction and the flames that continued to lick at what remained of his possessions, he sank to his knees and bowed his head.

"May Almighty God forgive your trespasses and mine," he whispered, "and may He grant you peace."

4. The Man

1

The cool tranquility of the abbot's office at the Sanctuary of Santo Domingo had not changed through the years, and there were moments, as Alvaro explained all that had happened in recent days, when he felt like a boy again. But the sensation was illusory, and he knew it. He had loved and suffered betrayal, he had held power and lost it, he had worked to achieve a goal that waves of unreasoning violence had destroyed. Friendship and honor, loyalty and even human decency were mere words that had lost their meaning, and when he finished his recital he stared at the smooth stone wall opposite his chair.

Father Sebastian, who had replaced the late Father Ramiro as head of the monastery, had listened quietly, and his old man's voice was clipped as he said, "The king whose government you reorganized and saved from the Moors was fickle to you. The wife you trusted gave herself to the man who was your friend, and you've come here because all is lost. You want to become a novice here, no doubt."

"Yes, Father." Alvaro was not surprised to discover that the priest could still read his mind so easily.

"Do you think Holy Orders are a refuge when a man can turn nowhere else?" Father Sebastian stood abruptly and tugged at his dark-red sash. "Do you believe God to be less demanding than man, or His work less important than the tasks at which you've failed?"

Startled, Alvaro was jolted out of his lethargy.

The old man smiled, and a note of compassion crept into his voice. "Your life has not ended at thirty-five, my son."

"You came here when the world turned against you."

"I came here when my conscience insisted that I fight the Lord's battles. I didn't creep away from my enemies like a beaten, frightened mongrel."

Alvaro leaped to his feet, his fists clenched.

Father Sebastian chuckled and patted his shoulder. "You have more spirit than you've imagined. Sit down, de Luna."

Alvaro obeyed reluctantly.

"You're bruised, and you need time to rest." The priest returned to his own seat and folded his wrinkled hands in his lap. "Then, when the time is ripe, you'll return to the world's battles."

"Never!"

"Have you forgotten that logic is the most powerful of all weapons?"

"It's because of what my mind tells me that I can't go on with the struggle, Father. Before I—found Teresa and Roderigo together, I planned to ride through Castile, rousing the people. The shepherds and townsmen and farmers know what I've accomplished, and I hoped they'd join me in a campaign to force the grandees to behave reasonably. But after seeing the irresponsible violence of the lords at my castle the other night, I've realized I was wrong. If I persuade the people to follow me, there will be a civil war, and the fault will be mine when Alfonso of Aragon and his brothers occupy the country."

The priest studied him in silence for what felt like a long time. "You've learned many lessons, de Luna, but there are some qualities you haven't yet acquired. Do you consider yourself blameless in all that has happened of late?"

"My victory against the Moors speaks for itself, Father!"

The old man ignored the interruption. "Your wife and

your friend betrayed you. Have you no guilt in their associa-
tion, either?"

"How was I to blame?"

Father Sebastian shrugged. "I don't judge you, my son, any
more than I would try to condemn the woman who lost her
life because of her folly. Nor will I raise my voice against
Roderigo. The Lord judges and punishes. We must strive to
hear His voice and obey His will." He leaned forward across
his desk, and his manner became brusque. "Power and wealth
were too potent for Doña Teresa. Did you take the cask of
brandy away from her at any time?"

"No, Father, I—"

"You were her husband, yet you permitted her to drink as
much glory as she pleased, and you were surprised when she
became intoxicated. You spent all of your days and nights ad-
ministering the affairs of Castile. Did it cross your mind at
any time that she might be lonely?"

"She had friends, ladies-in-waiting—"

"—but no husband. So she turned to Roderigo, who has
always shown a weakness for attractive women. And don't
forget that he's lived most of his life in your shadow."

Alvaro's lethargy disappeared, and he struck the desk with
the palm of his hand. "I heaped honors on him."

"You honored him. Did you give him opportunities to win
fame independently of you? I think not."

"Are you trying to tell me that I'm to blame for the affair
that my wife and de Pinar enjoyed?"

"Certainly not." The priest smiled and shook his head.
"I'm merely trying to persuade you to see that you must share
the burden of guilt, just as you must accept a measure of
blame for the revolt of the grandees against your rule."

Alvaro's anger faded, and he looked at his mentor thoughtfully. "I must admit that I accepted too many titles, too much
wealth, too many honors. I always claimed they were important to Teresa, but not to me, and that I cared about nothing

except the welfare of Castile. That isn't true." Spreading his hands out before him, he stared at them for a moment. "This emerald ring was a gift from King Juan. I've always said that jewels mean nothing to me, yet I've worn this gem for years." Twisting it off his finger, he dropped it onto the table. "Mohammed-ibn-Azar gave me this ruby after we signed our treaty." He removed it and placed it beside the emerald. "Accept both of them on behalf of the Sanctuary, Father, and take my golden scimitar, too."

Father Sebastian examined the rings, then thrust them into Alvaro's hand. "Don't tempt me, de Luna. Santo Domingo always needs money, but you'll want funds in the months ahead. Sell these so that you'll have enough money to buy food, but keep the scimitar. You'll use it, just as you'll have further use for Don Enrique's sword."

Alvaro tried to protest.

"I was going to suggest it might be to your profit to read and ponder the teachings of Ecclesiastes on the subject of vanity, but it appears that won't be necessary. However, you haven't yet curbed your impulsiveness."

"What makes you so certain that I'm going to fight again, Father?"

"You love Castile, de Luna, and when she calls to you for help, will you close your ears to her plea?"

Alvaro spent several weeks at the Sanctuary, recovering his health, and when he felt strong enough, he moved to his lodge on the outskirts of Madrid. He sold the emerald ring for cash, and through the long months of the autumn and winter, no one came near his remote house except the farmers who sold him food, which he cooked himself. He lived an austere life, read books that he borrowed from the Sanctuary and spent several hours exercising each day, riding out across the plateau on his stallion in the mornings and chopping firewood each afternoon. Every Wednesday he ate dinner at

Santo Domingo as Father Sebastian's guest, and he attended Mass on Sunday mornings at the Sanctuary chapel, but he discussed political affairs with no one, and the priests, respecting his self-imposed silence, refrained from mentioning matters of state to him.

However, no man who had taken such an active role in governing Castile could remove himself completely from the world, and in February, 1432, Francisco Cardinal Ruminez paid a surprise visit to his brother. They spent their first evening together amicably, confining themselves to the amenities, and Francisco praised Alvaro's cooking, which helped to bridge several embarrassing moments. The following morning, however, as they sat together at breakfast before a blazing fire in the tiny dining room of the lodge, the cardinal, who had been toasting a chunk of bread on a long iron rod, spoke suddenly, still facing the flames.

"I've kept in touch with you through Father Sebastian, as you've no doubt guessed."

"He said nothing to me, but I'm not surprised." Alvaro had grilled a fish and, splitting it deftly with his knife, placed the larger half on his brother's platter.

"He told me in some detail about the monastic life you've been leading. He's assured me repeatedly that you're enjoying good health, but he didn't prepare me for the change in your appearance. I was surprised to see that your hair is completely grey."

"I'm not a boy, you know." Alvaro's laugh was metallic.

"You're still bitter." The cardinal hesitated for an instant. "I'm not your confessor, Alvaro, but the bonds that tie us together can never be broken, so I'll speak my mind. You'll know only unhappiness until you forgive Teresa."

"Isn't it enough that I feel pity for her?" Alvaro speared a piece of grilled fish.

Francisco watched him, saying nothing.

"I saw her die. She paid for her transgressions."

"Perhaps," the cardinal said gently, "you've forgiven her without realizing it."

Alvaro shrugged. "I prefer not to talk about her."

"Naturally." The cardinal was tense behind a calm façade. "What of Roderigo de Pinar? Have you found it possible to forgive him, too?"

"I don't think about him, and I believe it unlikely that I'll ever see him again. I'm not certain what I might do if our paths should cross."

Francisco nodded and, seemingly satisfied, changed the subject. "You'll be pleased to hear that our house in the *Mozarab* district wasn't confiscated when your other property was taken from you. I wrote to the king, pointing out that you and I had owned the house jointly long before you had been created a knight and a lord."

"So you saved it. I'm grateful to you, Francisco."

"You can thank the king, not me. He showed unusual spirit when he stood up to Sandoual, I'm told, and members of the royal household guard, veterans of your campaign against Granada, I believe, stand outside the house at all times." The cardinal tasted his fish, then added carefully, "Juan paid me a visit only last week. His ministers keep close watch on all his movements, but there's no legitimate way they can prevent him from worshipping at the cathedral in his capital, nor can they prevent him from conferring privately with the priest who holds the Pope's seal as primate of Castile."

Alvaro, not bothering to toast his bread, broke off a piece from the loaf and ate it. "With all your wisdom, Francisco, you're naïve," he said, genuinely amused. "I'm sure the government has been in a ferment ever since you and the king met. Now the council's spies will report that you've paid me a visit, and the whole *Cortes* will be certain a major plot is being hatched to restore me to power."

The cardinal was not offended by his brother's patronizing

tone. "Juan misses you," he said quietly. "He told me repeatedly that you're the only real friend he's ever had."

"I'll be frank and admit I've missed him, too. He's a sensitive, honorable young man, and Castile is paying a high price for his mother's negligence. He was never trained for his position as king, and he needs help. However, I'm unable to give it to him." Alvaro poured himself a mug of mead.

"He was disturbed because of a long letter he received from his sister."

Alvaro stiffened. "When the Infanta married a traitor, she gave up her right to be considered a Castilian."

The cardinal's manner changed, and he looked straight at his brother. "Catalina has paid heavily for her mistakes in judgment, as have others."

Accepting the rebuke with unexpected meekness, Alvaro smiled wryly. "I deserved that, Francisco. I'm sorry."

"Her Highness is worried because of the preparations for an invasion that are being made in both Aragon and Navarre. Enrique tells her very little, but she writes to her brother that from what she has seen herself, Castile will be attacked in another month or two."

"There will be an invasion, but it won't come until June, at the earliest." The technicalities of the problem absorbed Alvaro immediately. "Juan of Navarre and Pedro would attack sooner, and Enrique has no military sense, either. But King Alfonso is a real strategist, and he won't move until the spring planting season has ended, the fruit trees produce their first yield and the mountain snows melt. He wouldn't be foolish enough to lead his army across swollen rivers."

Francisco neither knew nor cared about such details. "The king felt compelled to show Catalina's letter to his council, and Sandoual is worried."

"He has cause for concern." Alvaro's laugh was harsh.

The cardinal poured himself a small quantity of mead. "Our army has dwindled. Most of the grandees' retainers have insisted on returning to their homes, and recruiting parties that have been scouring the country have been unable to persuade men to enlist."

Alvaro ate the last scraps of fish on his platter. "When we were young, Francisco, and I looked up to the nobility, it wouldn't have occurred to me that most grandees are short-sighted, arrogant and stupidly ignorant. The shepherds who sell me meat and the peasants from whom I buy my vegetables and fruits tell me that the old taxes have been imposed on the poor again. So why should the people fight? Free men are eager to defend their liberties, but serfs know that one master is like another."

"The council is so alarmed that some of your friends are being called out of retirement, but the government isn't having too much success. General Huerrara sent his excuses, and Don Domenico refused to admit the council's delegation to his castle. I suppose you know his daughter has returned to Cuevas."

"I know nothing of the world's affairs, but I'm not surprised. Maria de Cuevas is a young woman of considerable stature, and I think she would find it repugnant to share her husband with Beatriz de Pimente."

It was the cardinal's turn to laugh. "For someone who claims to be ignorant of what goes on beyond the confines of your little estate, you show astonishing knowledge."

"The members of our family understand human nature. It's a trait we've inherited." Alvaro's eyes hardened. "Why have you come here, Francisco?"

"To tell you that your country is in danger, and to prepare you for the day when you'll be asked to contribute your services to Castile again."

Alvaro stood and jabbed at the logs burning in the hearth until the flames leaped high again. "The council won't come to me until the grandees are desperate," he said, and added softly, "and I won't listen to them until they've abandoned all other hope. You see, Francisco, I'll go back only on my own terms."

Officers of the cavalry escort paced up and down restlessly outside the little lodge, their horses nibbled the delicate shoots of early spring grass, and sentries were posted to prevent the pikemen from stealing the peaches and plums ripening on the trees in the small grove behind the house. The precautions were unnecessary, however, for no Castilian soldier would think of robbing Don Alvaro de Luna, and the men, resting after their long march, stood occasionally and stared at the lodge, hoping to catch a glimpse of the leader who had spent so many months in exile.

In the small, simply furnished drawing room of the house, King Juan bit his lower lip, drummed on the arm of his chair and shifted his weight constantly in a vain attempt to make himself comfortable. The minister-in-chief of the royal government, Diego Gomes de Sandoual, Count of Castro Xeris, tried to maintain greater dignity, but betrayed his anxiety by studying the relaxed face of the suntanned man who slowly read a long letter.

"My brother," Alvaro said at last, folding the parchment, "has a persuasive pen."

"His Eminence is a Castilian, Don Alvaro, and so are you." Sandoual controlled an impulse to tap his foot on the hardwood floor. "Aragon is mobilizing an army of more than seventy thousand men, twenty thousand more are being trained in Navarre, and our own people say they'll go to prison rather than bear arms for the *Cortes*."

"We need you, Alvaro," the king said desperately. "I need you. I should have more pride than to tell you this, but the Portuguese ambassador has postponed my marriage to Princess Isabella. It was a very unpleasant interview. He made it plain that Lisbon thinks I'm going to be deposed."

"We'll be attacked in a month, perhaps even sooner," the

minister-in-chief declared, "and you're the only man who can save us. I freely admit I did you an injustice, I'm willing to confess my errors publicly and I'll voluntarily submit to any punishment you believe I deserve."

Alvaro stood abruptly and the others rose, too. He looked around the room slowly, picked up the leather-bound, illuminated copy of Thomas Aquinas' *Summa Contra Gentiles* that he had borrowed the preceding week from Father Sebastian, and sighed. "It's been very peaceful here," he said, leafing through the volume, and added gently, "St. Thomas is right, you know. Reason and faith seem to differ, but they don't. They spring from the same source—God; therefore they can't be contradictory."

Sandoual, who saw no connection with the urgent problem that had brought him to Madrid, was confused, but Juan enjoyed a deeper understanding of his old friend, and smiled. "You'll help me, then?"

"If I hope to be true to the God in whom I believe, I must act according to the principles that guide my life." Alvaro planted his feet apart and looked up at the tense men. "Naturally, I must impose certain conditions."

"All of them are granted," the king said eagerly. "All of your titles and property will be restored—"

"I have no need and no desire for vast holdings of land. Personal wealth means nothing to me and rank is meaningless. Don Diego, would you be willing to serve with me and obey my orders?"

Sandoual was astonished. "You'd allow me to keep my freedom, Don Alvaro?"

"You're an experienced general, and Castile needs men who understand war." Alvaro held out his hand.

The count grasped it fervently.

"Will the members of the *Cortes* follow me?"

"Anywhere. They'll lose everything to the lords of Aragon

and Navarre if they oppose you, and they know they've been wrong." Sandoual's voice was hoarse.

Alvaro turned to the king. "Juan, if I'm to act effectively, there are two posts I must have, but only two. The council must be dissolved, and you'll have to issue a decree reinstating me as constable. I intend to remove the tax that has been imposed on the people, but that won't be enough to restore confidence. If I'm to raise an army in the course of a few days, I need the enthusiastic support of every man in the country capable of bearing arms. I'm afraid you'll have to make me head of the Order of Santiago again." Turning to the count, he smiled. "If the campaign is successful, I'll gladly return the honor to you. All I want is complete authority in the field for the duration of this war."

Sandoual, too moved to speak, removed his jewelled sash and dropped it over Alvaro's head.

"I'll send a courier to General Huerrara in Leon immediately, asking him to take command of the cavalry," Alvaro said, concentrating so hard on practical matters that he could not savor his triumph. "And I'll want every grandee who can raise a force of horsemen to report to Huerrara in the east. The enemy may attack prematurely when it becomes known that I've resumed command, and I must buy time."

Juan was confused, but the count understood. "Every extra day you can gain will make us that much stronger. You'll use the cavalry to harass the enemy and slow their march."

Alvaro nodded. "We may be forced to yield territory, but we'll recover it. And we can delay a meeting between the forces of Aragon and Navarre, too. That will give us a few additional weeks. Don Diego, there's no officer in Castile who understands the older type of warfare more thoroughly than you—I'll be obliged if you'll take command of the armored knights and the pikemen."

"You won't regret your decision, Constable. I swear to

you that the troops under my command will fight until the last man is killed."

"I hope it won't be necessary for you to fight at all," Alvaro replied briskly. "If I can, I'm going to reassemble the army that fought the Moors and place it under the command of Don Domenico of Cuevas. My archers will convince Alfonso that Naples and Sicily are safer hunting-grounds than Castile."

Juan laughed. "It appears that you've given a great deal of thought to this enterprise, Alvaro. Our visit today comes as no surprise to you."

"When a man lives as I have, he has many opportunities for reflection." Alvaro grinned at the king, then his mouth became thin. "When is my appointment as constable effective?"

"You hold office at this moment," Juan replied affectionately.

Alvaro stiffened. "One of my first official acts will be unpleasant. I beg to inform Your Majesty," he continued formally, "that although it will be my general policy to conciliate the members of the *Cortes,* I refuse to condone crime or permit acts of vandalism to be performed in Your Majesty's realm. The nobles who attacked and looted the castle that was my property outside Toledo will be punished immediately. Young Lerma and the others who assaulted the place will be arrested and held in prison until such time as Your Majesty can try them and judge their cases yourself. I charge them with the murder of my wife, the theft of my valuables and the destruction of my home."

Neither Juan nor Sandoual was surprised.

"Adelantado of Leon is neither more nor less guilty than the others, but he caused his father-in-law to suffer unjustly. I order that he be given into the custody of Don Domenico of Cuevas, who will judge and punish him as he sees fit."

Both of the visitors knew that, for all practical purposes, Alvaro had condemned Adelantado to death.

"The woman who encouraged him and whose morals have set a deplorable example in recent months will be punished, too. Beatriz de Pimente's head will be shaved, she will be whipped through the streets of Toledo and then sent to a nunnery, where she will be confined for the rest of her life."

Sandoual wiped a film of perspiration from his upper lip.

There was an uncomfortable silence, until Juan finally asked the question that no man except the king would have dared to express aloud. "What do you intend to do to Roderigo de Pinar?"

Alvaro became pale beneath his tan, and his eyes were cold. "Don Roderigo," he said, his voice desolate, "is responsible to God for his sins. He violated my personal trust, but he committed no act of treason against the state. Therefore I don't intend to bring charges against him." Dismissing the subject with a curt wave, he turned to Sandoual. "Don Diego, it will take several days to recall the members of my secretariat. In the meantime there are many decrees and orders to dictate—I'll be grateful if you'll permit me to utilize the services of your aides, who have nothing better to do at this moment than trample my flower beds."

When the officers hurried into the house a few moments later, he stood at a small table, scribbling reminders to himself on a scrap of parchment. The nobles saluted, and he acknowledged their presence with an absent nod. "Sit down, gentlemen," he said, his pen continuing to scratch busily, "and be prepared to work until dawn tomorrow, perhaps longer."

No one thought it incongruous that the short, balding man in an old woollen shirt, black breeches and shabby boots should be wearing the diamond emblem and sash of Santiago, or that King Juan looked happier, more relieved than he had in months. An invisible cloak of authority seemed to have settled on Alvaro's shoulders, and he took command quietly, efficiently. For the second time in his life he had become master of Castile, but he felt no elation. He had been given supreme power at the most critical period in his nation's history, and if his efforts to save her failed, the country would become a province of Aragon.

Bonfires were lighted in every town and city when royal heralds read a proclamation stating that Don Alvaro de Luna had been reappointed constable and that he had cancelled the tax obligations of all commoners. People throughout Castile celebrated at impromptu fiestas, and while the lutes still played and the castanets clicked, young men collected their bows and arrows, their pikes and their armor and set out for the little plateau town of Trillo, on the Tagus River northwest of Madrid, where water was plentiful and forests provided ample firewood and tentpoles. Alvaro established his headquarters in a cramped, eight-room house owned by the local baron, and so many secretaries, officers and aides filled the place that the constable, who needed privacy when he wanted to confer with his immediate subordinates, worked, slept and ate in a tiny chamber on the second floor, above the courtyard. The parish priest shared his house with King Juan, who enjoyed the luxury of a small sitting room as well as a bedchamber, but the growing army moved into tents on the high tableland, and the area it occupied increased rapidly, sometimes doubling in a single day.

Don Ernesto Huerrara, responding instantly to Alvaro's summons, came to Trillo and took command of the cavalry. As more horsemen volunteered to serve under him than he could use profitably, he accepted only veterans of the Granada campaign and others who proved to his satisfaction that they could ride rapidly, wield swords effectively and submit to discipline. Accompanied by a force of eight thousand, he set out for the border of Aragon in two weeks, and although there were rumors that King Alfonso planned to cross into Castile at any time, Huerrara's prompt arrival at the frontier caused the enemy to change his plans.

Don Domenico of Cuevas arrived at Trillo, solemn and purposeful, and although all Castile knew he had hanged his son-in-law, no one mentioned the name of Adelantado to him. There was a staggering amount of work to be done, and he plunged into the task of organizing the Granada veterans into regiments as they arrived at the bivouac.

Don Diego de Sandoual, anxious to prove that the constable's faith in him was justified, faced even more difficult problems as he dealt with grandees who were jealous of each other, who remembered details of ancient family feuds and quarreled violently when a rival was favored. Lords who were competent were given the command of companies of knights, but those whose talents failed to match their ornate shields and glittering armor were placed in units that would act as reserves. Older grandees, particularly men who were experienced in supervising the farms, orchards and grazing ranges they owned, were given the duty of providing the army with the food it needed. Sandoual proved himself capable of handling his temperamental subordinates, and after three weeks of training, only one knight had been placed under arrest for insubordination, a remarkable record.

King Juan of Navarre took advantage of the Castilian preoccupation to march south, his brother Pedro leading his cavalry vanguard, and after insolently cutting across a corner of Castile, the army of approximately twenty-two thousand disappeared across the border of Aragon. Some of the Castilian generals were bitterly disappointed, as they had hoped to dispose of the troops from Navarre separately, but Alvaro refused to become discouraged. Never had an army been formed so quickly or efficiently, he said, and he was satisfied with the progress that his commanders were making. It was preferable, he told them, to concentrate on the major campaign that had to be fought rather than to waste time regretting an opportunity that had been missed.

Even the grandees who had opposed Alvaro through the years and had contributed to his temporary disgrace were forced to admire his tireless energy. He started his day at dawn, read dispatches from civilian administrators, received provincial governors and sent enough letters to the heads of various government departments to keep a large staff of secretaries and assistants busy. He always found time to see the various Church officials who came to Trillo to pay their respects to him, and he made it a habit to dine at noon with the king and some visiting bishop.

He spent the rest of each day with the army, and no detail was too small, no question of policy too intricate to receive his complete attention. He worked out problems of supplies with quartermasters, arranged with his chief armorers for a steady flow of weapons into the camp and, rather than force peasants and swordsmiths to wait for payment, transferred a portion of the royal treasury to Trillo from the vaults of the Alcazar. There were so few buildings in the little town suitable for housing the gold that he took possession of the public baths, stationed a full regiment of household troops around the stone structure and insisted that everyone who sold arms, food or clothing to the army was to be paid in gold at once.

Don Domenico's archers readily accepted the constable's training suggestions, but the grandees and knights, although afraid to express open opposition, indicated in subtle ways that they thought they had a better understanding of their type of warfare. Alvaro proved otherwise by holding a tournament and, taking part in it himself, unseating three knights who had won the championships of their companies. Thereafter the lords and knights caused him no trouble and listened to him respectfully whenever he rode onto the fields where they were training. He won the respect of the pikemen, too, by removing his armor, dismounting and engaging in mock combat with several foot soldiers. Although he was at least a head shorter than his opponents, he defeated two who attacked him simultaneously and then held a heavy-set squire to a draw. After that day he was cheered whenever he rode through the camp.

Each night he and Juan ate a light supper with the generals, and grandees like Don Diego, who had been unfamiliar with Alvaro's methods, were startled by his informality. Free discussion was encouraged, disputes were aired and settled promptly, and anyone from a brigade commander to one of the constable's immediate subordinates could lay a vexing problem before the group, listen to the advice of his colleagues and then make his own decision. Alvaro urged every general to show initiative and imagination, for he felt that habits formed in a training bivouac would pay dividends on the battlefield. When he announced a ruling, however, he expected it to be obeyed without question.

After the evening meal he retired to his headquarters, where he received espionage agents who had returned from Aragon, read military and civilian reports and, on rare occasions, relaxed late at night with Don Domenico or the king, his only personal friends. On the day that he received word from Toledo that Beatriz de Pimente had been scourged publicly and sent off to a life of imprisonment as a servant in a nunnery, he retired behind piles of papers, refused to see anyone and read late into the night. In the days that followed, however, he recovered his equilibrium, and no one was foolish enough to remind him of the incident.

By June the army had grown into a powerful force of more than one hundred thousand men, and Huerrara's tactics of containing the enemy had proved so successful that Alvaro sent another eleven thousand horsemen to reinforce the cavalry on the frontier. Only the artillery and engineers were not yet up to full strength, and volunteers from the corps of archers and the infantry helped to cut down trees, build catapults and make scaling ladders. There was every reason to feel satisfied with the speed, skill and precision that had forged a powerful army in a short time, and even the cautious Cuevas agreed when Sandoual declared at dinner one night, "We've become so strong that Alfonso may be afraid to attack."

Alvaro worked later than usual when he returned to his headquarters that night. He studied reports on the state of preparedness of each unit, he pondered over long lists of supplies and arms that had been delivered to the camp, and he wrestled at length with a question that only he could answer. The first phase of the campaign was coming to an end, and he had to determine how soon the army would be ready to march against the enemy. Spirits were high, officers and men were confident, and everyone trusted him completely; in fact, he had heard some of the more superstitious say he had performed a miracle by delaying his foes until he was strong enough to move against them.

It was a temptation to give the marching orders immediately, and Alvaro weighed the idea carefully, finally rejecting it because he knew that, if a battle should be fought in the near future, Aragon and Navarre would still enjoy an advantage. But if he could delay for another three or four weeks, the Castilians would be ready to take the offensive, and it might even be possible to fight the war on enemy territory. Alfonso, who could have swept across Castile virtually unopposed had he acted early in the spring, had cause for regret, and could blame his brothers, whose quarrels and demands had created such dissension that the combined armies of Aragon and Navarre had been paralyzed.

Smiling as he read an espionage agent's account of a bitter argument between Pedro and Juan of Navarre, each of whom had insisted that he be appointed supreme cavalry commander, Alvaro realized he could thank his foes for the precious time he had won. He was still enjoying the account, relishing every detail, when an adjutant tapped at his door and came into the crowded chamber. "Lord Constable," he said, stepping over a pile of armor that had been left on the floor because there was no room for it elsewhere, "forgive the disturbance at this late hour."

Alvaro's subordinates were permitted to interrupt his night reading only when grave emergencies arose, and this was not such an occasion. Sensing the officer's hesitation, he became irritable. "What do you want?"

"A visitor is here to see you, sir, and refuses to leave."

"Tell him to apply again tomorrow, and if he refuses, the sentries can remove him. That's why we have guards stationed around the house." Alvaro returned to the report.

"If you please, Lord Constable, this visitor is a lady."

The chill in Alvaro's voice matched the expression in his eyes. "You should know by now that I receive no camp followers." The prostitutes who had taken up residence in the area were becoming too bold, and he made a mental note to curb their activities.

"This woman is no camp follower, Lord Constable," the aide declared nervously.

Alvaro's smile was cynical. "Have you become an authority on the subject, Don Luis?"

The young man reddened, but remained firm. "She's too old, sir. And her manner is that of a lady."

"What is her business with me?"

"She refuses to discuss it with anyone but you. I tried to get rid of her, sir, but she swears the matter is urgent, and something in her attitude has influenced me. She seems desperate, Lord Constable." The adjutant stood stiffly at attention. "I'm willing to accept full responsibility, sir."

Alvaro was touched, and his sense of annoyance lessened. The aide was a conscientious officer, and neither in recent weeks nor in the years prior to Alvaro's temporary retirement had he asked a personal favor. "She couldn't be one of our agents, Don Luis. We have no women working for us in Aragon."

"No, sir."

Feeling a trifle light-headed after his long day's work, Alvaro enjoyed teasing the serious aide. "On the other hand, she could be a spy whom King Alfonso has sent to kill me."

The adjutant's eyes widened. "I'll stay in the room with you, Lord Constable, and—"

"That won't be necessary. I can take care of myself." Alvaro laughed and dismissed the officer with a wave. "I'll see her, but if I find that my time is being wasted by some trivial request, I'll devise a suitable punishment for you."

Only vaguely curious, he returned to his report and did not look up again until he saw a veiled, grey-haired woman in a travel-stained gown of dark wool hesitating at the threshold. "You may come in," he said, stood and signaled to Don Luis, who closed the door.

She removed her veil. "Have I changed so much that you don't know me, Alvaro?"

"Catalina!"

She tried to curtsy, but there was insufficient space.

Alvaro caught her elbow before she could perform the clumsy act of obeisance. "I should drop to my knee before you, Your Highness."

Catalina smiled wearily. "I'm told that the Lord Constable of Castile bows his head to no man and kneels to no woman."

Hastily he offered her his chair, shoving a pile of documents aside. "Many of the stories told about me are false. Have I permission to sit?"

"You haven't changed, Alvaro." She was studying him openly.

He laughed without humor. "I'm sure I'd win the contest if we matched grey hairs, Your Highness."

Catalina slumped in the chair. "You're still young, Alvaro.

I'm tired and disillusioned, and I've grown old before my time."

He had perched on the edge of the desk, but rose quickly, pushed aside a stack of papers for a jug of wine and a cup, and poured her a generous quantity. "Forgive the way I live here," he said. "I entertain few people, and you're the first princess who has come to see me."

She sipped the wine gratefully.

"I hope Don Enrique will forgive my impertinence," he continued, "but I always believed Your Highness to be the most beautiful woman on earth. What I see now doesn't cause me to change my opinion." It was true that she had matured, but he returned her gaze frankly, and thought she was still lovely.

Catalina was pleased, and seemed less weary. "If you were a courtier who makes pretty speeches, I'd be unhappy. But I have reason to believe you're an honest man, and you certainly wouldn't flatter me." She pushed a stray lock of hair away from her face and smoothed her skirt. "After all, we're enemies."

"I have never regarded Your Highness as an enemy," Alvaro said carefully.

"You addressed me by name when I came into the room. I wish you'd do it again."

"Thank you, Catalina."

There was a soft tap at the door, and the adjutant peered into the chamber. Catalina quickly turned away, and Alvaro gestured curtly. "Get out," he said.

"Yes, Lord Constable." The bewildered aide closed the door.

Alvaro laughed. "Poor Don Luis. I joked with him and suggested you might be an enemy agent. How confused he'd be if he learned that I may have been right." His eyes narrowed. "Have you come here as a representative of our enemies?"

"I am a Castilian, Alvaro de Luna!" There was pride in her voice and she raised her head.

"You bring me no private message from King Alfonso or from your husband?"

"I bring no message from anyone. Enrique may think I'm still at the royal palace in Saragossa. If he's learned I've gone, he'll be very angry, although only his pride will be hurt."

The candid revelation that relations between Catalina and her husband were strained was embarrassing, but Alvaro felt surprisingly buoyant. He smiled, then sobered. "You've come to me for a purpose."

"I need help, and I can go to no one else."

He thought she was exaggerating, but kept his opinion to himself. Women, as he had learned, were not realists.

"I was afraid to tell your adjutant my name. I've taken great care not to identify myself to anyone, and only you know I'm in Castile."

"You've made the journey here alone from Saragossa?" He could not hide his astonishment. "You've traveled through country infested with the cavalry patrols of both armies?"

"I did what I believed necessary. I've spent years listening to Enrique and Pedro and Juan of Navarre plot against Castile. I've seen them infect Alfonso with their evil thinking. But I love Castile." She hesitated for an instant, then added bleakly, "I have nothing else. I've come home. I couldn't stay in a land of my country's enemies when we're at war, when a terrible battle is going to be fought at any time."

Her act of defiance had been sentimental and foolish, but Alvaro couldn't help admiring her for it. "Your brother will be delighted to see you, and the people will rejoice."

"Juan mustn't know I've returned," she cried in alarm.

"But his house is only a stone's throw away. Surely—"

"Alvaro, I've placed all of my hopes in you. Obviously you haven't thought about my problem or you'd realize that my position is critical. I'm a wife who has run away from her husband. If Enrique discovers I've come to Castile, he'll insist that I be returned to him."

"I'm afraid that legally, at least, he'd be within his rights."

"Archbishop de Pacheico of Saragossa would demand my return. And every official of the Church in Castile would be forced to cooperate with him. I wouldn't dare trust anyone, not even your brother."

"Particularly my brother," Alvaro replied wryly, frowning. "Francisco is a loyal Castilian, but he's a cardinal, and he places his duty first. I'm afraid you're right, Catalina. If Enrique finds out you've come home, the war will be suspended until you've been sent back to Aragon."

"I prefer to die," she declared fervently.

He wanted to soothe her, but realized that any personal gesture would be inappropriate.

Catalina sensed his reaction, relaxed slightly and looked straight at him. "You haven't yet understood that I've compromised you. Enrique has always accused me of loving you, and he'd be sure to see my flight as proof of his claims. To whom have I come? You."

Alvaro refused to let himself dwell on his growing certainty that there was cause for Enrique's suspicions. Hiding his own feelings, he said roughly, "His Highness couldn't hate me any more than he has through the years. Let him believe what he pleases."

"I wish I dared, but he's too clever. He'll use my escape as a weapon to help Aragon win the war."

"I don't think that even Enrique is that clever. I feel certain that our army will give a good account of itself."

"You don't know Enrique as I do, and you force me to speak bluntly, Alvaro." Catalina paused, twisted her veil for a moment and then regained control of her emotions. "If I hadn't given in to the frustration that had been growing in me for years, I wouldn't have left Saragossa, and I'm sorry my panic has brought me to you. It does no good now, though, to apologize and to confess that I didn't think of the complications I might cause for you."

"What can Enrique do to me?" he demanded, wanting to tell her she would feel calmer after a night's rest.

"He can ruin you and destroy the army's confidence in you," she replied flatly. "He wants to rule Castile, and you stand in his way. So he'll claim that you and I are lovers, that you care nothing about the country and that you've mustered your troops only to win me. My presence here will convince many people that he's telling the truth. The grandees will desert you again, and even the common soldiers who have loved you will lose faith in you."

"Would he blacken his wife's reputation with a gross lie?"

"If it becomes known that I've sought your protection, I'll have no reputation."

Alvaro hooked his thumbs in his belt and started to pace up and down, but the floor was so littered that he returned to the desk. "I'm pleased that you've left Aragon, and I'm honored by the extraordinary trust you've placed in me. I won't abuse it, but Castile must be saved, even if you and I are destroyed."

Catalina stood, her face deathly pale. "Are you suggesting that I return to Saragossa?"

"I'll place you under arrest and hold you as a prisoner before I'd permit such insanity!"

She was comforted, and her face softened. "I honestly believe you mean that."

"I advise you not to put me to the test." Her proximity made it difficult for him to think clearly, but it was vital that he concentrate. "You know, I'm tempted to detain you and announce that you've been captured. That would prevent Enrique from linking our names. Unfortunately, it wouldn't stop him from demanding your return, and I'd be helpless against the bishops. I don't mind defying the *Cortes*, but I want and need the help of the Church."

"I chose the worst of all times to run away."

Forgetting that she was a princess, he silenced her with an abrupt wave. "Let me think." He stared at the royal crest on a furled banner that was propped up against the far wall. "I don't see how we can keep your escape a secret from Juan—"

"He couldn't keep quiet, Alvaro. He'd brag to everyone, and then trouble would start. The only way to prevent complications is to tell no one what I've done, and that's impossible. I can't disappear from the face of the earth and hide indefinitely."

Alvaro looked at her sharply, then amazed her by chuckling. "You have great courage or you couldn't have made your way through the lines. Are you capable of showing even greater strength?"

"What do you want me to do?" she asked simply.

"Are you prepared to spend many days, perhaps several months living alone? I'm asking a personal sacrifice that you may not be capable of making. I know what I'm saying. I lived the life of a recluse for almost a year."

"I've been lonely for a long time," Catalina said quietly.

Alvaro stared at her again; their eyes met and neither turned away. He could feel his pulse pounding in his throat, at his temples, in his fingertips.

She sighed tremulously and tried to stifle the sound.

He knew that if he took her in his arms she would not resist him, but the memory of Enrique came between them. After what he himself had suffered, Alvaro could not forget that, regardless of what she might think of her husband, she was a married woman. "Are you certain that no one recognized you or followed you?"

"I'm positive. I planned my escape for many weeks, and I left no details to chance."

"It will be known tomorrow that a woman visited my headquarters tonight. Don Luis will be curious, and the sentries will gossip. So if you aren't too tired, I'll have to send you on your way tonight."

"I've placed myself in your custody, and I'm ready to obey any order you choose to give me. Where do you want me to go?"

"Toledo."

"But I'm sure to be recognized there."

"No, not if you follow my instructions. Do you have a fresh horse?"

"I sold my gelding to one of your quartermaster commissioners a short time ago, tonight, and bought a mare. There are so many horses in your army that I felt sure the gelding wouldn't be recognized by anyone trying to trace me."

"Good." He nodded approvingly, then climbed over his mattress to a map pinned on the wall. "You have a long ride ahead. Your first stop will be Guadalajara, the nearest town of any size, which lies twenty miles to the east. Go to the bazaar there and buy tweezers to pluck out your eyebrows, rouge to put color in your cheeks and on your lips, anything you find that will change your appearance. Buy a sleazy gown that will make you look like a strumpet. But wait until you approach Toledo before you transform yourself. You'll attract less attention traveling in drab clothes, and you won't be molested by military patrols. You'll need the disguise only in Toledo, where everyone except the young children will remember the Infanta."

Catalina was listening carefully, and unconsciously raised a hand to her greying hair.

"I've thought of that, too," Alvaro said. "The women of Granada color the soles of their feet and the palms of their hands with a dye they call henna. It also turns a woman's hair red. Harlots have used it for many years. I know," he continued, his voice becoming strident, "because my mother washed her head in a solution of henna and water when she began to lose her youth."

Catalina continued to pay close attention, and the scorn he expected to see in her eyes did not appear.

"You'll find henna at the bazaar in Guadalajara, too," he continued gruffly. "Apply it to your hair at some little inn near Toledo when you change the rest of your appearance."

"I understand." She drew in her breath. "Are you suggesting that I act the role of a strumpet after I reach the city?"

"No!" He realized he had shouted, and lowered his voice. "I don't want you to be conspicuous, that's all."

He seemed to be contradicting himself, and Catalina looked at him in bewilderment.

Returning to the desk, Alvaro wrote a brief note on a sheet of parchment, signed his name with a flourish and sealed the document with a blob of wax and his signet ring. "My brother and I own a house in the *Mozarab* district," he explained. "No one has occupied it for many years, but you'll find it comfortably furnished, and armed guards are stationed outside it at all times to prevent looting. This is a letter to the commander of the guard, authorizing him to pass you into the house. I'll send a letter to my brother, too, telling him that a friend of mine is going to take up residence there."

"Won't His Eminence be shocked?" Color was creeping slowly up Catalina's face.

"Probably, but he's a realist, and he's been worried because of my lack of interest in women. He'll probably be relieved. I'm sure," he added quickly, "that he won't call on you."

"I'll do as you've requested, but I don't understand your reasons for wanting me to change the way I look." Catalina was still perplexed.

"You won't be able to spend all of your time alone, indoors," Alvaro said patiently. "You'll have to go out to buy yourself food. The library is inadequately stocked, and you'll probably want books. Remember, you may spend a long time there. And I can think of no better disguise than that of a strumpet. The people of the *Mozarab* district would know a princess instantly, but they're so accustomed to prostitutes they'll pay no attention to you."

"I see. And thank you, Alvaro."

"This is only the beginning, a temporary measure. Assuming we win the war—and I intend to win it—we'll have to plan our next step. Meanwhile, you'll have ample opportunity to think about the problem."

Blinking away tears that came to her eyes, she accepted the letter.

"There's one detail we haven't discussed. Do you have enough Castilian money?"

"I've been accumulating Castilian *dolars* for more than two years."

It was obvious that anyone who managed her affairs so brilliantly could take care of herself in the difficult days ahead, and he was satisfied. Suddenly the thought struck him that, for the first time since Magdalena Ruminez's death, a woman with red hair would live in the *Mozarab* house. It was ironic that she should be the daughter of a king and wife of a prince, and he laughed, harshly and unexpectedly.

Catalina was startled.

Alvaro could not explain and, bending down, picked up her heavy veil, which had fallen to the floor. "It's a long ride to Guadalajara, and you won't want to be on the road when my infantry regiments march out at dawn for exercises."

"If I knew how to express my gratitude to you—"

"I want no gratitude." His manner became brusque, remote.

Catalina walked to the door, then hesitated. "There is one thing that I'd like you to know."

He glanced obliquely at her face, then braced himself.

"When I heard the news of Teresa's death, I wept for many days."

Unable to trust his voice, he made no reply and inclined his head awkwardly.

"I grieved for you, Alvaro, not for her."

Again they looked at each other intently.

Suddenly Catalina threw the veil over her head, and her face was hidden. "May Castile be victorious," she said softly, "and may God bless and preserve you." She raised the latch and left the chamber.

Alvaro stood silently for a few seconds, then walked to the window. Peering down into the street, he saw Catalina emerge from the house and take the reins of her horse from a sentry. Refusing an offer of assistance, she mounted the mare and rode off in the dark toward Guadalajara and the refuge in Toledo.

A tap at the door roused Alvaro.

The adjutant came into the room, saluted and stood at attention. He said nothing, but his eyes were curious as he waited patiently.

"You were wrong, Don Luis," Alvaro said lightly.

"Sir?"

"Perhaps, when you're my age, you'll become a better judge of women." Watching his aide's face, Alvaro knew that every word he spoke would be repeated in the morning. "Greying hair and the grand manners of a lady don't necessarily mean that a wench isn't a camp follower." Grinning, then yawning and stretching, he turned to the mattress in the corner, and the adjutant, excited by what he believed to be a juicy morsel of gossip, saluted again and took his leave.

Alvaro prayed for Catalina's safety before he went to bed, and for the rest of the night he remained awake, recalling every word she had spoken, every gesture, every expression that had crossed her face.

2

King Alfonso of Aragon and his brothers, patching up their quarrels because of their realization that the enemy was growing stronger, began to move early one morning in mid-June. Spies brought the news to Trillo in less than forty-eight hours, and Alvaro immediately gave the army of Castile its marching orders. Before dawn the cavalry vanguard was on the road, the regiments of archers left their bivouac and the knights, who needed more time to clothe themselves and their mounts in armor, brought up the rear. Each unit was accompanied by its own supply wagons, an innovation which permitted greater speed and mobility, and the main body of the army traveled almost sixty miles in three days.

Because the cavalry detachments at the border could not cope with their foes, whose numbers were multiplying, Alvaro, resigning himself to the inevitability of fighting on Castilian territory, sent word to General Huerrara to fall back. Huerrara's squadrons, tired but in good spirits, retreated so quickly that they prevented the enemy from cutting them off, and the entire Castilian army was reunited five days after Alvaro had begun his march east from Trillo. Alfonso, leading a force estimated by Huerrara's scouts as numbering more than one hundred thousand men, crossed the border without opposition, and after capturing the city of Cuenca, moved into battle formation on high ground west of the high-walled citadel.

Alvaro did not intend to let his foes choose a site that would put him at a disadvantage, however, and although he had been following the old Roman military road that led to Cuenca, he altered his route, cut across open country and halted on a plateau forty miles south of the city. The unorthodox maneuver startled his commanders, and Don Domenico pointed out to him that no troops stood between the invaders and Toledo. Alvaro, knowing the risks he was taking, was prepared to retrace his march if the enemy penetrated deeper into Castilian territory. But he was gambling on the belief that Alfonso would find the challenge irresistible; only a man of extraordinary vision would understand that it would be preferable to ignore the Castilian army and capture as much territory as it was possible to gain.

The following day Alfonso proved that, like his brothers, he still thought in old-fashioned terms that had been made obsolete by bowmen and lightly armored cavalry. Abandoning the heights outside Cuenca and seemingly unaware of the opportunity that awaited him on the road to Toledo, he marched south to meet the Castilian army. Huerrara's scouts reported that fifteen thousand nobles and knights in heavy armor were leading the column of invaders, and Alvaro made ready for battle.

He strengthened his outposts, placed his bowmen on the ridge, which overlooked a long, shallow valley, and, splitting his cavalry, placed half of the horsemen on each flank. Then, confident that Alfonso could not complete his march in less than two days, he ordered the army to relax and rest. The men slept, ate heartily and swam in a river behind the bivouac, but no one was permitted to leave the area, and sentries were instructed to shoot anyone who tried to make his way in or out of the lines.

That night the regiments were given rations of lamb, and while they cooked their meals over campfires behind the woods, Alvaro and King Juan visited each unit in turn, pausing to chat with the men and promise them victory. Juan lost some of his shyness when the soldiers cheered him and insisted that he share their meal with them. After taking a token mouthful of food at more than a score of campfires, he complained privately to his constable that he had eaten so much he was growing sleepy.

Alvaro, who had refused offers of food from the troops and instead had eaten some bread and olives he carried in a pouch, was enjoying himself. He took care to tell the sergeants of each unit that he planned to employ the tactics that had been successful against the Moors, and even the pikemen who belonged to companies maintained by armored knights understood his explanation. They realized they were members of a new type of army, and, sharing the optimism of their commander-in-chief, they felt certain they would send a disorganized rabble fleeing across the border into Aragon.

A courier from the headquarters staff found Alvaro as he and Juan were beginning to make the rounds of the regiments of archers. Dismounting quickly, the man saluted and drew Alvaro aside. "Sir, Don Domenico requests your return to your own tent as soon as possible. The sentries have captured a man trying to enter the camp from the west."

Cuevas, Alvaro thought, was becoming nervous as the battle drew nearer. "I fail to see anything remarkable in the capture of a spy," he said calmly. "I believe we've caught at least fifteen or twenty earlier today."

"All I know, Lord Constable, is that His Grace begs you to join him immediately."

Alvaro felt he had no choice, and leaving the king with the archers, he rode back to his own compound, which he had established in a small clearing in the woods. Armed guards raised their lances in salute, and the adjutant, a peculiar expression on his face, took Alvaro's horse.

"His Grace of Cuevas is waiting for you inside, sir," Don Luis said, and led the stallion away.

Puzzled and mildly irritated, Alvaro pushed aside the flap and entered the tent. Don Domenico was sitting at a small table, and standing on the far side of the enclosure, wearing full armor, was Roderigo de Pinar. Alvaro reached for his sword, but checked himself. "You sent a messenger to tell me that another espionage agent has been captured, Domenico?" he asked, trying to speak calmly.

Cuevas rose to his feet. "No, Alvaro. He voluntarily surrendered himself. He informed the officer of the guard that he wished to see you. I was told that the visitor was the Count de Pinar, so I took it on myself to intervene and send for you. If you wish, I'll withdraw."

"No, I prefer that you remain, if you don't mind."

Don Domenico bowed and, apparently aware of the purpose of Roderigo's unexpected appearance, withdrew discreetly into the shadows at the rear of the tent.

"I had hoped," Alvaro said distinctly, looking straight at the man who had been his closest friend, "that you and I would never see each other again."

"I knew how you felt, and I tried to respect your wish." Roderigo held himself erect, and only the hoarseness of his voice betrayed his tension.

Alvaro waited silently.

"I won't insult you by asking your forgiveness, nor will I try to excuse my past conduct. You have no reason to believe that I respect you—"

"I wish," Alvaro said, interrupting coldly, "to let the past remain buried. More important matters occupy my mind at the present time."

"That's why I'm here. Please, Alvaro, listen to me." Roderigo took a step forward, then halted, reddening. He tried to continue, but choked and coughed.

"I'm listening." Never had Alvaro shown such self-control, but even though he wanted to run his sword through the man who had betrayed him, the odd thought passed through his mind that he felt sorry for Roderigo. Teresa had soiled her lover as much as she had dishonored her husband.

"I am a Castilian." The night was cool, but Roderigo's face was wet. "I beg you to remember the fight to protect the king at my castle, and I'd like to remind you of my services against the Moors."

"I have an excellent memory."

"My country is in danger, and my king's enemies are marching against him. Regardless of the terrible wrong I did to you, I ask you to let me contribute my sword to Castile."

Alvaro stared at him for a long time. "We can use experienced soldiers," he said at last. "Don Domenico, please find a place in the ranks of the nobles for the Count de Pinar."

Alfonso's vanguard, which consisted of four brigades of Catalan light cavalry, supported by several battalions of lancers, reached the northern end of the valley late the following day. The Castilians watched them from the ridge, and a delegation of nobles called on Alvaro. They urged him to attack immediately, before the enemy columns could move into battle formation, but he rejected the suggestion, explaining that hundreds of knights, cavalrymen and squires would be killed in such an action, which would be inconclusive because the legions from Aragon and Navarre were too strong to be destroyed by such a maneuver. Only a full-scale battle, he said, could decide the issue.

The invaders continued to arrive on the plain through the better part of the night, and when dawn broke, the Castilians on the ridge were dismayed to see thousands of banners whipping in the breeze above a sea of tents. Alvaro remained calm, however, and after ordering his troops to move into the positions he had assigned them, he and the king rode to a forward position on the ridge from which they could observe the enemy's movements. Cuevas and Huerrara joined them, and by the time the sun rose it was obvious that Alfonso was planning to launch a frontal attack. Many Castilian grandees, clinging to their concepts of traditional warfare, felt certain the constable was making a mistake; he held the favored position, and they believed he should send his armored knights down the slope to strike first.

Apparently Alfonso couldn't understand why his foes were refusing to seize the initiative, for he sent several squadrons of light cavalry across the plain to investigate. Alvaro ordered the Castilians to hold back, and the bewildered horsemen rode up and down the valley unmolested. They saw the troops massed on the heights, and their officers carefully noted the disposition of the Castilian units. A few of the bolder men drew close to the ridge and counted the pennants of the grandees and knights massed on the right side of the line; when the observers finally fell back to report to Alfonso, it was no secret that the opposing armies were evenly matched in size.

The invaders hesitated until midmorning, certain that some type of intricate surprise tactics would be used against them, but when the Castilians continued to hold their lines, Alfonso finally lost patience. Trumpets sounded, thousands of pikemen formed a double line and, after a flurry of activity in the rear, the main body of the striking force of Aragon and Navarre moved forward. Thirty thousand lords and knights, all heavily armored, all riding war horses, moved in formation toward the valley.

As a spectacle, the prelude to the assault was impressive. Coats-of-arms were painted on shields, grandees of rank were followed by their personal standard bearers, and the majority of the knights had decorated their helmets with plumes or silk scarves. King Alfonso was conspicuous in a suit of gold chain mail, and Juan of Navarre, who rode on his right, was also dressed in gold armor. Pedro and Enrique wore silver, and the four brothers stared up at the ridge, trying to identify their foes.

At Alvaro's suggestion, King Juan raised his sword in salute, and his cousins, their faces hidden behind their visors, returned the gesture. The amenities had been observed, and the attackers increased their speed from a walk to a canter. Alvaro waited until the five hundred knights in the front rank approached the foot of the ridge, and for a moment he felt sorry for brave men who were relying on sheer strength to take them up the slope and enable them to overcome the defenders. Then he signaled to his bowmen, and a hail of arrows fell on the knights. The men of Aragon and Navarre were even slower than the Moors of Granada had been to realize they were facing an enemy fighting a different type of battle from that which they had expected, and at least half of the five hundred were either killed or wounded. King Alfonso ordered his army to pull back, and Alvaro instructed the archers to halt so that the dead and wounded could be removed from the field.

Alfonso, his brothers and a group of nobles conferred at length on the far side of the valley, and Alvaro, aware that no tactics they might devise could beat him, waited confidently for a fresh assault. The king of Aragon surprised him, however, by sending a courier forward under a white flag of truce. Don Luis was ordered to ride down the slope to meet the enemy messenger.

The adjutant returned in a few moments. "Their Majesties of Aragon and Navarre want to talk to King Juan," they said. "They propose that a meeting be held, under a truce, and that both sides be represented by their princes, dukes and counts."

The offer seemed hopeful, and certainly no lord would violate a formal truce and thus compromise his honor, but Alvaro pondered the suggestion before replying. "There's only one disadvantage that I can see," he said to the king and his principal generals, who anxiously awaited his decision. "As Alfonso knows, I'm not a duke or a count any longer. I couldn't take part in the meeting."

"But you think it would be helpful if we met them, provided you were there?" Juan asked.

"Our position here is impregnable, as Alfonso must realize by now, and his men-at-arms are helpless against our bowmen. He may want to negotiate peace terms. I can think of no other reason why he should seek a meeting, although I frankly don't understand why he wants the leading nobles to be present."

"We can overcome our disadvantage easily," the king replied with unexpected vigor, and smiled broadly. "We hereby restore your title of Duke of Truxillo."

Alvaro had no alternative, and accepted with a bow.

Don Luis rode back down the slope to tell the enemy courier that King Juan accepted the offer, and other aides hurriedly assembled the grandees of high rank. A page carrying a white flag started toward the valley on foot, followed by the king, who rode alone, his personal standard bearer on his left, a squire holding aloft the flag of Castile on his right. Eight dukes and twenty-three counts followed him. Alvaro remained behind for a few moments to confer privately with General Huerrara, whom he left in command of the army. He arranged to wave his scimitar over his head if Juan and the grandees were riding into a trap; in that event Huerrara was instructed to launch a cavalry attack, send his best squadrons to rescue the king and use the archers according to his own best judgment.

Spurring down the incline, Alvaro joined the procession in time to see Alfonso and Juan of Navarre leading their grandees across the field. The two groups halted within hailing distance of each other, and Alfonso, his gold armor gleaming in the bright summer sunlight, moved forward alone. The entire Castilian party advanced, and after a moment's hesitation the grandees from Aragon and Navarre followed their example, forming a solid line behind their monarch. Alfonso drew his sword and laid it across his pommel to indicate that he wanted to talk rather than fight, and Juan, who moved forward a few paces to meet him, did the same.

"Cousin, it pleases us that you consent to settle our grievances in this manner."

"Good morning, cousin," Juan replied cautiously, and glanced over his shoulder.

Alvaro moved up to join him.

"Our Constable, His Grace of Truxillo, will speak on our behalf, cousin."

His face grim, Alvaro laid his scimitar and his sword across his pommel, and saw that Enrique, who was sitting in the center of the enemy line with Pedro and Juan of Navarre, recognized the blade he had lost so many years earlier. The prince had grown heavier, but he was still powerful, and he clenched a mailed fist as he glared at his lifelong enemy. Alvaro wondered if he knew that Catalina had gone to the man her husband despised. It seemed unlikely that any news of her whereabouts had been discovered and, secure in the belief that she was safe at his house in Toledo, Alvaro concentrated on the business at hand.

"Your Majesty," he said curtly, and saluted.

Alfonso studied him for a moment. "You've climbed high in the world since our first meeting, de Luna."

"And you, Your Majesty, are in danger of losing your own place at the summit. My archers have given you one brief demonstration of their power, and they're prepared to do far more."

"I deserved that rebuke, Your Grace." Alfonso smiled and inclined his head.

His willingness to admit that he had been less than civil set him apart from his brothers, and Alvaro thought that, if an honorable peace could be arranged, the king of Aragon was the sort of man whose friendship he would seek. "I spoke brusquely, too, Your Majesty, and beg your forgiveness."

"On a day such as this," Alfonso replied gracefully, "all of us are short-tempered. Now, shall we proceed to the negotiations?"

"I've agreed to no negotiations, Your Majesty," Alvaro replied firmly. "Castile is willing to hear what Aragon may wish to propose, but our troops are prepared to resume the battle."

"If I sat in your saddle," Alfonso said, casting aside his air of formality, "I'd feel precisely as you do. I heard many reports of your victory over Mohammed-ibn-Azar, but I didn't believe the stories until I saw your archers in action. I congratulate you, Don Alvaro, and I assure you that I intend to reorganize my army before my next campaign."

Alvaro accepted the compliment with a grin, but said nothing and waited warily.

"In the meantime, my brother of Navarre and I must fight with the men and weapons at our disposal, if we are compelled to fight. You'll suggest that we can retire across our own frontiers, and that no one will force us to wage war against Castile."

"You read my mind, Your Majesty."

"Surely you realize, Don Alvaro, that I would lose my honor if I retreated without fighting a battle."

"I can sympathize with Your Majesty's predicament," Alvaro replied dryly.

"It grieves me that so many men will die if the battle is resumed. Your bowmen will inflict terrible losses on my army, it's true, but I won't surrender, I swear to you, and eventually we'll establish a foothold on the ridge. When that happens, you'll have to commit your knights and squires to the action, and before the sun sets tonight, there will be thousands of widows in Castile."

"There will be more," Alvaro declared pointedly, "in Aragon and Navarre."

King Alfonso agreed. "How much happier all of our people will be if there are no casualties." He paused, then raised his voice to speak directly to the Castilian grandees. "Aragon and Navarre are prepared to propose an honorable solution to the problem, a solution consistent with the laws of the code of chivalry under which nobles of every civilized nation live. Our champion will meet your champion in personal combat, on the understanding that all of us, on both sides, will accept the outcome of that fight as final."

Prince Enrique immediately moved forward. "I request the

honor of representing my brothers of Aragon and Navarre," he said, and glowered at Alvaro.

The trap was clever, but Alfonso's logic was absurd. Realizing he couldn't win a pitched battle against bowmen who would cut his army to shreds, he was appealing to the enemy grandees, hoping their acceptance of tradition would blind them to the reality of the situation. Alvaro scornfully started to reject the idea, but his words were drowned by a loud shout behind him, and a tall figure in armor rode forward.

"I demand the right to represent Castile," Roderigo de Pinar said.

Nobles on both sides were smiling, and apparently only Don Domenico of Cuevas realized that Alfonso had maneuvered his foes into a position that they were now forced to accept under the strict rules of the code of chivalry. Don Domenico looked dismayed, but Roderigo, proud and excited, sat erect in his saddle, and the dukes and counts of Castile applauded him. Even Juan, who loved tournaments, was pleased and, joining Roderigo, leaned forward in his saddle to speak a word of encouragement to him.

"It would seem, Your Majesty," Alvaro said to the king of Aragon, "that you've saved yourself from suffering a severe defeat. Regardless of the result, you've manipulated brilliantly."

"I appreciate your praise, Don Alvaro. The trick is worthy of the best you've played." Alfonso laughed, then sobered. "However, the result isn't in doubt. No one can beat my brother at the jousts."

Enrique glanced obliquely at Alvaro, then turned to his opponent. "I was hoping to meet someone else, but you're a satisfactory substitute, de Pinar. You and I have had some unfinished business to settle since a scuffle at your castle some years ago. And I've long suspected that you have more than a casual familiarity with my handwriting—I intend to make you pay for that incident, too."

"Save your breath. You'll need it," Roderigo replied rudely, pulling down his visor.

The Castilian grandees withdrew into the shadows of the ridge, and the enemy nobles rode back toward their own lines. Two knights from each side placed boulders on the field, marking the limits of the area in which the combat could be held. Each of the contestants was given a lance, and the Castilians rode past Roderigo, shook his hand and wished him well. Alvaro, furious because his former friend had placed certain victory in jeopardy, nevertheless realized that Roderigo was risking his life for his country. After the others had returned to their previous positions, he moved forward, removed his glove and held out his hand.

"Thank you, Alvaro," Roderigo said gruffly. "I hoped you'd do that."

"Think of nothing except the instructions that Father Sebastian gave us at the Sanctuary. You haven't fought in a jousting match for a long time, so remember to keep your balance, don't strike too soon and when you attack, aim high. May God ride with you."

Returning to his place beside the excited Juan and a dour Don Domenico, Alvaro saw thousands of men gathered at the ridge above. Enemy troops were pressing forward, too, trying to obtain a better view, and a tense silence settled over the field of combat.

Roderigo, sitting easily in his saddle, tested his lance, leaned down to tighten his stirrups and adjusted the strap of his helmet beneath his chin. Prince Enrique, looking confident as he waited at a line of boulders on the opposite side of the area, sat motionless, his lance poised.

The four knights conferred for a few moments, and after reaching an agreement that a young officer from Navarre should officiate, the others withdrew. A squire brought the knight his horse and a lance; he tied a square of silk to the point and raised the weapon high over his head. "Are you ready, Your Highness?" he called.

Enrique replied by pulling down his visor.

"Are you ready, milord de Pinar?"

Roderigo's words were unintelligible behind his iron mask, but he nodded emphatically.

The knight slowly lowered the lance, and when the silk touched the ground, the combatants started toward each other. Roderigo increased his speed slowly until his stallion was running at a slow canter, the pace that was considered proper for a jousting match, but Enrique recklessly spurred to a full gallop and headed straight for his foe. It was clear to Alvaro that the prince intended to win by utilizing a technique that, although ethical, was unorthodox. A single blow, accurately aimed, could win the fight for him, and Alvaro hoped that Roderigo had the sense to anticipate what his enemy was planning to do. The only possible defense, he thought, would be to swerve aside at the last moment, and he watched apprehensively as the space that separated the two men shrank.

But Roderigo had his own ideas about the technique to employ against someone who was going to risk everything on one strike, and to the amazement of every grandee and knight watching the battle, he deliberately slowed his stallion to a walk and waited for the prince to approach. The Castilians cried out, protesting, but Roderigo ignored them, and their moans turned to cheers when, using all of his strength, he struck first, his lance driving forward with an impact that threw Enrique to the ground.

The prince managed to strike, too, before he fell, but his blow appeared to be only a glancing one, and the Castilians applauded wildly as Roderigo, turning slowly, rode back

toward the ridge. Enrique was sprawled on the ground, and
the knight from Navarre, who rode forward, dismounted and
bent over him, crossed the prince's arms over his chest. The
officers and men of Aragon and Navarre were silent, and King
Alfonso, making no attempt to hide his grief, removed his
helmet and wept.

Roderigo rode up to King Juan, drew his sword and
saluted. Then, turning to Alvaro, he raised his visor, and the
grandees gasped when they saw blood streaming down his
face. "I've paid my debt to you, Alvaro," he said hoarsely, and
pitched forward.

He died before anyone could reach his side.

Nobles from Toledo and Saragossa toasted each other at
impromptu dinner parties, Castilian artisans from Avila and
Burgos shared cups of mead with workmen from Barcelona
and Huesca, pikemen and archers sat down together and
talked of returning home in time to harvest their crops of
wheat and barley. Fires burned brightly in the camps of
both armies, sentries allowed grandees and common soldiers
to pass back and forth freely from one side to the other, and
men who had been enemies sang and laughed together, exchanged anecdotes and rejoiced because their lives had been
spared.

But the atmosphere was solemn in the pavilion of silk that
had been erected at the base of the ridge, and the two men
who ate quietly by the light of flickering oil lamps were
thoughtful. Neither had much appetite, and they waved away
their stewards, who came to refill their glasses. King Alfonso
looked pale under his deep tan, and Alvaro's hand trembled
when he cut his meat, but in spite of their exhaustion they
shared a sense of rapport.

"I've decided not to give Enrique a state funeral," the king
of Aragon said. "A private service will be more fitting."

Alvaro nodded. "Roderigo will be buried on his estate at

Montalban. Juan and I will go, but there will be no public ceremony."

Alfonso stared at the nearest lamp. "We'll begin our withdrawal tomorrow morning. In three days there will be no foreign troops on Castilian soil. My brother of Navarre will sign a separate treaty with you, pledging eternal peace with Castile, and Pedro has given me his written promise to give up his struggle against our cousin. As for my own treaty with you, we can call in our adjutants right now and draft a document that will satisfy both of us."

"Castile needs no written peace treaty," Alvaro replied, his voice becoming firmer. "I'll gladly swear to you, privately, and repeat the oath publicly, that King Juan will never undertake a campaign to obtain revenge. Our troops will never invade Aragon or Navarre."

"I won't repeat my mistake," Alfonso said heavily. "If I had remembered the policies of my father and refused to listen to my brothers, I wouldn't be violating the peace that has bound our countries together. I'll gladly make you the same promise, Don Alvaro. Castile need never again fear an invasion from Aragon."

They shook hands solemnly, and the sounds of singing drifted into the pavilion. Alvaro listened, then smiled faintly. "Some day, Your Majesty, though not in your time or mine, our people will be united. They share so many traditions and customs that Castile and Aragon must become one."

"My father often said the same thing, but I made the error of trying to use force to bring them together. Perhaps I can help to achieve the goal that both of us envision by meeting with you next winter, when the passions of the present unpleasantness have cooled. There are many agreements we might reach that would be beneficial to both of us."

"I'm always ready to serve Castile in any way I can."

Alfonso raised his glass in a toast. "I wish it were possible to appoint you Constable of Aragon, Don Alvaro. I've never known any man more devoted to his country, and I wish you happiness. You deserve your share."

Alvaro remained in the field until September, supervising the slow demobilization of the force he had raised, paying each man a bonus in gold and, after the regiments of volunteers had disbanded, directing the transfer of troops who were remaining in service to various garrisons throughout the country. He controlled the operations of the government from his tent, received visitors and, having won the confidence of the grandees, appointed many of them to administrative posts.

He corresponded frequently with Catalina, whose disappearance puzzled both Castile and Aragon, and he repeatedly urged her to appear openly at her brother's palace, as she no longer had any reason to remain in hiding. She replied stubbornly that she preferred to remain in seclusion for the present and that she was enjoying her life of solitude. He respected her wishes and told no one her secret. His desire to see her became overwhelming, and in late September, when he finally returned to Toledo, he slipped away from the honor guard that was scheduled to escort him in triumph to the Alcazar, and rather than wait until morning for the ceremonies in which King Juan and members of the *Cortes* would appear, he rode alone from the camp that had been established for him in the hills and, arriving after dark, made his way quickly to the house in the *Mozarab* district.

Handing his reins to the astonished sentry stationed outside, he cautioned the man to tell no one he had arrived. He mounted the steps quickly and tapped at the door. After a brief wait, he heard a bolt slide, the door opened and he stepped inside. Catalina, looking remarkably young in a gown of green velvet, smiled at him.

"No one in the city expects you until morning," she said as he took her hand and kissed it.

"I wanted to see you tonight." Alvaro was puzzled. "You don't seem surprised."

"I felt sure you'd come here tonight. After all these years, I've begun to understand you."

He stared at her, and she raised a hand to her hair, which was piled high on her head.

"The henna hasn't faded yet," she said. "It won't disappear for a few more weeks."

Alvaro followed her to the drawing room on the second floor. "You look as though you belong here."

"I feel more at home in this house than in any other place I've ever lived. I'm grateful to you for letting me use it as a sanctuary—I'll be reluctant to leave." Reaching out absently, she stroked the tapestried back of a chair.

Alvaro had planned to make a speech to her, but found it easier to say, "It would be a mockery to offer you condolences on Prince Enrique's death."

"I can only repeat what His Eminence said to me. God chose His own way to punish both Enrique and Roderigo de Pinar."

"Francisco knows your identity?"

"I believe he guessed it from the first, but he's been very discreet, and I haven't questioned him, naturally. He paid his first call on me a few days after the jousting match, and since then he's come to see me frequently. We've discussed many things," she added suddenly.

Alvaro saw she was tense, although she continued to smile.

"His Eminence and I have talked about the past and the future."

He took a step closer to her. "I've been thinking about the future, too, wondering how an illegitimate nobody could dare to hope that a princess would marry him."

Catalina relaxed, and a mischievous light appeared in her eyes. "The Lord Constable, Duke of Truxillo and head of the

Order of Santiago is hardly a 'nobody.' " She stood and faced him.

The barriers were disappearing, but a few remained. "Only members of royalty may sue for the hand of a princess."

"Cardinal Ruminez says I no longer rank as an Infanta of Castile, and I was never given a title in the hierarchy of Aragon. He assures me that if it should be necessary, which is unlikely, Pope Eugenius will issue an edict to clarify my status."

His impossible dreams had materialized, and he rejoiced, humbly and quietly.

"I've grown too fond of this house to leave it," Catalina said. "I want my children to be born here."

Alvaro kissed her, and for the first time in his life knew complete contentment.

At last they drew apart, breathless and self-conscious, realizing that they were just beginning to know each other. "Tomorrow," Alvaro said, "I shall not ride in the parade alone."

EDWARDS
    MASTER OF CASTILE